D1713668

Ordering information: james@jameshartman.net

Acknowledgments

Many thanks to many people:

To those in law enforcement, whose lives and careers intersected mine in a variety of ways over may years: Ken Dupaquier, Carole Dahlem, Tom Buell, Charlie Tynes, Jerry DiFranco, Jack West, Wayne Mayberry Jr., Jack Strain, Randy Smith, Mike Core, Al Strain, Tim Lentz, Rick Richard, Gerald Sticker, Kathy Sherwood, Mike Rooney, Lenny Pfleider, Kathy Sharp, Wendy Wicker Talley, Wayne Wicker, Ernie Fussell, Huey Davis, Jimmie Estes, Lenny Thompson, Donovan Livaccari, Sean Beavers, Bobby Golding, Matt Lewis, Hal Taylor, Jimmy Richard, Fred Oswald, Cathy Porter, Joe Jarrell Jr., Mark Arroyo, Ron Ruple, Richard Palmisano, Brad Hassert, Danell Gerchow, Daniel Seuzeneau, Tommy Benasco, Jennifer Boyet Harper, Ronnie Frey, Jayme Toncrey, Tiffany Tate, Michael Ferrell, Mike Boyet, Barney Tyrney, Randy Caminita, Marlene Nicolas, Gene Tyrney, Freddy Drennan, Albert Cromp, Donald Sharp, James Weary, Leslie Bourg, William Hart, Chris Vicari, Clint Mathews, Ronnie Jones, and many others.

To those who gave me some insights into Coroner's Office work through our professional interactions, from crime scenes to office procedures: Jim Hamler, Dr. Peter Galvan, Joy Raybon, Melanie Hughes, Rebecca Caminita, Doreen Mittlestaedt, Dr. Charles Preston, Dave Morel, Ken

Fielder, Mark Ford, Dr. Mike DiFatta.

To those who give me spiritual growth that extends beyond Sunday worship into the real world, no matter how ugly it gets: Rev. Elder Rachelle Brown, and Revs. Tom Howe, Clinton Crawshaw, Gail Minnick, Alisan Rowland, Keith Mozingo.

To those who have worked with (and, sometimes, against) me in the pursuit of journalism: Ashley Rodrigue, Faimon Roberts, Sara Pagones, Kim Chatelain, Norman Robinson, Melanie Sheubrooks, Kris Fairbairn Fortunato, Ken Jones, Michael Hill, Jason Allen, Susan Roesgen, Kendall Francis, Robert Rhoden, Kevin Chiri, Paula Ouder, Mike Scott, Margaret Pierce, Barbara Danahy, Mike Ross, Doug Mouton, Helena Moreno, Mike Bland, Jane Boulen, Kia Callia, Rob Masson, Paul Rodgers, Chuck Gay, Heath Allen, Bob Noonan, Paula Pendarvis-Milham, Glynn Boyd, Nancy Parker Boyd, Curt Sprang, Angela Hill, Dionne Butler, Scott Burke, Deepak Saini, Belinda Hernandez, Lee Zurik, Tanzi Jones, Richard Boyd, Ron Thibodeaux, Paul Rioux, Andre Trevigne, Liz Reyes, and many others.

To friends, some already included in the above lists, who provide immeasurable encouragement, often without realizing it, and some of whom provided additional inspiration for this story: Dana Lafonta, Jennifer Boyet Harper, Adam Eversole, Sam Nguyen, Zel Angelle, Jerod Dunbar, Richie Hollis, Kathy Sherwood, Cindy Starbuck Leonard, Brian Jones, Ellen Waguespack, Patrick Rouse, Marshall King, Alisan Rowland.

To my family, all of them, for too many things to count.

To God Almighty, because if this is any good it's not really mine. "Every good gift and every perfect gift comes down from above." – James 1:17.

Dedication

To the women and men of law enforcement, including Coroner's Office investigators and District Attorneys;

To the unnamed crime victims who are never discovered or identified, and their families;

To the victims of hate crimes;

To the clergy who care and to the ones who should be involved, but aren't;

To the media personages who do the job right;

To those who fight monsters;

To my Gerflufterflaffen. She knows who she is.

Author's Note:

The people represented in this story are products of my imagination. Although some of these characters may bear resemblance to actual individuals, and while some characters and their actions may be inspired by specific people, absolutely nothing in this book is meant to represent the actual behavior, lifestyles or personalities of anyone.

The events described in this story are, likewise, products of my imagination. Any similarity to actual events is purely and unintentionally coincidental.

Some events in this story are presented in a very realistic manner, while with many I have taken artistic license for the sake of storytelling. If the reader has experience or knowledge in law enforcement or forensics, she or he should take extra care to suspend disbelief.

Prologue

Sunday, August 7, 6:15 a.m.

Karly was not happy about being at work this early. As captain over the 911 call center, she usually worked Monday through Friday, 9 to 5. In emergencies she filled-in, and in hurricanes and other crises she lived at the Emergency Operations Center where her people were housed. Only in the direst of circumstances did she pick up a weekend shift to cover for a dispatcher.

This was different. Her nine-position shift was down to six already; the rest had caught the stomach virus that was running roughshod over the entire community. And for the last two weeks – on Sunday mornings – they'd gotten calls from someone calling himself "O," reporting the location of a body and confessing to the crime. At least in her mind it was a confession, but she was neither a detective nor a lawyer, so whenever they caught the bastard – and she knew they would – those tapes would be priceless evidence for the prosecution. It was vital the calls were handled perfectly.

She could've called in other dispatchers to cover the empty positions, paying from her meager overtime budget. But in times like this, when they could be almost certain a body was about to surface, she wanted to oversee things herself.

Morale was low and tensions were high. The inauguration of a new sheriff a year ago, the first new one in two decades, had left some people rattled – including, at first, Karly herself. New executives always change upper rank and management. They have to. There had been a minor purge, but she had been spared. Now, 13 months later, things had settled into relative comfort and routines. But as far as she was concerned, she was a one-year employee who still had to prove herself.

Unlike the previous sheriff, this one was very hands-on. They heard him on the radio more frequently, and he showed his face at crime scenes and in often-ignored divisions like hers. In his first year in office, when crimes occurred he responded to the scene. They heard him on the radio and saw him on TV. Recently, he had taken a back seat. This was part of his style, Karly knew, and she admired him for it. He stepped forward to reassure the public and then stepped back to the let the professionals do their jobs.

She looked around. The room was quiet, still, with only an occasional phone ringing, which was typical for an early Sunday morning. People were sleeping, and many – at least around here – were getting ready for church. But she could see her staff on-edge, waiting for the call they all knew – or at least expected – was coming. It was beyond what most of them had ever experienced. She understood.

In her 30-plus years of 911 and dispatch work, she had handled many bizarre and violent calls; she had never handled a serial killer case, let alone spoken to such a person herself. Still, she was confident in her abilities and experience. It didn't really cross her mind to worry about it. It would happen or it wouldn't, and they would rise to the occasion as they always did. They had been through Hurricane Katrina, for God's sake. They could handle anything.

She had listened to the first two recordings herself before handing over copies to detectives. That was part of her job. They were chilling.

"911, where is your emergency?"

"Listen carefully," said a voice, almost mechanical but calm, smooth, soothing, powerful. "There's a body in the Middle Pearl River. You'll find him just off Highway 90, under the bridge. Do you understand?"

"What's your name sir," the dispatcher asked after only a second of hesitation.

"My name is O," he said.

"Are you with this person now, sir?"

O laughed, gently.

"Oh, no," he said. "I rather like my freedom, and my work is far from finished."

"Where are you?" she asked.

"I'd rather not say," he responded with perfect calm and almost aristocratic tone. "Enjoy your day."

Then he hung up.

The second call, a week later, had been virtually the same. That time, the body was to be found in Bayou Lacombe, just under the bridge on Highway 190. His directions had been perfectly accurate, just as they had been the first time.

In her position, Karly wasn't usually privy to the details of an investigation. She only learned what came over the radio, what her dispatchers or deputies told her, and what was discussed at the weekly ComStat meetings. She had managed to glean that the tapes had been sent to the FBI lab in Quantico for vocal analysis, but the backlog of federal cases meant they'd be waiting weeks. The number from which he had called, which appeared on the operator's screen automatically, had been a disposable cell and different each time. Reality wasn't like TV cop shows where everything was tied-up neatly inside of an hour.

One of the dispatchers broke the silence.

"Captain?" she asked. It was one of the newer ones, only on the job six months or so. "What if he calls again today?"

"What if he does? We do our job," Karly said, calmly and as reassuringly as she could. "Get all the information you can, keep him talking as long as you can without getting personal, and send it to the dispatcher 10-18."

The woman sighed heavily.

"In here, we can't do what they do," Karly said, referring to deputies and detectives. "It's frustrating. It can be scary. But what you do on that call could make a difference for a lot of people and help them catch this son of a bitch."

They had all been listening. They said nothing.

A few minutes later, the phones lit up sequentially at almost all the call stations. A major accident on the interstate had caused at least one death. There was a flurry of activity as they notified the ambulance service, the fire department, State Police and their own deputies for traffic control. Interstate 12 was going to be closed for a while, and she knew it was bad when the supervisor asked for the Crime Lab and the Coroner. That could mean any number of things, but in this case it meant at least one fatality and, quite possibly, a criminal element to the accident that went beyond DWI or reckless driving. She had no way to know. That was frustrating, but after decades she was used to it.

Her team performed admirably. Just as things were settling down, the 911 line lit up on a sole screen – hers. She pushed the button on the console and tightened her headset. She couldn't miss a word.

"911, where is your emergency?" she asked.

"This is O," he said.

"Good morning," she said, calmly and respectfully. "We've been expecting your call."

That seemed to catch him off-guard. He was used to being in full control. He paused for a few seconds and then spoke again.

"Today's present for you is in Lake Pontchartrain."

"Sir? Could you give me your location?" She knew he wouldn't, but she wanted to keep him talking.

"Of course not," he said. "But tell your divers to look off the east side of the northbound span, about 20 yards from the pilings, right by crossover 3."

His specificity was unique.

"What should they look for?" Karly asked.

"My work, of course. Another one. Another one of them."

For the first time in his three calls, she felt a little emotion in his voice when he said "them." She decided to run with it.

"Sir, who is 'them'?"

He hung up. Apparently, he didn't want to say.

Chapter One

Sunday, August 7, 8:45 a.m.

Fred leaned over the stern of the boat and heaved again, the choppy waters of Lake Pontchartrain splashing a foamy spray back at him, as if spitting on his face in retaliation for something. He recoiled slightly, wiped his face with his sleeve, and leaned back. It was unlike the boat rides of his childhood, the fond memories with his grandparents on the Tchefuncte River. He shook his head, banishing the memory and shaking his own vomit from his face.

If he could've seen himself, he'd have been astonished at the greenish hue that colored his face. It was day seven of a stomach flu that had afflicted hundreds – if not thousands – in the Parish. Unlike many of them, though, he couldn't stop to rest and recover. The now-expected Sunday boat ride wasn't helping. Combining the virus with the motion of the waves was bad enough; adding the circumstances made it worse, as it always had. Recovering murder victims from any environment had never been his favorite thing.

Beside him, a few feet to port, a figure emerged from the water, pushing himself up with muscular arms that belied the 50-plus years of sun and wrinkles on his face. Without seeming to pause for breath after being underwater for 20 minutes, Fitz practically threw his giant frame into the boat. He looked at his superior.

"It's good, Major," he said. "Another one."

In 30 years of police work, Fred had never gotten used to the word "good" to describe reported or alleged crimes that turned out to be legitimate. There was nothing good about it.

Fred turned away and heaved again. There was nothing left, just the abdomen-straining effort itself with nothing to show for it but more nausea, pain, and a sinking feeling that had nothing to do with Fitz's report. He composed himself and turned again to face the diver.

"More?" he asked, with his usual calm tone.

He commanded 100 detectives, but Fred never raised his voice, never let anxiety show, never let his rank go to his head. His illness would not change his demeanor. He would never allow it. He couldn't disallow the symptoms of his illness but knew there would be no judgment of his ailment from the others.

"Hard to see much down there, Major," Fitz said. "Feels like a male subject, based on the size."

In the murkiness of this lake, feeling one's way was often the best or only way to make a discovery authentic. The water wasn't deep, but it was colored from a silty bottom made worse today by high winds above. Constantly changing salinity made the wildlife as variable as the weather. From manatees to bull sharks, Lake Pontchartrain – more an inland sea than a lake – contained it all.

"His ankles are tied to a cinderblock with some sort of chain," Fitz continued. "I couldn't tell what injuries he had sustained, not down there, not in that light and this weather. The waves have the silt all stirred up."

Fred took a deep breath and glanced upward. Police officers serving the world's longest over-water bridge were huddled against the rail, watching, assuming – as were they all – that what they found down here had begun up there. Fitz waited.

"Hand me the radio," Fred said. Fitz went into the cabin where the deputy piloting the boat had remained at his station, and returned with a hand-held.

"7101 to Central," Fred said into the mic. "Contact Causeway PD and ask their supervisor to give us a report by 1200 hours."

"10-4, sir," the dispatcher responded.

The previous sheriff had long ago wanted to build a more complex radio system that would allow all 10 local agencies to communicate directly by radio, but had been stymied by both technology and provincial political minds. Now, 50 feet below the officers Fred wanted to reach, he had to relay a message through a dispatch center 20 miles to the north. He had no patience for the absurdity but no time to dwell on it. He turned back to Fitz.

"Where's the C.O.?"

"Major Douglas said he has two investigators and a body bag standing by," Fitz said. "Waiting to confirm what we had."

The Coroner's Office was yet another agency with which he could not directly communicate via radio, and out here on the water cell signals were iffy, at best.

Fred took a second to process that Douglas himself was at the harbor, but didn't have time to dwell on it. It was odd.

"Get them out here and let's get this over with," Fred said. "You have the tools you need? Bolt cutters?"

"Yessir."

"Good. Take a breather until they get here, but have your gear ready to get back down there."

Fred knew Fitz, like himself an athlete and long-distance runner, didn't need a breather. He also knew the Coroner's Office investigators were as fed up as he was. Three weeks, three murders, all the bodies found in waterways on Sunday mornings, and all of them announced by the killer himself through a voice-altered and anonymous call to Central.

They were working around the clock, a third of them sick, and had almost nothing to lead them to the killer. They had, in fact, almost nothing to lead them to the identities of the victims. In St. Tammany Parish, murders weren't ordinary – and this case was the most extraordinary Fred had ever seen.

Dora was tired. Christian was even more so. Although death investigators at the Coroner's Office – "inspectors," the new coroner had dubbed them -- rotated shifts like firefighters, with one day on and two off, in times of crisis they all worked what seemed like all the time. There were cots and showers at the office, and lately they had been used, a lot. The last month had been grueling. In addition to the normal volume of suicides, increasing heroin overdoses, vehicle crashes and other unclassified deaths, the two homicides – now three – had taken everyone's attention and focus. She was spent; her partner had succumbed to the virus plaguing the area – non-fatal but beyond unpleasant – and, like many emergency responders, had kept working, or trying to. Somehow she had so far avoided catching it, but the commitment of many had left even more stricken with it through basic exposure.

Standing in the warm summer rain at the Mandeville Harbor, she was ready for it to end and was surprised it hadn't. Dealing with dead bodies and grieving families day in and day out was hard enough. Handling a serial killer – although no one, for whatever reason, would yet put that label on him – was something they had never handled before. It was over the top, too much.

Major John Douglas, commander of the Sheriff's Special Operations Division, was in the cutter tethered to the piling. He didn't usually respond to such things personally; the chief detective and chiefs of patrol divisions would, but his job didn't really require it. This was different, for more reasons than he could share. Lt. Dan Moreau was also there, and a deputy she didn't know was in the boat.

Christian sat in the van, air conditioner streaming at high speed on his face, his head leaned backwards; Dora leaned against the driver's door, smoking a cigarette and trying not to think. Her face was impassive.

She heard the crackle of a radio and saw Moreau reach for the field mic clipped to his jacket collar. She couldn't hear what was said.

"Inspectors," Douglas called from the deck. "It's time. Let's go."

Dora turned to her partner and didn't need to say anything. He hadn't been sleeping, merely resting, and slowly exited the van. They met at the back doors and grabbed their kits, two body bags (just in case), and boarded the boat without saying a word.

Moreau tossed them each a life preserver. She wrapped on hers and fastened it; Christian moaned at the idea of something around his neck, but did it anyway. The pilot gunned the engine and the boat took off fast – too fast. Christian grabbed the rail and vomited into the wake.

"Christ," she said under her breath. Between the motor and the wind, no one heard her. It didn't matter. It was as much a prayer as a blasphemy.

She couldn't see the speedometer but the deputy piloting the boat wasn't going very fast, despite his abrupt departure. She was glad he had at least some respect for the weather, if not for his passengers. In about 20 minutes they could see the other Sheriff's Office vessel up ahead, anchored only yards from the Causeway Bridge. Half a dozen officers and other bridge personnel stood on the span, looking down.

Dora shook her head, thinking, "vultures" – a term she usually reserved for reporters. Causeway cops craved excitement, she knew – or so she had been told. Driving 24 miles in one direction at a time and only being able to make left turns for 12 hours in a shift drove them crazy. At least that was the law enforcement lore. A body in the lake that did not seem to correlate with a smashed railing up above – a serial killer – was unique. She couldn't blame them for their interest, but they weren't stuck with the stench and the rot and the pressure to bring a killer to justice. They mostly worked accidents and breakdowns, and only an occasional "overboard," as they called it – a car that jumped the rail and landed in the lake. Those were very rare.

The boat pulled alongside the other vessel as Moreau threw bumpers over the side. She didn't see Douglas, and only then realized he had remained at the Harbor. She didn't have the time or focus to wonder why. As the pilot brought the vessel about, maintaining an even distance in windy weather and choppy seas wasn't tenable and every precaution had to be taken. Thankfully, there was no need for them to board the other boat.

Once they were more-or-less stationary, she saw the diver – Fitzmorris, she remembered, although she blanked on his first name – take a backwards plunge off the Sheriff's Office boat. He held what looked like bolt cutters. From the bow, she heard more than saw another diver make the plunge. This was good; it would take two able-bodied men to haul the dead weight of a waterlogged corpse to the surface and into one of the boats. From there, she'd need help getting it in the body bag and in his very sick state, Christian would be little help.

It seemed to take forever but it was only a few minutes. Fitz and the other diver surfaced between the boats, which struck her as unsafe, given the weather conditions. There wasn't time to question it and it wasn't her place. She grabbed her partner by the arm and moved him towards the rail. The divers held the body flat on the surface of the water, supporting him with their own strength, and with a fluid motion heaved it onto the deck. It was indelicate, to say the least. On a normal crime scene – a land-based one – that would've been unacceptable. It was disrespectful to the dead and evidence was easily lost. In an underwater scene, it was inevitable. There was no graceful way to extricate a body from beneath the surface and place it onto a boat – not to mention in a body bag – without such indiscretions. Losing evidence from an underwater crime scene was inevitable, if there was any to begin with.

Christian moved to help, but the movement itself took him aback. He turned away. He was a veteran death inspector and wasn't bothered by the sight before them, but that didn't matter. Dora literally pushed him away and motioned to Fitz. He hopped into the boat and, without words, helped secure the deceased into the bag. She thanked him with a gesture and watched as he went back into the water.

When the divers were clear, the pilot took off towards the Harbor. In their wake, she could hear Fred's boat follow.

Dora Jenkins had been investigating deaths for the coroner for more than a decade. She knew how to respect precision while not wasting time, particularly when she, herself, was pushed to the point of exhaustion and frustration. She pulled off the latex gloves she had worn to load the body and nonchalantly tossed them into the lake before donning another pair.

She hadn't closed the bag completely, not only hoping for the wind to remove some of the stench but also to give herself access. Now, she leaned over, held onto the rail with one hand and pulled back the bag with the other. She didn't touch anything, not at first. She knew better. She just looked. She had been at this long enough to know some things the pathologist would record.

The state of decomposition suggests the subject has been dead for two to three days, she recited in her head – not only from experience and observation but from the autopsy reports on the first two victims. Both orbital bones are fractured, making facial reconstruction difficult or impossible. Due to decomp and exposure to the elements, including aquatic life, both eyes are gone and lips are damaged.

She leaned closer and pried open the mouth.

Most teeth are missing, she thought as if reading the report out loud; whether the loss of dentition is from trauma, pre-mortem conditions or decomposition cannot be determined -- although loss of teeth due to decomposition would be unlikely after only a few days. There appears to be significant blunt force trauma to the head and neck. By all indications, the subject had light hair, cut short, military style.

She unzipped the bag a little more and pulled back the flaps to examine the limbs.

On the left arm, someone – presumably the killer – had excised a three-inch square in the mid forearm. At least that's how it appeared to her. This was new, unlike the other victims.

The victim's clothing – dark-colored gym shorts and a t-shirt – were mostly intact. Given the wound on the arm, she felt compelled to look further. She unzipped the bag all the way and gingerly lifted the sides, examining the corpse as best she could without touching it. On the right ankle, another three-inch square of skin had been excised. Under these conditions she couldn't determine how deep it was, but it was more than a scratch, more than an accident, and not the sort of marks a surgeon would leave when removing a cancer or a keratosis. Again, this was new.

Her eyes scanned the length of him. Nothing else stood out, but she had to know.

She cautiously grabbed the waistband of the shorts just below where his navel would have been and pulled them back.

He was like the others. His genitals had been removed, too.

From the distance of a few dozen yards, Fred could tell Dora was inspecting the body, bent over as she clearly was on the deck. He only hoped she was as reliable as the coroner said and would keep what she saw to herself. This was no time for leaks.

Ahead, on the shore, he could see Leveque, the public information officer, standing at the harbor. Fred wondered if he would be followed by the phalanx of photographers who seemed to trail him to every crime scene in the Parish.

He didn't have to wait long. His radio crackled but he could barely hear it.

"7101," he said into the mic. "10-9 your last transmission."

"Major Walder, 1120 here," Leveque said. "Just wanted you to know word is out and this scene is no longer 10-35. I've requested MPD send units to assist."

"Fuck," Fred said, although not into the mic. It wasn't Leveque's fault. Media do what they do, although sometimes how they did it was a mystery.

"10-4," Fred said. "How many are at the harbor?"

"All four," came the reply. "Plus some newspapers. MPD is 10-97 now, putting up tape."

That was some relief, Fred thought. Mandeville Police knew how to manage this; they would set up a perimeter and keep the gawkers – both reporters and the general public – at bay. How everyone else responded remained to be seen. He could only hope.

Jerod Leveque was surrounded by onlookers and reporters but he took a moment to be alone in his own thoughts. While always attuned to the radio in his hand and the phone in his pocket, he also had the wherewithal to know when and how to withdraw and focus. He had only a moment.

"Central, 1120." His radio crackled in the wind.

"1120," he said.

"Do you need our units to assist MPD?"

His patience was thin. He wasn't Fred.

"I need whatever units are necessary to secure this scene. All other units are on the water and I'm flying solo," he said, with more hostility than he intended.

9

"10-4, sir," the dispatcher responded.

Dispatchers were trained to keep transmissions as short as possible. They weren't supposed to punctuate transitions with "sir" or "ma'am" or even someone's rank. That she did so suggested that she sensed his annoyance. It didn't matter. At the moment, he didn't think much would assuage the aggravation that had been rising from frustration to near-rage. He didn't like this aspect of his job, these kinds of cases, but it wasn't the crime itself that was enraging him. It was the unsettling knowledge that things had changed and would never be the same. These sorts of things don't happen here, he kept thinking, over and over. They just don't.

Leveque had been PIO for only a year, hired by the newly elected sheriff. His background was as an investigator, but in his new role he had learned to be hands-off with detectives, hands-on with reporters, and as proactive as possible. He hadn't called the media about this report, but he had been ready to respond and had been there as fast as anyone. It was Sunday, after all, and this is when "O" liked to reveal his work.

Like all of them, he was tired.

Within what seemed like seconds, three Sheriff's Office cars and two from the Mandeville Police descended on the scene. Jerod didn't wait. He walked towards them all, fast.

"We have boats on the way to this location with a 30 victim," he said, using the signal number they all knew meant murder – and which they had all both assumed and expected. "I have four TV stations already here, other reporters, and the public. I need this area secured from there – "he pointed to a piling 80 feet off to his right – "to there" – another, 20 feet to his left. He didn't wait for acknowledgment, but turned around and walked back to the dock. He spoke on the authority not only of his rank, but of the sheriff himself, and no one had to know the sheriff was incapacitated at the moment. So far, no one did.

It took less than two minutes for the deputies and officers to comply. Jerod noted it, although he'd never remember who actually strung the "CRIME SCENE" tape, or who moved the media and civilian onlookers back. He hated that he had to exert that level of authority in these kinds of circumstances. He hated that he wasn't one of them anymore. He hated that he wasn't on the boat. He was pleased, however, that he had the command authority to get done what he needed done. He wasn't going to give that up.

The boat carrying the body and the Coroner's inspectors arrived first. Fred's boat was right behind them, and the major took land first. He walked straight to Leveque.

"Explain," he said.

"Sir?" Jerod asked. Fred outranked him by one level, but on any other day they'd have been on a first-name basis.

"Why are the media here?"

"I don't know, Major," Jerod answered. "They started calling me the same time Central sent the text."

Jerod's assumption that Fred was angry, that he assumed Jerod was the leak, was quickly assuaged.

"That son of a bitch is calling them, too," Fred said, frustration in his voice.

Jerod thought he had a good relationship with the press. He realized he needed to test it.

"Maybe so, major," he said.

Fred fastened his gaze on him, his body smelling of lake water, his breath of vomit.

"Find out," he said.

Fred turned and went back to the boat. As indelicately as they had removed the body from the water, it had to be done with care and respect at this point. Not only were there civilians and TV cameras - and the ubiquitous smart phone cameras, too - all around, but while evidence preservation in the water was almost impossible, now that

11

they had the body contained they had to keep it intact, undamaged, and as preserved as possible. Dropping or sliding the body bag was not OK. It had to be done right.

Fitz hopped out of the boat and headed to the gurney waiting at the dock by the vessel that carried the corpse. While Fred appreciated the diver's muscle, he also knew he was as spent as the rest of them. He looked around for the Crime Lab van, cursed under his breath that they weren't there, and then remembered they were tied up on the Interstate. The Coroner's Office SUV was in place to transport the body, but he would've preferred his own lab units immediately examine the body and debrief Dora. It wasn't to be and it was his own fault. He should have anticipated the need for more resources. It was the new normal, this type of Sunday morning.

As Dora and the frail Christian – Fred wondered why he was even there, as sick as he was – talked with Fitz and Moreau about how they were going to lift the body onto the gurney and into the van, Fred scanned the crowd. That's another thing he wanted the Lab detectives for – to shoot photos of the onlookers. Detective TV show lore that perpetrators sometimes like to watch the frenzy they created was no fiction. He cursed under his breath again, and glanced at his watch. On a normal workday, if he called for the lab they'd be there in 15 minutes. On a Sunday morning at 9 a.m., with a fatal accident already clogging traffic, that wasn't going to happen; it could be at least an hour or more, and that wouldn't do.

He grabbed his radio from his belt. He needed to say something to Moreau but didn't want to be seen conveying it in person.

"7101 to 9202," he said into the mic. From 100 feet away he saw Moreau look up at him, then back to his radio, understandably puzzled.

"9202. Go ahead, major."

"I need you to 10-23 on the 29."

"Sir?"

"Go to iCall."

iCall, a separate channel setting, allowed the two of them to converse by radio without anyone else hearing it over the channel. It also required less formality.

"Go ahead, Fred."

"Listen," Fred said. "The Lab isn't here yet. I need photographs of the crowd. I also want to examine that body myself once it's in the CO van. I'm going to need help."

"Name it," Moreau responded.

"First, standby on removal of the body. Once it's in the van, if the perp is in this mob, he'll be gone. As long as he has a show to watch, he's not leaving. Second, you have an underwater camera on board, right?"

"Yessir."

"Can you modify the settings at all so it'll take decent shots in this light?"

There was a long pause.

"I'm not sure, but I'll do my damnedest."

"Good. Thanks. Act like you're photographing the body but take candid shots of these people. As many as you can get from that distance and angle, but try not to act like you're doing it."

"You got it."

Fred turned his radio back to the regular channel and scanned the crowd himself. No one stood out, except for one of the officers whose car was serving as one anchor for the perimeter. He walked towards him, fast.

"Officer Cone," Fred said, loudly, as he approached. The tall blond turned with a military precision that matched his appearance.

"Sir," Cone said.

Fred neared, got close enough to see Cone blink twice at the smell of vomit, and took a step back.

"You used to work in our Crime Lab, right?"

"Yes, sir," Cone said.

"I need you."

Fred motioned to the next uniform over, the other Mandeville officer, and beckoned. The officer came without hesitation, and Fred was reminded how much he liked working with that agency. There were no egos and no jealousy over jurisdictions. Crime was crime and they needed to work together to solve it, especially now.

"Yes, Major?"

"Can you shift this way and man two positions for a bit? I need Cone to help me in the van."

"Of course, sir."

Fred noted his name tag, "Rooney," and hoped he'd remember it when he next saw the city's chief.

"Thanks," he said. "Cone, come with me."

As they approached the van, Fred saw Moreau doing his best to accomplish some surreptitious photography. He didn't know how much it would help. As far as any onlookers would know, he borrowed Cone from the perimeter for extra muscle in moving the waterlogged corpse; in reality, he had a different need.

Leveque stood at the edge of the perimeter in an area cordoned off specifically for media. He had done his best to get them a good shot for the body bag coming out of the boat, but there were no guarantees given the movement of personnel and vehicles. Responsible journalists never showed actual bodies, but they would show body bags. Jerod knew these people and trusted most of them. Rather than a formal press event, they had an easy dialogue. He assumed everything was on the record and measured his words.

"Jerod, can you tell us if this body was weighted down?"

"At this point, no I can't. Please understand we're only now getting the remains to the Coroner and I won't release any details about how he was disposed of until the autopsy is complete."

"He?" asked another reporter. "So it's another man."

For a split second, Jerod thought he had screwed-up. He hadn't.

"Yes," he said. "I'll confirm that."

No one had yet said it – internally or publicly – but most serial killers preyed on women. This one had a different agenda and they had yet to figure out what it was.

"Are the Causeway Police involved in the investigation? Since the body was so close to the bridge it seems logical he'd have fallen or jumped –"

"Or been pushed," interjected one of the other ones.

"We have a good working relationship with the Causeway Police Department and if we need assistance I'm sure they'll provide it," Jerod said.

"My producer talked to someone at the Causeway and they said the bridge railing isn't damaged. So can you confirm the victim was not in a car?"

"Yes," Jerod said. He knew they had to do this, but his patience was wearing thin. Murders were awful, but give him an open-and-shut domestic homicide any day over this monstrosity.

As if on cue, all the reporters' eyes – and cameras – turned back towards the dock. Jerod stepped aside to clear the shot, but stayed close. Dora, Fitz, Moreau and Cone were lifting the body as carefully as possible – but with great strain – onto the gurney. Jerod felt for them. It was no easy task to lift that much waterlogged dead weight in any case. He had done it in his previous life. With many sick and all of them exhausted, the rain and slick decks made it worse. When they lowered the body successfully onto the cart and strapped it down, Jerod released a breath he hadn't even realized he'd been holding.

They all watched as the gurney wheeled to and into the back of the Coroner's Office vehicle, an SUV specially outfitted for this use and with windows heavily tinted.

From their angle, they couldn't see any more. That was how Fred had wanted it.

Blair Francingue turned her head and shot a subtle look at Clarence. He felt her gaze instinctively, one reporter to another, and glanced back. She gently moved her head to the left and shifted her eyes simultaneously, a subtle gesture. He knew what she was asking him to do.

On a major crime scene like this one, it was TV crews that drew the notice. Not only were the reporters themselves easily recognized, but the mere presence of a photographer with a tripod and large camera captured the attention of law enforcement and bystanders alike. That was Blair's place, but as a newspaper reporter Clarence could move about more easily, unnoticed, blending with the crowd. TV reporters were also always dressed to go on-camera, regardless of the day or hour; news reporters like Clarence could show up on a Sunday morning in shorts and a T-shirt and no one batted an eye. Often, too, newspaper writers could remain virtually silent, simply writing down the answers to questions the TV folks posed.

By virtue of professional courtesy, the print media gave way to those who needed space for cameras and the right angles. Clarence and one other writer from a small local weekly stood at the back of the media gathered at the harbor this wet Sunday morning. Stealthily – but without appearing to be slick – Clarence stepped further backwards, slowly, until he was out of the media group and among the onlookers. There weren't hundreds of them, as there might've been only 30 miles away in New Orleans. Mandeville was more concerned with propriety and discretion, and the people were willing to wait until the news actually made it online or on TV. Most weren't even following Facebook or Twitter, though he and Blair had both been sending out brief updates on social media.

He walked slowly through the crowd, away from the lake and towards the northern end of the perimeter Leveque had set up. The "crime scene" tape was tied to one of the pilings, and although deputies and officers had spaced their vehicles and themselves at fairly regular intervals, he knew they wouldn't be bothered by him unless he tried to cross the line – something he would never do. At the northernmost point of the yellow plastic boundary, he found himself away from most of the crowd, as people had naturally gathered where the TV cameras were. He almost chuckled, enjoying the advantage he had by virtue of his medium, the only daily newspaper left in the New Orleans market.

A deputy was posted at the piling, but Clarence didn't get close. He stood back, quietly observing, his notebook folded and tucked in his waistband at the middle of his back. He looked as inconspicuous as anyone in the crowd of civilians. He wished he smoked, as it would've given him something to do with the hands that usually held paper and pen. Awkwardly, he stretched his arms in front of him, interlocking his fingers and pulling at his own shoulders, hearing his knuckles crack slightly.

The deputy – one he didn't recognize – had his back turned, watching the action at the rear of the Coroner's Office SUV. It was exactly the vantage point he wanted and precisely why Blair had silently asked him to relocate. Now, the task was to not be noticed by Major Walder or Dora what's-her-name from the Coroner's Office. They would recognize him, and that wouldn't be good. He didn't seem to be at risk of that.

Although Fred and company had led the gurney to the back of the large vehicle, they hadn't yet loaded the body inside, as he suspected they wanted people to perceive they had. It made sense if Walder wanted to examine the body immediately. Climbing inside the vehicle would've limited both space and light. Even in the gray sky and drizzle, there would be better visual access out of doors. But to avoid detection, Fred would have to hurry.

He wondered, only briefly, why they were allowing the corpse to get wet in the rain, and then realized: A body that had been underwater for hours or days – or even less – had already lost most evidentiary value. Some raindrops wouldn't hurt.

He was only about 30 feet from them, maybe 40, but they didn't notice at all. Even the deputy still had his back turned, watching the goings-on at the back door of the SUV. Dora stood on the far side of the gurney. A deputy he did recognize – Cone was his name, although he couldn't recall or didn't know his first name – was beside her, holding a flashlight. Both were fixated on the body inside the opaque black bag. Fred had his back to Clarence, on the near side of the body, and was hunched over. Even from this distance, he could see both fatigue and frustration. Fred had a bad color, and Clarence deduced without even consciously thinking about it that he, too, had fallen prey to the local epidemic. He was sorry for that. Although reporters have a reputation for being heartless, Clarence had worked hard in his 15 years as a journalist to never lose his humanity. For that matter, he was sorry for the guy in the bag.

At the moment, that didn't matter. He would deal with his humanity later, or at church – if he ever had a free Sunday morning again.

He could see Fred and the others' movements but he couldn't hear them. That was OK, for now. He saw Fred reach up and grab Cone gently by the wrist, redirecting the flashlight in the deputy's hand. He said something to Dora and she reached in her bag and handed him something that looked from this distance like a small wooden stick – a tongue depressor, maybe?   Fred reached into the bag with it and slowly withdrew. Then, as if he suddenly realized an error, he spoke to Dora again and tossed it to the ground. She handed him surgical gloves, bright green ones, which Fred quickly donned. Then he reached into the bag with both hands. Cone's light followed the detective's movements.

As Fred began to wrestle with what Clarence thought was the victim's left arm, actually pulling it out of the bag, Clarence reached into his back pocket and pulled out his smart phone. As subtly as he could and without raising it to his face for a perfect shot, he aimed it at the scene and started video recording. It wouldn't be much. It would be grainy, soundless, lacking in clarity, but it would be more than the others had. Holding it steadily in front of him he slowly glanced to his right, back to where Blair and others stood. She was watching him. He looked at her and gently nodded. She smiled back.

Chapter Two

John Douglas was at a loss.

He had driven home from the third murder scene – the only one of the three to which he had responded – in absolute despair. The house was empty. Donna was long gone – months, actually, although it seemed like longer. Thirty years of marriage and she was done. He hadn't heard from her since she had left. He hadn't heard from her lawyer, either, which gave him hope. The children, both in college, were always silent. They didn't concern him. At the moment, in fact, no one concerned him but himself.

He sat on the sofa in front of the big-screen TV mounted over the mantle and watched the breaking news. He couldn't help it.

The first reports showed a broad shot of the harbor. He could see himself in the footage, and beat himself mentally for even responding. This was not his scene. It was Fred's. Now, he had shown his interest out of instinct and he was afraid.

The first murder, two weeks ago, had rattled everyone. He knew who the victim was, but couldn't say. He knew who the victim's wife and children were, but couldn't say. He had to wait. And the waiting was killing him. Then it came again. And now, again. He couldn't help but feel it was directed at him.

He poured another cup of coffee, sat down, and cried.

Margaret sat at her desk and looked at the two reporters across from her. Usually, they were planning, plotting, preparing their next joint expose, a combined talent of television and print journalists that others in this market didn't yet rival. Today, they were debating how and when to reveal what they knew. Margaret was the senior member of the bureau, with 40-plus years of journalism behind her – and, she hoped, a lot more to go.

Her Greek features belied her graying hair. She was still a pretty woman at 63, with steely eyes, a calm voice, and a mind that forgot nothing.

Blair and Clarence sat across from her, the joint progeny of the unification of television news and newspaper reporting that had evolved from cutbacks, mergers, and the utter stupidity of corporate forces.

She listened more than she talked, like a good reporter. Like a parent, in fact.

"We have the video, so why not use it?" Clarence asked.

"I agree," Blair said. "No one else has this. We can be the first."

"But it's crap," Margaret said. "There's no focus, no audio, only shady images of –"

"It was the best I could do," Clarence said.

"And no one else has it," Blair said. "Something is better than nothing."

"But what does it show?" Margaret asked.

The younger journalists paused.

"It shows the chief detective examining the victim's limbs," Clarence said.

"So what?" Margaret asked. "Isn't that to be expected?"

"Of course it is, but we have the video," Blair said.

Margaret sighed and leaned back in her chair.

"What else do you have?"

"Not a fucking thing that's unique!" Blair was in her late 20s, pretty and blonde and all about getting the scoop. She used Twitter more than should be allowed by law, in Margaret's opinion, but it was what sold these days.

Clarence glanced at Blair. He was used to her youthful outbursts, but still, he wished she would calm down. He had been 29 once, eager and enthusiastic. Now in his early 40s, it was a job. He wanted to do it well, of course, but he had his limits when it came to fighting with editors and producers. He would plead his case, but when a boss said "no," he was used to just rolling with it.

Margaret wasn't fazed by Blair's outburst at all. She sat in silence and pondered, then looked at Clarence.

"Write the story that will accompany the video and I'll consider it. Do it fast."

Dora pulled the van into the Coroner's Office bay, backing in to make it easier to offload the body they carried. Beside her Christian shifted in his seat. He seemed to be better than he was just a few hours earlier, but the way this virus had attacked people she didn't trust it. He might rally now and collapse in an hour. She respected his effort to keep working but he wasn't really much help at this point. Thank God for the others – and thank God it had finally stopped raining.

She opened her door, began to step out, and then recoiled, pulling back into the vehicle and shutting her door. Across the parking lot, across the grassy area behind it, almost hidden in the piney tree line, she saw the reflection of sunlight on a camera lens. She squinted to gain more focus. It was a woman, she thought, with a tripod and video camera. She muttered a profanity. Christian turned to her, speaking for the first time in hours.

"What did you expect?" he said. Dora was surprised he was lucid enough to have noticed.

She shook it off, literally, shuddering a bit in her seat.

St. Tammany didn't have this. They didn't have media hiding to get a good shot, they didn't have serial killers, they didn't have epidemics. This place was a suburban paradise and she was suddenly very pissed off that it wasn't any more.

Dora reached for her phone and dialed Leveque. He worked for the sheriff, not the coroner, but he was her only option. He answered on the second ring.

"Hey, Dora," he said. "What do you need?"

From anyone else, "What do you need?" might've seemed abrupt. From Jerod, she knew, it was meant to be helpful. She sighed.

"We just got to the office with the body," she said. "I'm in the bay. There's a photographer in the woods across the yard."

"Is he –"

"She," Dora interjected.

"Is she on our property?"

"Negative," she said. "At least not that I can tell."

"Is she interfering?"

"No."

"Let her shoot," he said. "We have no legal right to stop her and no reason, really. Are you backed into the bay?"

"Yes."

"Good. Then she won't see much anyway. Fred is on the way and that's what she's really after," he said. "She knows her station can't show pictures of the body. She's probably staking it out for B-roll."

"So just ignore her?"

"Yup," he said. "But let Doc know. Talk to you later."

He hung up. Dora stared at the phone. This was all new to her, the attention. She didn't like it.

"Christian, you OK?" she asked.

He nodded, weakly.

"Let's go," she said, as she reached for her phone again.

Fred drove fast but carefully to the Coroner's Office. Built in the center of the Parish, it was truly state-of-the-art. The morgue and autopsy suites were completely contained, and even had separate water and air filtration system in case a body came in that contained or was contaminated by airborne bacteria, viruses or other toxins.

He knew they were being watched. Of course they were being watched. Dora's call a moment earlier had confirmed it, although in this particular instance he wasn't sure who the watcher was. As long as it wasn't the killer, he also didn't care.

He pulled his SUV to the bay, beside Dora's vehicle, and without hesitation walked to the back door by the morgue. He pressed the buzzer and waited. In seconds, the door buzzed back and the first set of glass doors opened. He paused as they closed behind him and the second set slid apart. It reminded him of "Get Smart," but he considered it necessary and far from comical. Now, he was truly in what they all called "the death center." He had been here before, far too often in recent weeks, and already knew the autopsy suites lined the right side of the hallway. At the second one he found them.

The body bag had been resealed and lay atop a stainless steel table, above which were mounted a Stryker saw and multiple light sources. The hum of the fan – turned extra high given the condition of this body – overlapped with the hum of the cooler. As soon as Fred walked in, Christian looked up in relief and left him alone with Dora and the corpse. This being an obvious homicide, no one would be left alone with the body, lest an aggressive defense attorney later accuse someone of planting or altering evidence. Christian was sicker than Fred was, but Fred was starting to feel suddenly worse.

It wasn't the body, the smell, the hollow sterility of the autopsy suite, nor even exhaustion. He was sick and getting sicker, despite his best efforts. It was infuriating, and Fred wasn't used to rage. It sapped his energy even more. He had to rally. He knew it, so he just did it – or he had until now.

Dora said nothing, and they were left in impatient silence while waiting for the pathologist. Ordinarily, at least one case agent would've been here, as well, but Fred had ordered everyone to stay away. There was no need for a bigger circus, he had more experience than just about anyone at the Sheriff's Office, and he needed everyone rested and well. At the moment, however, he was questioning his own wisdom. He wished Nick was here, or someone she designated.

Suddenly, the room began to spin. He didn't remember the last time he felt this bad, but at the moment, he didn't remember much. He staggered backwards, leaned into the wall, and slid to the floor. It seemed like minutes, but Dora was at his side in seconds. She was used to dealing with the dead, but as a paramedic she also knew how to tend to the living.

Dora grabbed his wrist with one hand and placed the other on his forehead, tilting his head backwards to ensure his airway stayed open if he vomited again and resting the back of his head gently against the wall. In the closed suite, Christian wouldn't hear her if she yelled and she didn't want to step away from her impromptu patient – even to the phone across the room. When she was sure he was breathing, she did, quickly, pressing the intercom button. She didn't know for sure where he was, but she had a guess and pressed the "staff lounge" button.

"Christian! I need you! Bring my kit!"

She heard mumbling, but that was sufficient. She went back to Fred. His color was slowly returning, his breathing was steady. This was, she thought, a combination of exhaustion and dehydration, in addition to the virus that had afflicted so many. It wasn't life-threatening, but he needed more treatment than he was going to get in an autopsy suite. There was a hospital three miles away and her instinct was to call for an ambulance.

She hesitated. If the photographer was still outside, which was a safe bet, how would it look to see the Sheriff's Office chief detective carted off on a gurney? She shook her head abruptly, and gave herself a mental slap. She was trained to save lives, not reputations. That was someone else's problem.

Christian walked in as quickly as he was able, and seemed startled alert by what he saw. Without a word, he handed Dora her bag and squatted beside her.

"What do you need?" he asked.

"Go to that phone and call 911," she said, indicating the wall phone with a jerk of her head, her eyes never leaving Fred. "Do we have any IV needles? Saline?"

"I think so."

"Bring them."

She barely listened as he dialed the phone, and was equally unaware when he left the room, returning moments later with a sterile needle, tubing, and an IV bag. She didn't know where he had gotten them or why they even had them, but she didn't care.

"Alcohol," she said.

Christian looked around until he spotted swabs and handed her one.

"Gloves," she said.

She wasn't concerned about catching anything from Fred, but protocol was strict, and she certainly didn't want him catching anything from her.

Christian tossed two universal-size latex gloves to her, which she seemed to put on within a second.

"While I get this needle in his arm, find me something to hang this bag on," she said. "Something portable, ideally."

She heard him leave again and cursed the lack of a tourniquet. She looked around, saw nothing, then pulled off her left shoe and sock. In short order, the sock became a tourniquet on Fred's upper arm – a feat that surprised her given her small feet and Fred's lean, muscular frame. Still, it worked. As his veins began to bulge, she inserted the needle in his left arm. Unconscious, he barely winced.

Christian came back at the same time, a wheeled chair in front of him and an old-fashioned overhead projector on it. There was a wire coat hanger in his hand, a bag of fluid on the cushion. She looked at him, incredulous.

"It was the best I could do," he said, "but it will work."

While she taped the needle onto Fred's arm, Christian connected the tube to the bag, hanging it by a bent wire from a projector.

They had not taught this in paramedic school.

She realized the back door was secured and they wouldn't hear a siren in here.

"Go see if that ambulance is here."

He ran from the room.

"You're gonna be OK," she said to Fred. His face was darkening again, blood flowing. He was semi-conscious. "We're gonna get you to a hospital."

He opened his eyes halfway.

"Call Nick," he said. "Someone needs to be here. Call her." And then, as he began to fade further, "Thank you."

It was like him, she thought, to always remember common courtesy.

Nicole Brooks was literally pacing in her living room dodging, as she stepped, her children, all of whom were playing on the carpet. Her husband stood in the kitchen but he knew better than to say anything when she was like this, in what he called "cop mode."

She had been like this for days – or at least since Friday. Major Walder had ordered everyone to stand down, but as second in command of the detectives, she was antsy, anxious, wanting to work. She had been kept abreast of developments in the case of "O," but as a woman in the man's job of law enforcement, she'd had to fight for it.

She was used to it, but that didn't mean it was OK. It also didn't mean she could ever stop fighting for it. Clay admired her for it, for never giving up but never letting the struggle make her hard.

Nick was every bit as good a mother to their children as always, but the frustration was mounting. Three murders, three crime scenes, and she had been banished from all but the first, once they realized a serial killer was at work in their parish. That wasn't Fred being sexist, she knew; he had banished everyone – a decision with which she disagreed but which she supported because he was the boss. But her cop instincts were in high gear and she wanted to catch the killer more than anyone.

"Nick," said Clay from the kitchen. "Can you calm down? You're unsettling the kids."

She looked at the young ones, ranging in age from 4 to 10, playing happily, and pointed to them.

"Really?" she asked, both incredulous and a bit insolent. "They look fine to me."

He knew when to back off, and he did.

"Charley, you need some more juice, sweetheart?" Clay asked.

The youngest of the brood looked at him and nodded. Charley didn't speak much.

"Come on," he said. "I'll get you some."

The child awkwardly stood and ran to the kitchen, sippy cup in hand.

Nick rolled her eyes in a direction no one could see. This was him being demonstrative, trying to prove she was neglecting the children in favor of her career. She hadn't. She wasn't. She never would. She continued pacing.

The phone on her hip rang, and she retreated to the bedroom. The number on the Caller ID was unfamiliar, but local.

"This is Captain Brooks," she said.

"Nick, this is Dora at the C.O. Fred is really sick. I just

sent him to the hospital. We need you."

"On my way," she said. "Standby."

Nick waved at her husband, kissed her children on the way out the door, the put the phone back to her ear.

"Dora? Still there?"

"Yes, ma'am."

"What have we got?"

"Another water kill, as you probably know."

Nick nodded, although no one could see her as she climbed insider her office-issued Taurus. Any other captain would've had an SUV, but she was a woman. She knew better than to complain.

"10-4," Nick said. "Any details?"

"I did a preliminary examination on the way to the harbor," Dora said. "Same as the last two. He's been in the water about two days. Gym clothes. His ankles chained to a cinder block, so obviously ligature marks on lower extremities."

"What else?" Nick turned onto the highway, headed for the Coroner's Office.

"Weird thing. It's unlike the others. He had several areas of skin removed. I can't tell how deep until Dr. DeMarco gets here and does the autopsy."

"Tattoos," Nick said.

"That's what I thought, too," Dora answered. "The removals weren't really surgical. I mean, it doesn't look like a trained clinician did them."

Nick filed that away.

"Go on."

"Nothing else, really, at least not until autopsy."

"OK. What's up with Fred?"

She heard Dora sigh.

"He was vomiting on the boat and really struggling out at the scene, but he held it together. Once we got here, he collapsed. I had no choice but to call an ambulance."

"Crap."

Since having children, Nick had taught herself not to curse like the average cop, but it was hard. The situation warranted profanity, but she was trying not to give in.

"I know. Look, Nick, I didn't have a choice. He was unconscious and dehydrated on the floor in the fucking autopsy suite. I got a makeshift IV in him but what was I supposed to do?"

Nick was calm, but not pleased.

"You couldn't have taken him yourself?"

"And leave the body unattended? You know what that can cause in court. Not to mention that I hadn't sterilized my unit since I brought in this corpse, so God knows what I would've exposed him to."

Nick sighed again.

"You're right. I get it. Any media?" Although handling reporters was Leveque's problem, it was a question detectives had learned to ask. The new administration was so media-friendly it was just another factor in every case.

She was on the interstate now, only a few miles from her destination.

"One. In the woods by the office. She probably got it all."

"Fuck." Her parent filter was off now.

"I know," Dora said. "I know. But that's Leveque's job. Mine was to keep him alive."

"I get it. You did what you had to. Where's DeMarco?"

"On his way," Dora said.

"Why the fuck wasn't he there already?" Nick asked. "It's not like we couldn't have predicted this."

"I cannot advise, captain."

Dora had slipped into respecting-rank tone, which meant Nick had pushed farther than she wanted to.

"OK. I'll be there in 20," she said, and hung up.

She put her phone in the drink well and plugged it in. This was no time to risk losing phone power. Anything could matter. Everything mattered.

Headline: Third Victim of Serial Killer Pulled from Lake

Dateline: Mandeville, Louisiana

"As divers brought the body of the third victim of an apparent serial killer to Mandeville Harbor Sunday morning, the Sheriff's Office and Coroner's Inspectors hauled the body as gently as possible from a Search and Rescue watercraft to the SUV bearing the markings of the Parish's chief death investigator.

"Onlookers were contained by yellow 'Crime Scene' tape at a distance as Chief Detective Fred Walder pretended to load the corpse into the van, but it turned out Walder was actually concealing his own visual inspection of the body from reporters and onlookers.

"This reporter has obtained exclusive amateur video of the seasoned detective examining the body before it was loaded into the Coroner's vehicle, including particular attention to the victim's limbs."

Margaret leaned back from her computer and took off her glasses. It was, Clarence knew from experience, a contemplative pose and not a contrived one.

She paused.

"It's good, Clarence," she said. "But it's nothing but click bait. We can embed the link in your coverage and, yeah, it's exclusive, but what does it really mean?"

He shrugged.

"It means Blair and I were quick enough on our feet to get something no one else has, and that's what everyone wants us to do," he said, calmly.

She went back to reading.

"Although Walder didn't come close to the area where reporters were confined, Public Information Officer Jerod Leveque confirmed the subject is male and is likely the third victim of a serial killer working on the Northshore of Lake Pontchartrain in the last month."

Margaret sighed, pausing again.

"Is that true?" she asked.

"Essentially," he said.

She scoffed.

"Essentially?"

"Well, yes," Clarence said. "Leveque confirmed ... enough. Look, no one is calling this a serial killer yet, but what the fuck else is he? Three murders, three men, all found on Sunday mornings, all tipped off to law enforcement, all found in water – I mean, what the fuck?"

Blair sat beside him, silent for a change, content to let him fight the battle.

Margaret sighed again, leaned forward, and read aloud.

"Although a casual observer might assume a body found in Lake Pontchartrain only yards from the world's longest overwater bridge had ended up there from above, the Causeway Police Department declined to comment on the lack of damage to any of the northbound span's rails."

She looked at him again, this time over her lenses.

"True?"

"Absolutely," he said. "True and accurate and documented."

Margaret's gaze unsettled him, although he knew that wasn't her intent. She was thinking, probing, balancing getting a scoop with the ethics of journalism -- or the standards of journalism she had learned decades ago.

Her gaze darted between him and Blair. She sighed heavily again and said, "Do it. Run it. Air it. Get it up online ASAP."

Roxanne didn't usually work late on Sundays unless she had to - and today, she had to. Church work didn't stop for weekends, and although she had a week until the next service of worship to lead, she still had administrative and pastoral tasks to handle. Today, it had been the budget.

She sat at the outdated computer in her office, staring at the slagging offering figures as if she could raise them herself through prayer and sheer willpower. Before long, she realized she had been staring at them mindlessly. They weren't horrid. The church would survive. They could pay the rent and her. But could they grow? She just didn't know.

The phone rang, a rarity at 2 p.m. and, unfortunately, a rarity at this church entirely. Caught off-guard she let it ring three more times before she answered it.

"Metropolitan Community Church," she said. "This is Pastor Roxanne."

There was, at first, no response, but she could hear breathing.

"This is Pastor Roxanne," she said again. "Is everything OK?"

More breathing before, finally:

"Is this the gay church?" It was a man's voice, asking what was, for her, a common question.

"Well," she said, laughing affably and gently, and immediately regretting it. "This is the church that accepts and affirms LGBT people. We just celebrated our 48h anniversary, and I'd be more than happy to give you some literature and websites to visit."

"I don't want all that," he said.

She paused. As pastor of a church with a majority LGBT congregation, she was ultra-sensitive. People reached out blindly, sometimes, seeking comfort anonymously. Her pastoral instincts kicked in. Whoever this was, he was troubled.

"OK," she said. "How can I help?"

She heard a heavy sigh, then another.

"Is this strictly confidential?" he asked, finally.

"Of course," she said.

"Do you have caller ID?"

She almost laughed again. The church was in a rented space, hardly adequate for its needs, with a 10-year-old desktop computer and one step up from rotary phones.

"No, sir," she said. "We don't. I assure you, this conversation is strictly between us."

More silence. She watched the clock on the wall across from her desk as the caller pondered her word. Twenty seconds.

"Do you promise?" he asked. "Swear in the name of Jesus?"

It was her turn to pause.

"Well, I do promise, but swearing on Christ's name is a bit much," she said before adding, gently, "We don't have Caller ID and I assure you that even if we did, whatever you tell me stays between us."

He didn't pause this time, blurting out, "I know who the dead man is."

Roxanne paused. Three years of seminary and six years as a pastor hadn't prepared her for this. With the crime rate in New Orleans, "the dead man" could mean any number of people.

"I'm sorry," she said after a moment's hesitation. "Which dead man?

"The one in the lake," he said, almost angrily.

"I'm sorry," she said again, although she didn't really know why. She had seen something on the news about it before church this morning, but she didn't know details. Sadly, New Orleanians had become inured to such things. "I hadn't heard about that."

She heard him breathe again, deeply.

"This morning," he said. "We pulled another body. This one was in Lake Pontchartrain. The others have also been in the water."

"Ah, yes," she said, reaching into the recesses of recent memory to pull up news stories in her mind. "I'm so sorry. Were you close?"

"Yes, we were close!" he said, loudly and angrily, so loud that Roxanne pulled the phone an inch from her ear out of instinct. "We were lovers!"

"I understand," she said, although she was only beginning to. "I'm sorry for your loss."

This time his deep breath was punctuated with sobbing.

"You loved him," she said.

"Yes," he said, through broken breaths. "I did. But he loved her more." He broke down in sobs.

Roxanne was in full pastor mode by now.

"Who?" she asked.

"His wife, dammit. He loved his wife more than me."

This relationship dynamic was not new to her, but the circumstances were. She had counseled married men and women who were in the frightening process of coming out, and had once been married to a man herself, but this was unique. She needed to learn more but this call was tenuous and she knew that if she lost him she might never get him back.

"I'm very sorry," she said. "I know how much that must have hurt you."

She waited. He sobbed some more.

"Do you know who killed him?"

It was a bold question, but she was flying blind. Segues were hard to concoct.

"If I knew who killed him, don't you think I'd have arrested the son of a bitch by now!"

She paused, her head instinctively tilting to the side. It was the second implied reference to working in law enforcement, but she didn't dare broach that subject.

Closeted cops were not unusual. She had some in her congregation, and she desperately wished she could reach one of them right now for guidance without violating this caller's privacy.

"I understand," she said. "What about his wife? Does she know what has happened?"

"She's dead, too," he said. "They just haven't found her yet."

"Wow," she said, calmly, and for lack of anything else to offer. "How can we help you? We are here to help."

In response, he hung up. Roxanne sighed, put her head in her hands, and prayed.

Simon DeMarco swiped his pass card and the first set of glass doors slid open. When they closed, he swiped again, and he was inside the morgue area of the Coroner's Office. He walked down the hall, whistling calmly, and turned into the second autopsy suite. Dora and Captain Brooks from the Sheriff's Office were inside, seated, quiet, brooding.

"Good afternoon, ladies," he said, affably. "What've we got?"

Dora looked downward at her notes. Nick glowered at him and he caught her gaze.

"Problem?" he asked.

"Only that this was a predictable crime and we've been waiting an hour for you to get here," she said, evenly but probably more forcefully than she intended.

He met her eyes, cocked one eyebrow and tilted his head to one side. Then he turned back to Dora.

"So what've we got?"

"White male victim, approximate age 40-45. Found underwater, ankles chained to a cinderblock. Blunt force trauma to the head and face, particularly around the eyes. Multiple fractures are apparent in the head and face. Ligature marks around the ankles. Victim has three

37

excision wounds, probably postmortem, possibly tattoos – one on the left arm and one on each leg. COD pending autopsy."

When she finished, she looked up. Nick was still glaring at the pathologist, who was choosing to be oblivious.

"OK," he said. "Let's get started."

"Don't you want to know where Fred is?" Nick asked.

He looked at her and smiled slightly.

"I don't question the Sheriff's Office in who they decide to send to autopsies," he said. "I'd prefer you not question the Coroner's Office on the timing of them."

Dora took in a breath, quickly. Nick stood her ground.

"Fair enough," she said. "But you might want to know that I'm here because Major Walder is in the hospital. He collapsed right here."

He raised his eyebrow again.

"Has the room been cleaned since then?" he asked.

"No, doctor," Dora said. "The body was already here so it seemed like we'd be spreading contamination one way or another."

He sighed. She was right. If they moved the body to clean the room, they'd be spreading more of the fetid rot of the corpse and wasting a lot of time, too. He could only hope whatever Fred was carrying wasn't airborne and hadn't contaminated the body.

"True enough," he said. "So, again, let's get started. Y'all staying in here or watching through the glass?"

"I'm staying," Nick said.

"Me, too, doctor," said Dora.

"Then suit up," he said. "We're taking no chances with this one, either way."

Roxanne paced through her office and into the conference room, around the table and back again, asking herself over and over aloud, "Who can I call? Who can I call?"

The conversation with her anonymous caller an hour earlier had been unsettling, to say the least. As trained clergy, she knew that anything said to her was confidential unless the penitent admitted suicidal or homicidal intent. In such cases she was obligated to act. This was different. The caller had admitted neither. He had admitted being a closet homosexual in love with a married man. He had admitted to having a broken heart and to withholding information – but what that information was, she didn't know.

"What do I know?" she asked herself aloud. "The victim was a man married to a woman and having a love affair with a closeted man, possibly married himself." She paused. "That's it. That's all I know."

No, it wasn't.

"The caller, the lover, is most likely a cop. He had said 'we' pulled the body from the lake and 'don't you think *I* would've arrested him by now.' Was there more?"

She replayed the call in her head. The most important part leapt to mind.

"He knows the victim's wife has been killed but hasn't reported that," she said. "Who can I call?"

Desperate to help, to keep confidentiality, but also to let police know there had been another murder, Roxy was conflicted more than she had ever been.

She had to do something. She went to the ancient computer on her desk, called up TheNewOrleansAdvocate. com and waited impatiently while it loaded. The top story was about this case. She read it, quickly. Then she opened Google and searched for the Mandeville Police Department. She dialed the number.

"Mandeville Police, this is Marlene."

It was a woman's voice with an unusual accent which, without even realizing it, Roxy found somewhat comforting.

"I just got a call about the murder that might be helpful to you," she said, realizing as she spoke that she hadn't thought this through. She was suddenly nervous. "Could I speak to an ... um ... a detective?"

"Hold on, ma'am," the officer said. "Let me see who's available."

Marlene was not used to working Sundays. She was a secretary, not a cop, but because she had the badge and uniform and the title "officer," and because all hands were on-deck right now, she was helping handle the phones. It was a Sheriff's Office case, technically, but this body had landed in Mandeville's front yard. She pushed the intercom button to the back of the Police Department building, a structure too old and too small to accommodate them. Two months until retirement, she didn't care.

"I have a caller with information about the 30," she said into the speaker. "Call is parked on line 10. Anyone here?"

"Rooney here," said a voice back to her. "I'll take it."

She didn't respond, but watched the blinking light on the phone until it became steady, indicating it had been picked up.

"This is Officer Rooney," he said into the phone. "Who am I speaking to?"

Roxanne breathed deeply.

"I'd rather not identify myself," she said. "But I will if I have to."

"Well," he said, "I'd prefer that you do, but go ahead."

"Are you a detective?"

"No ma'am," he said. "Not yet. But from your lips to God's ears. I'm a patrol officer. I was at the harbor this morning when they brought in the body. What is it you want to report?"

Roxanne paused. He sounded affable enough, approachable, even.

"I got an anonymous call a few minutes ago," she said.

"The caller said he knows who the victim is."

"Great," Rooney said. "Who is he?"

"He didn't say."

Rooney sighed and rolled his eyes. Another one of these. There had been a few like this already.

"Well, ma'am, what did he say?"

"He said the victim's wife has been murdered, too, but no one has found her yet."

Rooney was caught up short. He hadn't expected that.

"Wow," he said calmly, without meaning to. It was unlike him and ran against his training and instincts to express even that level of emotion. "Interesting. Did he say where we could find her?"

"No," Roxy said. "When I tried to ask questions like that, he hung up on me."

"I see," he said. "Did he leave a name? Number? Do you have Caller ID?"

"No," she said. "No. And no."

Then her stomach churned. She had called a law enforcement agency. The call would be automatically traced.

"Do you have Caller ID?" she asked.

"Yes, ma'am. We have to. Someone will be in touch, so would you like to go ahead and leave your name?"

Now, her stomach churned and her blood pressure dropped at the same time.

"My name is Roxanne," she said. "Roxanne Clement. I'm a pastor."

"Yes, ma'am," he said. "Thanks for calling. I'll make sure a detective calls you back ASAP."

She hung up, reached for the trash can by her desk and heaved into it. This wasn't how things were supposed to happen.

Chapter Three

"911, where is your emergency?' Amanda answered.

"Well ... I'm not sure there is one and I feel kind of foolish for calling ...."

"That's OK. What's going on, ma'am?"

"We haven't seen our neighbors in a few days and when we went to go to church this morning and drove by their house, there was a stack of newspapers on their porch. With everything going on, I just figure anything like that might matter."

"Yes, ma'am. What's the address?

"71429 Middle River Road, Slidell."

"Yes, ma'am. Do you know the family name?"

"Prescott. Phil and Mary. They have two children, too. Teenagers."

"And when did you last see them?"

"Um ... Friday before last, I think."

Amanda entered the caller's phone number into the system.

"We'll send someone out to check on them. What's your name, ma'am?"

There was silence as the caller hung up. Seconds later, Amanda's entry appeared on the dispatcher's computer screen.

"Central, 2317. 10-65?"

Sean was tired. Only two hours into the night shift this Sunday, his third night shift in a row, usually a quiet time, he had been overwhelmed with calls. Most of them had been bullshit. Paranoia was high as the third murder in three weeks and an unsolved serial killing was afoot and the news media were all over St. Tammany at full throttle. He didn't blame them, but it was making everyone jittery, if not paranoid. He didn't want to deal with any more nonsense.

"10-71," he said, indicating that he was ready for a call in his assigned zone.

"Welfare check, 71429 Middle River Road, called in by a neighbor."

He sighed in relief. This should be an easy one. Most welfare checks turned out to be phone lines disconnected for non-payment, families on vacation, or inattentive neighbors who didn't notice an absence until it was weeks old. It took him less than ten minutes to arrive, during which time he did his best not to think about the case the higher-ups were working, hogging, keeping way too much to themselves. It wasn't that he thought he necessarily had anything to add, but with so much secrecy lately, he worried that his coworkers were starting to lose faith in the new sheriff already. Solving crimes takes collaboration. Collaboration requires sharing information. That wasn't happening very much lately. He tried to convince himself there were reasons for the secrecy that he just didn't know.

He pulled into the driveway of a large house backed up to the river. Properties like these were commonplace in St. Tammany, an enclave of white flight and upper middle-class wealth that made the Parish itself rich – not just statistically, but visibly.

"2317 Central, I'm 10-97." He was on the scene.

"10-4."

He parked his unit in the driveway, headlights on, and scoped out the house. It was a two-story Acadian. In the dark he couldn't say for certain, but it looked relatively new and very large. There was no garage, which he found odd for a home this big; in the driveway were three vehicles – a new-ish dual-axle pickup truck, a BMW convertible and a Toyota sedan. He immediately knew this kind of family: father/breadwinner, mother/trophy, semi-spoiled teens. He exited his vehicle and approached the front door. The porch light was off, but even in the dark he could see at least a week's worth of newspapers in a pile on the doormat.

As he stepped onto the broad front porch, a stench caught him. It was the smell of death, of rotting flesh. He had smelled it before, more than once.

"2317, Central. You might want to get a supervisor rolling, and a detective in this direction, and the lab."

He was overstepping, he knew. It was a supervisor's job to call investigators and the Crime Lab, but he held back, at least, on calling for the Coroner. His lieutenant was paying attention, for a change.

"2301, Central. Belay that 2317, what do you have?"

Sean tried the door and found it open. He pushed it gently and recoiled from the smell.

"2301, you'd better 10-19 my location," he said into the shoulder mic, and then, he thought, "if you were even listening to know where I am. Then you won't belay anything."

With supervisors on the way, Sean returned to his vehicle and waited, despite his professional inclination to be a detective and his personal curiosity to explore the house. Anticipating what was ahead, he popped his trunk and took visual inventory. There were masks, gloves, and evidence bags. He knew they would be necessary, even before the Crime Lab unit arrived. A house didn't smell like that without death inside, and a lot of it. He was glad he had left the door open. It might help with the odor.

Impatience and youthful impulse got the best of him. He was determined to be right. He had to be. He donned a pair of gloves and a mask and headed back towards the front door. He knew better than to touch anything, but he also knew better than to wait 20 or 30 minutes for rank who had been sitting at the office drinking coffee, and who may or may not have read the day shift's briefing reports.

With his foot, he gently pushed the door open farther than what he had a few minutes ago. Even through the mask, he could sense the stench again. This time, though, he didn't recoil. He steeled himself and took a gingerly step inside. The floorboard creaked and he almost chuckled. It was a horror movie soundtrack, and a bad one. There was no hockey-masked machete killer inside. He knew that. Killers didn't sit around and wait for days, and based on the smell alone – not to mention the stack of Advocate newspapers at the door – he knew it had, in fact, been days. Still, it was both amusing and disquieting. As a 20-something, he couldn't help being a product of his generation and the cultural fluff of horror films.

He stepped again. No creaking this time. He reached, finally, for his flashlight, realizing he should've done it well before now, and grabbed it in his left hand as he was trained to do, keeping his right free for his weapon. He half-chuckled to himself again. This was silly, prowling through a dark crime scene when overhead lighting was readily available. He reached towards the wall and felt for a light switch. His fingers found it through his glove and he switched it on. He almost wished he hadn't.

Seeing it, even though expected, made it somehow worse. Even through the paper mask, the scene and the smell combined to push him backwards to the front porch and down the stairs, and he landed on his back on the sidewalk. He was embarrassed, humiliated. As a veteran cop, with seven years under his belt, he should've been able to withstand it. He was thankful no one had seen his reaction, but he wasn't done. He rolled to his side, lifted his mask, and retched into the grass. Now, he would have to tell. In theory, there might've been evidence there. The lab would have to know his own vomit was on the crime

46

scene.

His head reeled and spun, his vision blurred. He thought back to academy training. Preserve the scene. Call superiors and the lab. Keep your composure.

He had done all of that, but he had also been human. He also saw his future ahead of him, and that did not involve being a puking bitch. It involved being a homicide detective, maybe even rank or chief detective someday. He forced himself to his feet, still slightly dizzy, and made his way again to the front door. The smell was better; opening the door had helped. The four minutes on his back had helped more. Turning on the overhead light and the ceiling fan had helped. He stepped inside, carefully, and surveilled the room. The light was still on. So, he realized, was the television across from the sofa, although its volume had been lowered to almost nothing.

On the sofa, a woman was prone, arms across her chest, her brain in a scatter plot across the cushions. She had been sleeping when the killer struck, he thought. Behind her, near the staircase, two more bodies lay. Sean approached, carefully, using his flashlight as much upon his feet as on the corpses ahead of him, not as much to see but to avoid stepping in evidence. The male, maybe 16 or 17, was on his back, with what appeared to be a bullet wound in his chest. The girl, a bit younger, was on top of him, face-down. Her fatal wound appeared to be in the back of her head.

They all appeared to have been dead for days, starting to bloat and rigor long gone. That accounted for the smell. A fly buzzed by his face. He heard the sound of an air conditioner running but the house was hotter than it should be.

He had seen enough, and retreated to the porch. His rank appeared not long after.

His lieutenant had been his friend for years, his supervisor for only a few months. They had a calm rapport, but he was surprised the sergeant or corporal hadn't come first. Perhaps they were too far away.

"What've you got, Sean?"

"Three fatalities. All GSWs. One adult female, two teens, one male and one female. I didn't venture past the initial scene in the front room. There may be more."

"Christ," he said, grabbing his radio. "2301 Central."

"10-71."

"Better go ahead and call the Lab and a 7000 unit – whatever detective is on duty and his supervisor. At least three victims with gunshot wounds, all 10-7. Call the Coroner, too, and make major notifications."

"10-4. What signal?"

Signals were the numeric codes used to describe any call. Dispatchers needed them for the computer records and whoever would be dispatched needed them to know what he or she was coming to.

The lieutenant thought for a second; Sean listened intently, staring him in the eye.

"29U, for now," he said.

Sean had briefly considered in his haste that it was a 30/29S – a murder-suicide. Family annihilations happened. But even if there was one suicide in there, the rest were clearly 30s – straight-up murder. Calling it a 29U – unclassified death – was misleading and disingenuous, but it would also slow down the gossip and, maybe, the time it took media to find out what was going on. It was the only reason he could think why his lieutenant would've chosen that signal. It wouldn't matter, really. They would change it in official reports.

If it was a murder-suicide, a family annihilation, there had to be another body in there – unless he was in the bayou that flowed behind the house, and that seemed unlikely, atypical. Sean hadn't seen a weapon, so if the father of the family were responsible and had offed himself, too, he was almost certainly somewhere else in that house, probably with a gun in his hand and a bullet in his head. If he wasn't, the situation was even worse – a triple murder with a missing would-be victim or an unknown suspect at large, and three rotting corpses. It was the last thing any of them needed.

Karly walked into her office as she usually did lately – surly, tense, and generally angry. She put down her purse and laptop, slammed the door, then sat at her desk. There was a lot to do, too much, and she wasn't happy about being at work at 10 p.m. on a Sunday night when she had already spent much of the day there. When a major crime happened, though, almost everyone with the rank of captain or above went to work. It was part of the job, and it was a job she had been doing for more than 30 years.

She grabbed her desk phone and pressed the intercom button for the shift supervisor.

"My office, now," she said, without waiting for a reply to the tone. "I need a report."

Brandi was at the door in seconds.

"Hi," she said. "What do you need, captain?"

As the lieutenant on duty in this division, she was responsible.

"Sit down," Karly said. Brandi did. "Do you have the 911 call recordings?"

"In progress," Brandi said.

"Good. I need them on my desk before your shift ends. Radio logs?

"Same."

"Good. What's the mood on your shift?"

"They're kind of fucked-up, captain. With the 'O' serial killings and now a triple murder, everyone is freaked out."

"I know all about 'O,'" Karly said. "I was here this morning and talked to him myself, remember?"

It sounded more snarky than she intended but at the moment, she didn't care. Brandi said nothing.

"What's call volume like?"

"High. People are on-edge. They're calling about everything. Anything. A car backfires and our phones ring off the hook."

Karly started to answer and then realized what Brandi had said.

"You said this is a triple 30," she said. "My page said 29U. Who changed the signal?"

"Officially, nobody," Brandi replied. "The logs still say 29U. But we all know that we don't do notifications or call detective supervisors if it's really unclassified. You're not the only one with experience and instincts, captain."

Karly recoiled a bit, her expression perturbed and her posture defensive.

"Sorry," Brandi said. "I didn't mean that how it sounded. I just meant –"

"I know what you meant," Karly said, forcing herself to deescalate. "Go back to your station and get me those recordings. I said by 0600, but sooner would be better. I need to hear them for myself."

"10-4, ma'am."

Karly put her elbows on her desk and rested her chin in her hands, staring at nothing, lost in thought.

In her decades of law enforcement work, all of it in 911/dispatch and most of it in St. Tammany Parish, she had worked plenty of homicides from this end of the radio and phone. She had listened to tapes, read reports, even taken calls herself about a wide variety of mayhem and carnage. She'd seen the Parish change from mostly rural with a few suburban enclaves to sprawling housing developments and fewer and fewer rural areas. Through it all, as the population surged from 50,000 to nearly a quarter million, the murder rate had remained almost unchanged, with only 10-15 homicides a year. Most of them were domestic, many were drug-related, almost none of them random. And unless some madman had been working quietly and without detection, they'd never had a serial killer before.

She sighed. She was using words in her head that almost no one was saying out loud: "serial killer." Even tonight, no one was saying "triple murder." It was as if they were all in denial, the cops themselves, refusing to admit what was right in front of them. She wasn't a detective, but even she knew that was a dangerous way to think. It would only slow down the investigation, making them think twice about every step – or even to step in the wrong direction. It wasn't good, and there wasn't a damn thing she could do about it.

"What the fuck is going on?" she asked aloud to her empty office. "And where the hell is the sheriff?"

Leveque pulled up on the scene to find a dozen Sheriff's Office vehicles, some of the marked units with their roof lights still swirling. The result was a dizzying cascade of red and blue that made it difficult to see as he navigated on foot between the vehicles towards the house. When he finally had his bearings he stopped and gave his eyes a moment to adjust, as he grabbed his radio.

"1120, Central, I'm 10-97," he said, and immediately wished he hadn't. Some reporters had scanners that could access their high-tech radio system, and they knew "1120" was him. They also knew the public information officer didn't respond to unclassified deaths. "Fuck," he said under his breath.

"10-4, 1120," Central replied.

Checking in on a crime scene was important, not only to let other deputies know where you were but for legal purposes. Everyone who set foot on a crime scene was logged into the computer and on a paper log at the scene. Any of them could be called as witnesses. Public information officers at some agencies – and even one of his predecessors – had been subpoenaed in murder cases before, and in change-of-venue motion hearings. Who would know better than the PIO that an accused killer had gotten excessive press coverage, too much to find an unbiased jury? Still, he should've used the phone to check in with Central and signed only the paper log on-scene. Too late now, he thought, as his cell phone rang.

He recognized the number, and cursed again. He thought for a second, then sent the call to voicemail. Clarence would have to wait.

Deputies had set up crime scene tape around the entire house, using their vehicles to anchor it. As a former detective, he knew not to cross the tape without authorization. Despite his rank and position, he still couldn't just barge into what he imagined was a bloody crime scene. The more feet on the scene, the easier for someone to track evidence in – or out – or leave a bloody footprint that could be mistaken for evidence. He didn't see Fred, but that wasn't surprising; in the dark, with the strobes, and amid all the activity, he might not notice the chief detective. Fred would find him when he was ready and his job, right now, was to be still and wait.

He surveilled the scene. Nice house, three vehicles, the stack of newspapers on the porch, a few potted plants that looked like they were dying from lack of care. A breeze – rare on an August night in Louisiana – cooled him for a moment, but carried with it a familiar stench.

"Christ," he said. "How long have they been dead?"

"Neighbor said they last saw them nine days ago, captain."

He startled, not having realized he had spoken aloud. In the dark beside him, a uniformed deputy stood solemnly. He seemed to be the only one on the scene without something in his hands – a clipboard, flashlight, something.

"Deputy Sean Baxter," the deputy said, extending his hand. Jerod shook it.

"You were the first on-scene," Jerod said.

"Yessir."

"Fill me in," Jerod said, withdrawing a small notebook from his pocket.

"Worst thing I've ever seen," Sean said.

Jerod looked up at him, impatience in his gaze.

"Sorry," Sean said. "Three victims that I saw. Adult female was apparently sleeping on the sofa. Head shot. Teen boy on his back at the bottom of the stairs, shot in the chest. Teen girl lying on top of him, shot in the back."

"OK. What else?"

Before Sean could answer, a figure approached rapidly, flashlight in his left hand aimed directly at them. Within seconds, they both recognized it was not a man, but a woman. Captain Nicole Brooks.

"For future reference," she said to Sean brusquely, "you should be debriefed by a detective before talking to the media."

"I'm not media, Nick," Jerod said, just as brusquely. "And it's not Baxter's fault."

She turned to him and set her steely eyes on his.

"Maybe not," she said. "But close enough." Without averting her eyes, she said, "Baxter, start over."

"Yes, ma'am," he said. "Three bodies. Adult female. Apparently shot in the head while sleeping on the sofa. Two teens. Male, chest shot, on his back at the bottom of the stairs. Female, shot in the back of the head, on top of the boy. Looks like the boy came running when he heard his mom get shot, and the killer took him down. Girl came next, turned and tried to run."

"Thanks for the speculation," she said. "What else?"

"A stack of newspapers on the door mat –"

"How many?"

"Ma'am?"

"How many newspapers?"

"I didn't stop to count them, captain, but I'd guess about seven."

"Close," she said. "Go on."

"TV was on, but volume turned very low. No lights on in the lower part of the house. Air conditioner was on – I heard it – but it was hot as hell in there. Severe stench."

"What else?"

"Well, ma'am, as I already told the Crime Lab investigator, the smell knocked me down and I ... I, um ... I vomited in the grass at the bottom of the porch." He pointed as he spoke.

"OK," she said. "Understandable. Inside, did you go past the front room?"

"No, ma'am."

"Were there any lights on the second floor when you arrived?"

"I didn't notice, captain." That was an odd question.

"Where's the r/p?"

"Reporting person is MIA," he said. "Gone on arrival."

"Did Central get her name?" Nick asked.

"I don't know, ma'am, and I didn't ask. I was waiting for instructions. I didn't want to get in the way of your team."

She looked at him very directly, staring upward at his lanky frame to make eye contact in the glow of her flashlight. She assessed him briefly. He was young, late 20s, she thought. His tone was earnest, and she didn't want to beat his spirit down. Some might've said he didn't have enough observations, or that he was a pussy for losing his dinner in the yard. Those were her initial thoughts, too, but she stifled them.

"OK," she said. "I'll track that down. Find another uniform and tell them I said to look for other neighbors. Thank you, Baxter. That's all."

"Yes ma'am." He departed quickly.

She turned to Jerod and sighed.

"Sorry about that," she said. "Lots going on today."

"It's cool," he said. "I've had days with too many crime scenes, too. This is one of them."

"Yeah," she said. "I know. Sorry again."

"Media are already calling me, Nick."

"I'm not surprised, since you went 10-97 on the air," she replied.

His face flushed. Nick was sharp – both her mind and her tongue. He took a deep breath, suppressing both his pique and his embarrassment.

"What can I tell them?"

"Tell them they can fuck off," she said. "After what they did this morning, I have no reason to help them."

"Wait, what?"

"You haven't seen the story they posted online tonight?"

"No."

"Grab your smart phone and take a look, cowboy. Then do a better job minding your cattle."

She turned and walked off, and he saw her talk to the Crime Lab tech, then heard a motor rev as the flood light atop the vehicle began to extend. It was going to be a long night. As he reached for his phone, he heard Nick yell at some deputies to turn off their "goddamned overheads." As he opened the news app, the flare of red-and-blues was replaced by the more helpful glow of a flood light. He read Clarence's story, watched the video, and his jaw dropped. Then he looked at the time: 9:55 p.m. In five minutes, half the viewers in greater New Orleans were going to see that.

Roxanne's usual bedtime was 10, especially after a long Sunday, but tonight sleep was the last thing on her mind. She felt like she had screwed up bigtime by losing the caller, but she also felt trapped between conflicting obligations. The ethics of her profession said she kept things confidential. The ethics of simply being a human said she shouldn't be silent. No detective had called yet, so she hoped they had blown off her call as the rantings

55

of a lunatic and would ignore her. But that wouldn't really solve her problem, the conundrum of conflicting obligations.

She had practically paced a hole in the living room of her Uptown New Orleans duplex. Even the cat had grown weary of watching her move about and had taken a spot on the back of the sofa to watch his mistress without having to turn his head.

Roxanne glanced at the clock on the wall, an old fashioned one with a gold pendulum. It was almost 10 o'clock, she realized. Her habits said to sleep, but she suddenly realized she could be missing something simple. Maybe this had all been resolved by now and that's why no detective had called her. She threw herself on the sofa, grabbed the remote and turned on the TV to local news.

It wasn't good.

"Our top story tonight is the recovery of yet a third body from waters on the Northshore, but first we have some breaking news from Slidell. Bureau Chief Blair Francingues is live." The screen shifted to a somewhat grainy picture of Blair, mic in hand. "Blair, what's going on?"

"Mike, we're on the scene of what may be another murder in St. Tammany Parish, and it's made more mysterious by what we don't know. Earlier tonight, deputies were dispatched to the scene of a 29U – that's what cops call an unclassified death." The picture shifted to the scene, as red-and-blues went dark and a bright white light took over from the top of a Crime Lab van. "A scene like this isn't usually newsworthy, Mike, since a 29U can turn out to be anything, but what grabbed our interest was the volume of emergency personnel who started responding.

"Because we're the only station with a Northshore bureau, our scanners can pick up radio signals from law enforcement in the area. What we heard after the initial call were more than a dozen deputies responding. Then detectives – including Deputy Chief Detective Nicole Brooks – along with the Crime Lab and Public Information

Officer Jerod Leveque, who we also saw earlier today in Mandeville. Just now, not one but two Coroner's Office vehicles have arrived."

The shot went back to Blair's face, with the Coroner's units pulling in behind her.

"We're being kept far from the crime scene, but as you can see over my shoulder, whatever happened here is a really big deal. No one at the Sheriff's Office is answering our calls over here – not even Public Information Officer Jerod Leveque – but we're the only news agency here so we're going to stick it out until we have some answers for our viewers. Back to you in the studio."

"Thanks, Blair," the anchor resumed. "Keep us posted. Our other top story tonight, also from Blair and our partners at the Advocate, was the discovery of yet another murder victim this morning. Blair filed this report earlier."

The screen cut to the daylight scene at the Harbor, and Blair's face popped up again. She looked the same but with a different outfit, Roxanne realized, wondering how reporters could manage to look fresh and alert no matter what time it was.

"A man's body was pulled from Lake Pontchartrain just a few miles from the Mandeville Harbor this morning, the third such victim in as many weeks," she said into the camera, then the view cut to shots of Sheriff's Office boats coming to the dock. "Sources tell us law enforcement was tipped off by a phone call this morning. Interestingly, all three bodies in the recent spree have been found in waterways on Sunday mornings, and all three were men." The screen went to shots of the previous two crime scenes.

"Officials are still very tight-lipped about the case, and despite the similarities, authorities are not yet calling these crimes the work of a serial killer," she said.

They cut to an interview with Jerod, who spouted the usual platitudes with his usual charm.

"What we did find today was Chief Detective Fred Walder examining the victim's body before placing it in the Coroner's Office vehicle," Blair said. "Major Walder seemed to pay particular attention to the victim's limbs." The screen cut to amateur video. "While it's not at all unusual for an investigator to do a thorough examination of a murder victim, it is unusual for it to be conducted on the crime scene – or, in this case, the scene of recovery – especially outdoors and in the rain.

"Making this case even stranger, although the body was recovered several miles from shore and adjacent to the Lake Pontchartrain Causeway, there was no visible damage to the bridge railing above." Cut to footage of the bridge, shot from a car and focused on the rail of the northbound span. "Leveque gave only vague answers this morning, and said reporters – and the public – would have to wait until after an autopsy is complete and investigators have more time to review the case. The answers have been the same on each of these cases. As always, we'll stay on top of it. Reporting from the Northshore, I'm Blair Francingues."

Roxanne grabbed the remote and clicked off the TV. This was worse than she thought.

"Leveque! Hey, Leveque!" The voice was unfamiliar and Jerod barely heard it over the hum of the Lab van's humming light and the Mobile Command Center's generator. He looked up and squinted in the darkness. "Better get over here." He still didn't know who it was, but he could tell the direction from which it came and walked swiftly in that direction. Behind him, Crime Lab investigators were entering the crime scene dressed in biohazard suits.

He walked towards the perimeter, his eyes scanning what seemed like a growing crowd and his vision blurred by stress and fatigue like he had never experienced before.

"Leveque. Over here."

Straight ahead was another uniform. He rubbed his eyes and refocused, recognizing, finally, a familiar face.

He approached quickly, but the uniformed deputy didn't leave his post at the perimeter. Jerod neared and extended his hand.

"I'm Captain Leveque," he said.

"I know, sir," he said. "We went to the LSU Academy together."

"Holy crap," Leveque said. "Tommy. Where've you been?

"Livingston Parish S.O.," Carmichael said. "I just started here last week. Sorry I haven't had time to say hello until now. Not to be short with you, Captain, but I called you because I wanted to be sure you knew there were reporters here."

"Yeah," Jerod said. "Where?"

"Over there." Tommy pointed to the end of the driveway.

Jerod squinted. Blair and her photographer were packing up gear and putting it in a van bearing the station logo.

"What the fuck," Jerod said under his breath. "That bitch did a live shot without talking to me."

Tommy said nothing as Jerod reached for his phone. He glanced at the screen and cursed again. Clarence had called once, which he knew. Blair had called three times and texted twice. He had been so wrapped up in the scene he hadn't even realized. He had been doing detective work instead of media work. There was nothing to be done now. He was still livid about their subterfuge this morning, although he could've prevented it if he'd known what Fred was doing. Tonight was unavoidably his own fault. He needed to talk to the major.

He turned to walk back to the center of activity, paused to wave perfunctorily to his old classmate, and suddenly realized how completely exhausted he was. He was barely functional and clearly unfocused. Fortunately, the news cycle was done for the day and he was off the hook for at least five hours. He needed sleep. He did not need to talk to another reporter – especially Blair or Clarence – until he had calmed down and had time to think. He didn't even need to go home; the cushion in the Command Center would do if necessary, and it wouldn't have been the first time. But he needed to see Fred first.

He approached the house again. Nick was standing on the front lawn, watching the comings and goings of lab techs. He went and stood beside her. Her demeanor was different than before. She was still focused – she was always focused – but she no longer seemed hostile. She was just watching, observing, thinking. He said nothing for a moment. She broke the silence.

"You need sleep," she said, without looking at him.

"Yes," he said. "So do you."

"You've been up since dawn," she said. "I haven't. Go home. Just please come back early. I'm going to need you."

"You know it, ma'am," he said.

She turned and looked at him.

"Ma'am?" she said, chuckling.

"I'm beat," he said. "I don't have the energy to be insolent."

She chuckled.

"We have the same rank," she said. "And we're friends."

"Yeah," he said. "Both true. Speaking of rank, where's Fred?"

She looked at him again, eyebrow cocked.

"I was wondering when you'd ask."

"So what's the answer?"

"He collapsed at the morgue today. He's in the hospital."

"Christ," he said. "Why didn't you tell anyone?"

"No reason to cause any more crisis of confidence," she said. There was a pregnant pause. "So where's the sheriff?"

He sighed, deeply.

"I'd tell you if I could. I'll tell you when I can. Maybe tomorrow."

She didn't look at him, didn't respond. She accepted the answer more graciously than either of them would've expected.

Jerod turned and walked away. He got in his car and drove home – just a few miles away. Terry was in bed already, which he expected. They hadn't seen each other in days, it seemed. He set the alarm, set his phone to sleep until 4:30 a.m., brushed his teeth, and crawled into bed as quietly as he could.

George Stewart King rolled over in bed and moaned. The pain of withdrawal was unbearable, worse than he would've imagined, and in the haze of detox he felt a twinge of sympathy for the addicts in his jail. He shouldn't be here. He was a sheriff, for God's sake. It wasn't his fault.

He wondered how many of them said that.

It was dark, but not dark enough. The IV in his arm was uncomfortable enough. The periodic visit from nurses taking his vitals in what seemed like 10-minute intervals was exhausting. He just wanted to sleep. He wanted to get better. He wanted to get clean and get back to work. His top staff was good, but how good he just didn't know yet. He'd been sheriff for less than 14 months and many of them were untested, hired on instinct and experience. They hadn't yet been through a major crisis together.

Worse, still, he hadn't named a chief deputy yet. He had chosen not to structure his agency with deputy chiefs, as his predecessors had. He had appointed majors and had weekly meetings with them. Without him, the Sheriff's Office was being governed by committee, if at all. There was no single person in charge.

He felt his blood pressure rise and heartbeat increase. This was his stress, his job, his calling. And he had ruined it with addiction.

It had started with the wreck. An 18-wheeler rear-ended his car – his personal car, a high-end SUV – while he and his wife were on their way home from their anniversary dinner, celebrating 32 years together. It was an unusually long marriage in general, and virtually unprecedented for cops. He had suffered four broken bones and a ruptured spleen. His wife had suffered a shattered skull, and was dead on the scene. His physical pain was unreal, the loss of his wife unbearable. Regimented pain meds led to addiction. Addiction led to pharmacy shopping. Forged prescriptions led to a federal investigation, a quiet confrontation in the Coroner's Office, and remand to a recovery facility. They said he'd be here for 90 days. He was four weeks in. It seemed like too long and not enough. He just wanted to go home, go back to work. He had no idea what was going on and it was killing him. All he could do, instead, was accept the treatment and try to rest. He rolled over and cried himself to sleep.

Chapter Four

Jerod woke before his alarm. He climbed from bed, brushed his teeth again, and went to the kitchen. He reached for the coffee to prep the pot and realized it was already done.

God bless Terry, he thought, and just pushed the start button. While the coffee brewed, he went to the garage, occupied not by vehicles but by exercise gear. He had no mind for weights this morning, but grabbed the jump rope. He stretched, briefly, then started. It wasn't so much muscle-building as aerobic, but that's what he needed: blood to his brain. He needed his brain. Dear God, he needed his thoughts straight. He needed to focus, think on his feet, balance his cop instincts with his media training. He thought he was being quiet.

He had lost count of his jumps when the door from the house to the garage opened.   He stopped jumping.

"Hey," Jerod said. "I'm sorry if I disturbed you."

Terry only smiled.

"It's OK. I'm happy to see you. Coffee's done. I didn't know if you'd need your uniform today, but I pressed it and the brass is on. You also have suits ready."

"You're amazing," he said. "Really amazing."

Terry just smiled.

"How was church?"

"It was great, as always," Terry said. "Attendance was a little down, but Roxanne's sermon was super. So was the music."

"I miss it," Jerod said. "I hope she understands."

"We haven't really talked," Terry said. "But when we do, I'll let her know. She doesn't watch the news, you know. She probably doesn't know who you are – professionally, I mean."

"I'm OK with that," Jerod said, smiling. "I go for you, not her."

"I know," he said. "And I'm glad, although I hope you find other reasons, too. Whatever happens with all this, I'm here for you. I told you I would be. Finish your workout." Then he went back inside.

Roxanne woke with a start. She couldn't remember what, exactly, she had dreamed, but it wasn't pleasant. She grabbed her phone; there were no missed calls. She sighed and rolled back onto her fluffy pillow. It had been a gift from an ex. The woman was long gone but she still loved the pillow.

She still wasn't sure what to do. She wanted to do what was RIGHT, but what was that? It was hard to tell. She laid in bed and prayed for discernment. There was a TV in her bedroom but she knew there would be nothing new at this hour, and she relied on an antenna instead of cable so she never knew what signals she would even receive. There would be a newspaper on her doorstep soon, but she also knew it wouldn't have anything she hadn't already seen.

She hated that she was at the mercy of the media in getting information. She had to act, but she didn't know how. It was Monday, her day off, but she had long known that as a pastor, there was really no such thing. No one needed a day off more than pastors, she thought – except, maybe, for police officers – but no matter what day was designated as a day of rest, it just didn't happen. People had needs. Congregants and even perfect strangers were distressed, addicted, afflicted, depressed.   She couldn't stop. She wouldn't.

Then, suddenly, she had an idea, and knew what to do – sort of.

John Douglas barely knew who he was. He hardly knew who anyone was. He had started drinking at noon on Sunday and hadn't stopped until he passed out. When he woke on the floor at midnight he moved to the sofa. When he woke up there at 2 a.m., he moved to his bed. He woke again at 5 a.m., still dressed, redolent, and half-drunk.

When he was able to focus he looked at his phone. 21 missed calls. That wasn't good.

"Fuck," he said. He reached for the eye drops on the nightstand and administered one to each eyeball. Then he blinked vigorously and tried to center himself. It didn't work. Instead, his anxiety only increased.

Whatever was on his phone could wait a few minutes. He went to the kitchen and threw a small plastic cup into the Keurig, realizing as he did that his hands were shaking, badly. He shoved the cup into the machine with more force than necessary, then headed for the shower, tossing his uniform and brass into the hamper on the way; he'd deal with separating them later.

Jerod arrived back at the Slidell crime scene a little before 6 a.m. As expected, the Crime Lab vans were still present and Crime Scene tape still surrounded the house. A scene like that would require hours, if not days, to thoroughly scan for evidence.

As he also expected, Blair's report from the previous night had brought out her competition. What had been a single TV news crew was now five – including one from Mississippi. God only knew how many print reporters were there, too. They flocked together, some holding coffee cups and some cigarettes. He shook his head as he drove past them and as close to the house as he could get. A uniformed deputy lifted the Crime Scene tape to let him in.

He didn't use his radio this time; that had caused enough trouble. He grabbed his cell and called the non-emergency number for the 911 Call Center.

"Radio Room."

"Hey, Karly," he said. "Good morning."

"Morning, Jerod," she said. "You 10-97 again?"

"Yes, ma'am," he said.

"Thank God," she said. "Our phones have been blowing up all night. Apparently every reporter in the world watched Blair's report last night and they're racing to play catch-up. We didn't tell them anything."

"You probably don't know anything to tell them," he said. "I'm not sure I do, either."

She sighed.

"You're probably right. But, listen, I have some thoughts. I know you're really busy but when you have time please come by my office or give me a call."

"Absolutely will do," he said, and he meant it. Although he was newer to the agency, a recent hire by Sheriff King, his background as an investigator with a local police department meant he had interfaced with Karly and her staff innumerable times in the last decade. They were friends. Others might have dismissed her suggestions. She worked in a closed room and had probably never been on a crime scene in her entire career. To some street cops, that invalidated her insights; to Jerod, it made them more valuable, more detached, based solely on information at-hand. "I'll call you later today," he said. "If I forget, you call me."

"10-4," she said. "Be safe – and please, please, catch this motherfucker."

He let out a dramatic breath.

"Believe me," he said. "We're trying our best."

"I know," she said. "I've got you logged on the scene again. Talk to you later."

He went to the door of the house, the closest he'd gotten to these deaths. He hesitated, stifling his instincts, before entering. In his moment of reluctance, he was saved as Sgt. Yolanda King walked out. Tall, physically strong and smart, he loved working with her. She saw him and stopped.

"This one is crazy," she said, looking him in the eye.

"The scene or the killer?" he asked.

"Both," she said. "What do you need?"

"Whatever you can tell me."

"On or off the record?"

"Either," he said. "Both."

She hesitated. He could see her reluctance in her eyes.

"Tell me," he said. "Where's Nick?"

"She left about an hour ago," Yolanda said. "She said she was getting her kids off to school and then she'll be back."

"Good," Jerod said. "So ... what've we got?"

"Three dead in the living room. Mom and two teens. Nothing else. It sucks."

"Damn right, it does," he said. "Father? Weapon?"

"Negative on both," she said. "He's either in the wind or he's also a victim and we haven't found him yet."

Jerod's mind swirled.

"Or maybe we have found him and just don't recognize the connection," he said.

"Huh?"

"Yesterday was O's third victim, right? We don't have IDs on any of them. What if this family is connected to victim number two. They were last seen 10 days ago, right?"

"Right," she said.

"That victim appeared in the water two days later. No ID. No m/p report."

"No missing person report doesn't mean …."

He let the silence hang between them for a moment, until she got it.

"Call Nick," he said. "Someone needs to go to the morgue now. Any family pics in there?"

"Yeah," she said, and then her jaw dropped again as his idea of what had happened sunk in further.

"Bring me one," he said. "And anything else you've got I can carry. I'll go. Media can keep dangling. They're almost to the point of making up shit anyway."

Dr. Leslie Wilson was confounded. Three years of medical school at Tulane, 25 years of practice in emergency medicine – including 11 in New Orleans, the murder capital of the country – and she had never seen anything like this. Dora and Dr. DeMarco sat across from her at the conference table in her large office. She had looked over Dora's report from the scene, now held in her right hand, and at DeMarco's quickly written autopsy report in her left.

"What. The. Fuck." She said.

DeMarco's look was steely. Dora was demure.

"Could you be more specific, doctor?" DeMarco said.

Dora looked up, clutching her coffee cup in both hands, and said nothing.

The Coroner took off her glasses, which seemed to always rest on the end of her nose, and rubbed her eyes.

"Let's just talk," she said, and put both reports on her desk. "Cause of death?"

"Which victim?" DeMarco asked.

"Let's start with the most recent one," she said.

"You have my report," he said.

"I do," she replied. "And I've read it. Now. Let's just … talk."

He hesitated for a moment.

"COD is multiple blunt force trauma to the head and neck," he said.

"That's cause of death," Leslie said. "What's manner of death?"

"Well, clearly, it's homicide," he replied.

Leslie glanced up at him.

"Nothing is 'clear' in this whole case," she said. "There's nothing fucking clear about any of it."

Leslie cursed like a sailor, often. Dora sunk back in the chair and tried to be invisible.

"Look," Leslie said. "I've got to meet with the Sheriff's Office, the D.A. and the goddamned media in a few hours. What the hell am I telling them?"

DeMarco looked at her, still smug.

"Cause of death was blunt force trauma with an unknown instrument. Manner of death is homicide. What else do you want from me?"

Leslie let out a breath and continued staring out the window. The fountain behind her was a small distraction, and one she didn't welcome. She hadn't been coroner when this building had been constructed and it wasn't what she would've done anyway. Among other things, there was no reason for a pond and a fountain outside the fucking Coroner's Office.

"Speculate," she said, without turning from the window.

"About? The weapon?" DeMarco asked.

"Yes," she said.

"The breaks – or shattered bone, actually – seemed to be caused by a cylindrical object. Something hard, obviously."

This time, he wasn't being snarky. He was grasping at straws. He was a scientist, not a cop.

"Keep going," Leslie said. "Something solid or hollow?"

"I can't tell for certain but I'd guess hollow."

"Good," she said. "Size? Something large like a

baseball bat or small like a crow bar?"

"Probably something in-between," he said. "Maybe a pipe. Probably about an inch and a quarter in circumference."

"Ligature marks?"

"Only on this morning's victim – I mean yesterday's morning's victim – and only around his ankles. He had been weighted-down with a cinderblock. At least that's what I heard from the cops. I haven't examined the weight."

"Restraint was ...?"

"Chain," DeMarco said. "Link. Large links. They left bruises and indentations around his ankles, so the shape is relatively clear, especially thanks to the bloating of the body."

"I assume you photographed those marks," Leslie said.

"Yes," he said.

"Toxicology?"

"Pending."

"DNA?"

"Samples have been drawn. They'll be sent to the State Lab later this morning."

The Coroner paused, out of questions for the moment.

"Dora," Leslie said. "What do you have to offer?"

"Well, ma'am, he had three areas on his extremities that had been excised," she said. "They weren't medical and the obvious guess is that the victim had identifiable tattoos."

"Sheriff's Office people know that?"

"Yes, ma'am," Dora said.

"Then why the fuck don't I?" she asked, her eyes back on DeMarco.

"Sorry, Doctor," he said. "I failed to mention that part."

"Fail," she said. "That's a great word. Is there anything else you've failed to tell me?"

"No, ma'am."

"Is there any way to tell what those excised tattoos were?"

"No, ma'am."

"Fine," she said. "Get out."

They both stood.

"Not you, Dora. I have more questions for you."

Dora sat down slowly. DeMarco's eyes widened, but he said nothing as he made for the door.

"Simon," Dr. Wilson called after him.

He turned to look back at her.

"Don't fail again," she said. "Don't start the autopsies on the three new murder victims until a detective is here, but don't even think about leaving until they're done. Are the bodies here yet?"

"No," he said.

"Fine," she said. "Let me know when they arrive. And Simon... when you know something, I need to know it, too."

"Yes, ma'am."

"Otherwise," she said, "I can start doing the autopsies myself and save a shit ton of taxpayer dollars. I want an update on the autopsies from this morning ASAP. Don't make me ask. Now, get out."

Roxanne's clericals – banded collar, casual pants, white collar – were crisply ironed and starched. For Sunday worship she usually wore red or green ones. She had selected the black ones today, thinking it added credibility. She sat in her Saturn sedan in the parking lot of the Mandeville Police Department and took a deep breath. It was time to be strong. She had prayed the entire way across the Causeway, and now she felt ready. To practice being firm, she slammed the door of her car when she got out. Then she walked briskly through the single glass door.

The lobby was stark. To her left was a door with no windows, clearly locked and boasting a large sign, "AUTHORIZED PERSONNEL ONLY. VISITORS MUST BE ACCOMPANIED BEYOND THIS POINT." Past the door, a thick glass window shielded a lone dispatcher from whoever walked in. A slot to pass documents was at the bottom and a grated metal circle was embedded in the center. No one was there, so she turned to the outer wall, to her right. A bulletin board held notices of Neighborhood Watch meetings, a canned food drive, hurricane preparedness, and a few community events. She realized what was missing: There was not a single "Wanted" poster. Suburban life, she thought. It was supposed to be safe.

She heard a noise and turned to see a woman walk into the dispatch room. She was older, probably near 60, Roxanne thought. She had short blonde hair and was wearing not only a uniform but a windbreaker with "Police" across the back. Roxanne moved to the window.

"Good morning," she said.

The woman turned abruptly but didn't lose her composure.

"Oh, hi," she said. "I mean, good morning. Sorry. We don't have a lot of walk-ins. How can I help you?"

She had an accent Roxanne couldn't quite place, but it was endearing and she felt at ease.

"My name is Roxanne Clement," she said. "Is Officer Rooney here?"

"I'll check," the woman said, "but he isn't scheduled today."

Roxanne's face fell a little, but she rallied and smiled again.

"Hmmm," she said. "Well, it's kind of important."

"OK, hon," she said. "Let me see."

She turned to her phone – and a console of technology Roxanne didn't recognize. She couldn't hear clearly through the glass, but the woman picked up the phone and spoke a few words, then looked up at her. Roxanne smiled, which was hard to do at 6:30 a.m.

The woman turned back to her computer – or whatever that was – and Roxanne focused on the television mounted on the wall. She couldn't hear, but captioning was on. A somber-looking anchor pitched to a reporter in the field – or what they liked to pretend was a live broadcast – and Blair was on the screen again, talking about the murders. It was why Roxanne was here, but she couldn't watch. She went back to the bulletin board. There was a Lakefront cleanup coming up, and although two months away, a city-wide free Halloween party. So, this was suburbia.

"Excuse me, Ms. Clement?"

The woman was at the window. Roxanne turned and smiled, expectantly, eyebrows raised.

"Officer Rooney is here," she said. "He'll be out in a few minutes."

"Awesome," Roxanne said. "Thanks so much."

She wondered at – but was not offended by – the woman's choice to call her "Ms." Instead of "Reverend" or "Pastor." Some people, regardless of their religious backgrounds, couldn't grasp the concept of female clergy. It bothered some of her colleagues; Roxanne just took it as part of the job and not worth fretting about.

About a minute later, the door opened and a man she took to be Officer Rooney walked into the lobby. She turned to him, expecting to be invited to the back. Instead, he let the door close and approached her. He was tall, handsome, and she guessed him to be in his mid-30s, with dark hair only beginning to gray around the temples. His uniform was crisp, but his demeanor was a balance of a policeman's notorious hardness and the eyes of someone who was genuinely compassionate.

He was sizing her up as she was him. He was taken aback by her collar, but tried not to let it show. Her name had sounded familiar to him, but he hadn't placed it yet.

"Good morning," he said, extending his hand. "I'm Officer Rooney. And forgive me, but is it 'Reverend' Clement?"

She smiled.

"Yes," she said. "Reverend or pastor, whichever makes you most comfortable."

"I'm here to make you comfortable, ma'am," he said affably. "Please, have a seat." He gestured to a narrow bench that lined the wall. They both sat. "What can we do for you?"

Her mood fell. She had assumed he would remember talking with her the previous afternoon, but suddenly realized how foolish that was. The previous day he had worked a murder scene, and had probably taken dozens of calls from people just like herself – tipsters who knew less than they thought they did.

"I called yesterday afternoon," she said. "I got a call at my church around 2 o'clock from someone who said he had information about the murder. Well, actually he DID have some information. But he also said your victim's wife had also been killed and you just hadn't found her yet."

His eyes lit up as he remembered the conversation.

"Yes," he said. "I remember now. I'm sorry. A lot happened yesterday."

"It's OK," she said, and she meant it. "I do understand."

"So what brings you in today?"

The question caused her to literally stiffen her back. It surprised her. Why wouldn't she be here? He spotted her discomfort.

"I mean ... did a detective call you to make an appointment?"

"No," she said, "and that's exactly why I'm here. I didn't think it could wait. I asked for you because you're the only person I know here. I mean – not that I know you – but, I know your name and you were very kind on the phone and –"

His brain swirled a little. It was frustrating being a cop in an age where everyone thought cases were solved in an hour's time with four commercial breaks, and where victims and witnesses lost all concept of time. It was hard to be annoyed with someone wearing a priest's collar, though. It didn't occur to him that she had thought of that, too.

"Well, reverend, I did pass on your message to the detectives but we got so many calls yesterday ...."

"I understand," she said. "But since he told me there's another dead body literally rotting in someone's house right now, I thought you might prioritize my information." She smiled as innocently as she could.

Rooney realized he was disarmed not only by her clerical collar but by her charm. She was pretty, he thought. Green eyes, red hair that looked natural, and just a smattering of freckles across her nose.

"Well," he said, "I think all the detectives are out right now, but if you'd like to wait...."

"Why don't you take my statement?" she asked. "I remember you told me you hope to be a detective yourself soon, so I'm sure you know what you're doing."

That disarmed him even more. He didn't even remember having said that.

"Well," he said. "I suppose I could, given the circumstances. It would really be better if you'd come back later, though."

She made her eyes sad.

"Really? I live in New Orleans, so that would be really inconvenient. And I have a meeting at church tonight." The last part was a lie.

He took a deep breath – not quite a sigh – and stood up.

"OK," he said. "Please follow me."

They walked to the door and he waved at the woman inside the glass enclosure – who, Roxanne just realized, had been watching them the whole time. The door buzzed open and she followed him down a long corridor.

"I'm not a detective, so I don't have an office," he said as they walked. "We'll have to do this in the squad room."

They turned a corner and walked into another stark room, much larger than the lobby. Narrow desks and built-in seats lined one wall, with a Breathalyzer machine at one of them. All had a built-in handcuff for restraining suspects, and she hoped she wouldn't be in one of those. A large table occupied the center of the room, and one other officer sat at it, typing slowly on a laptop. Chris motioned for her to take a seat on the opposite side and sat down next to her, turning his chair sideways to face her. She turned hers, as well, wanting to keep eye contact.

"OK," he said. "My notes from your call last night are in the detectives' tip file, so would you mind repeating it?"

"Sure," she said. "I was working in my office after our church service and the phone rang."

"What time was it?"

"Around 2 p.m., I think. We don't have Caller ID and I was so flustered I didn't note the exact time."

"OK. What did he say?"

"Well, first he asked if he had called 'the gay church.'"

"The what?"

"Actually, I get that question a lot. Our church was founded almost 50 years ago specifically to do outreach to the LGBT community," she said. "Most of our members are gay, so it's a common question. Lots of people call us 'the gay church.' I always respond that we're a CHRISTIAN church that welcomes and affirms LGBT people."

She paused and realized he had stopped taking notes.

"What's wrong?" she asked.

"I've just never heard of that," he said.

"That's not surprising, really," she said. "You probably don't have a lot of LGBT friends."

"Actually, I have a few," he said.

She thought for a moment that she might've offended him. She realized that perhaps she had stereotyped the suburbs. Perhaps these folks, too, resented being thought of as intolerant.

"I'm sorry if I offended you," she said. "Most of us in the LGBT community have a negative stereotype of police. We haven't always been treated well."

He frowned.

"You're a lesbian?"

She almost giggled.

"Yes," she said.

"Sorry," he said. "It's just – you're just telling me a lot of things I didn't know. And I don't mean any offense, but you don't look like a lesbian."

This time she did giggle. Some would've found it offensive. To Roxanne, it was another opportunity to knock down stereotypes.

"Yeah, I've heard that before, too," she said.

Chris literally shook it off.

"OK. So, anyway. After you confirmed for him that he had called the 'gay church,' what did he say?"

"Well, he said he knew who the victim in the harbor is, but couldn't tell me. He told me they had been lovers, but that he – the victim – loved his wife more. And he told me the wife was also dead somewhere."

Chris jotted it all down.

"Did you try to get him to tell you his name? Her name? Where her body is?"

"Well, yes," she said. "Of course. I didn't ask it so directly, but I did try to probe a little bit. He dodged every question. And when I asked if he knew who the killer is, he said – and this is almost a quote – 'Of course not. If I knew, don't you think I'd have arrested him by now?'"

That was her moment. The denouement of the story.

She looked up to see his reaction. It seemed to take a minute for him to understand, and he glanced up from his note pad, finally.

"The caller was a cop?" he asked, incredulous.

She paused for effect.

"That's how it sounded to me," she said, gently. "Doesn't it sound that way to you?"

John started to wake up again. He was still disoriented, but this time he was uncomfortable, too. It wasn't just the throbbing headache he had self-induced with over-drinking on Sunday, but something else was causing him pain. He struggled into consciousness and realized he was on his bathroom floor. The shower was running, the room was filled with steam, and he was still wearing his boxers and one sock.

"Dammit," he said, wondering how long he had been there. He peeled off what was left of his clothing and climbed in the shower. The water was too hot – maybe all hot – and he screamed as he braved the burn and reached through it to turn it off. Then he slid down the wall into the tub and laid his head against the wall.

He couldn't stay like this. Someone would wonder where he was and why he wasn't at work like the rest of them undoubtedly were. More to the point, he simply couldn't stay like this. He had to get up and be human again. He had to face the day and whatever horrors awaited – whether internal or external, time would tell. That was something he had learned in the Program, during his brief participation. He hadn't stayed long. Neither did Donna after he started drinking again. When she hacked into his email and read about 10 months' worth of personal emails while he was passed-out drunk one weekend, she left, quietly. She had left his secret email account open on the computer and had said nothing else. It was enough. He understood.

He hadn't understood how she'd found out, and he

didn't understand at all what had happened later – what was happening now. He also couldn't believe that what he was thinking could actually be true. He had descended into more despair, depression, and bourbon. His inability to understand is what had drawn him to the harbor yesterday. It's what had led him here, again, to the bathroom floor.

Jerod walked into the lobby of the Coroner's Office with an evidence bag in his hand. It wasn't sealed, so it wasn't official. It was a caddy of convenience.

At the glass-enclosed reception desk, a middle-aged woman sat, busily shuffling papers and files. She looked up when she saw him at the counter, but didn't say anything, as if trying to place his face. It took only a moment; before Jerod could identify himself she stood up and saw the badge clipped to his belt.

"Oh, Captain Leveque," she said. "Good morning. Who are you here to see?"

"Dr. Wilson. DeMarco. Dora. Christian, if he's still alive. Whoever," he said. "But I need to see whoever it is, quickly."

Her eyes widened.

"OK," she said. "If I could get you to sign in" – she pointed at a binder on the exterior of her glass confinement – "I'll see who's available."

His gaze was icy. He resented the hell out of having to sign in, but he did it, his grip on the pen so hard that he realized he was probably creating indentions four pages deep. It was procedure, he thought. It was not her fault.

Name, agency, here to see, time in …. When he finished, he threw the black ballpoint back on the counter and looked up. She was on the phone, but looking straight at him.

"Dr. Wilson will see you," she said. "I'll come escort you to her office."

He started to tell her that he knew the way to the

fucking Coroner's office, but realized that security in this building was so tight – tighter than his own office – he would need her to swipe her ID to open magnetic locks. He was surprised you didn't need one of those key cards to flush the urinals.

She emerged from her perch and led him down a short hall, past the restrooms and into a large classroom with rows of desks and a low stage. To the right was the door to the inner sanctum. Jerod resented that, too, but it wasn't this coroner's fault. Her predecessor had designed this building – before going to prison – and had made it so his very large office was as difficult as possible to access. The receptionist swiped her card and opened the door, then closed it after he went in.

To his left, 30 feet away in this palatial and political enclave, Dr. Wilson sat at her desk. Behind her, a large window looked out on a manmade pond with a floating fountain in it. Jerod hated extravagance, especially on the public dime. He took a deep breath and reminded himself that Dr. Wilson did, too.

As he approached her desk, she rose – a sign of respect not all elected officials would offer to someone who was essentially subordinate, he thought. Politicians treated voters with respect, but for some reason cops weren't considered voters in their minds.

"Good morning," he said, his voice deep from lack of sleep and his tone respectful.

"Good morning, Captain," she said. "They said this was urgent, so I can only assume it's about the 'O' murders. Please, sit down."

He seated himself in a wingback across from her desk – the chair itself another symbol of her predecessor's opulence.

"Dr. Wilson," he said. "I have an idea. A theory, really. I haven't even talked to my superiors about it because I'd like to confirm that it's even possible first."

She studied him for a moment, both as a physician and

a woman. About 5'10", she thought. Maybe 185 pounds. Low body fat. Fit, but not over-muscled. Olive skin that reflected his southwest European heritage. Black hair. It was a damn shame he was gay, she thought.

Jerod waited in the silence. He knew from her reputation and from experience that one did not speak aggressively to Dr. Wilson. One might not choose to speak at all, unless spoken to. He wasn't intimidated by her, but he was on a mission and he wasn't going to ruin it with a personality conflict.

"Go ahead," she said finally.

"May I speak confidentially?" he asked.

"Go ahead," she said again, more emphatically. She hated repeating herself.

"You're aware, of course, of the three murders attributed to the killer who calls himself 'O,' and I know you're aware of the triple murder we discovered last night," he said.

She looked at him with a mixture of condescension and curiosity.

"Of course," she said.

"Ma'am, what if they're related?"

She paused, took off her glasses, and swiveled in her chair to look at that damned fountain. He hated talking to someone's back, but as an investigator he was trained to know that some people listened better without eye contact. She was one of them.

"What are you thinking?" she asked.

"Ma'am, we can't find the father, the man of the house, from last night's killing. I mean, not last night's killing, since they were probably dead for nine days. Last night's discovery."

She spun in her chair to face him again.

"I'm not a cop," she said. "Is that unusual in a family annihilation?"

"Yes, ma'am, it is. But what if that's not what it was?"

She cocked her head, her glasses still in her hand. Her eyes told him to continue.

"Ma'am, none of the 'O' victims has been identified. There aren't even any missing persons reports. What if the killer is obliterating the victims' families at the same time so it takes us longer to ID them? Or for some other reason we don't know yet?"

"That's interesting," she said, with a lilt in her voice that he found discomfiting. She seemed more interested in the mystery itself than in the lives lost, the dead bodies in her morgue. "How can we pursue this theory, Captain?"

"Well, ma'am, I've brought some family photos from last night's crime scene. Could we try to match them to the second 'O' victim?"

"Match photos? How? The 'O' victims' faces are almost gone from the fucking fish, not to mention being underwater in the summer heat for two or three days."

"Well, maybe the faces will tell the tale," he said. "But maybe there will be something else. Clothing he wore in the photo. Jewelry."

She nodded, digesting his thoughts.

"I like this," she said. "I really like it."

She hit the speakerphone button on her desk device and dialed three digits.

"Yes, Doctor?"

"Tell DeMarco and Dora to appear in my office ASAP."

"Dr. Wilson, Dr. DeMarco is in autopsy with last night's victims right now."

"He'd better not be," Leslie said. "He was supposed to tell me when they arrived. Anyone from the S.O. here?"

"Yes, ma'am, but it's a detective I don't know. I didn't get his name."

Leslie sighed.

"OK. Get Dora in here with whatever she has, and page DeMarco to get in here as soon as he's done. It shouldn't take him long. Those bodies were so bloated he could dissect them with a tongue depressor."

Leslie hung up with the push of a button.

"Good work, Jerod," she said. He hadn't even realized she knew his first name until now. "And now we wait."

"Yes, ma'am," he said.

"When we're alone," she said, "please don't call me 'doctor' or 'ma'am.' Use those in public or in front of staff. When we're alone," she said, "my name is Leslie."

Chapter Five

Monday, 7:30 a.m.

Chris Rooney scanned his report from his interview with Rev. Clement. It seemed complete. His aspiration to have a badge that said "detective" made it imperative that when he overstepped as a patrol officer he did it correctly and thoroughly.

Mandeville had a small Police Department. With a total staff of only about 60, half of them in patrol, he had a limited window of opportunity to advance. He had come to New Orleans from New York, then to Mandeville from New Orleans P.D., frustrated with mismanagement, high crime and low pay. Now, he was frustrated with the lack of openings. It was no one's fault. This was police work in a city of 10,000 people, but it was worth the trade-offs. Still, he was determined to prove himself, and show that his "big city" experience would be valuable to this place and these people.

He had totally overstepped by taking Rev. Clement's statement on his own. That wasn't OK. But on the other hand, he had shown initiative and had filled the gaps. What she had told him had the potential to be explosive, if it was true. He didn't doubt her, but he had to be cynical about the caller she reported. On the other hand, whoever had called her hadn't said, "I'm a cop and I know something." He had inadvertently implied that he was a cop. That changed it. It changed the tone. It changed everything. Someone trying to manipulate the situation for personal gain – or just for publicity – would've taken a more direct approach.

As a small agency, MPD didn't have a chief detective. It just had a chief. There was a lieutenant over detectives, but he wasn't around. He wasn't sure what to do.

He walked back to the lobby, where Marlene still sat at the reception desk.

"Hey there," he said.

"Hey, Chris," she said.

Marlene had emigrated from France more than 50 years ago and her English grammar was perfect, but an accent lingered. He liked her.

"Is the lieutenant here?"

"No, sir. Out at the Harbor," she said.

"Chief?"

"On his way," she said. "I have a stack of messages for him."

He chortled.

"I bet. Can I get first crack at him?"

"Sir?"

Five decades in America, 29 years at the MPD, and she still didn't get idioms.

"Can I see him before he gets tied up on the phone?"

She smiled.

"It's up to him, but I can let you know when he gets here – and let him know you want to see him."

"Thanks, doll," he said.

"Chris? Why are you here? You're off until Wednesday."

Rooney shrugged.

"I care too much," he said.

She smiled at him.

"I know," she said. "Me, too. That's why I love you."

When Marlene said that, she meant it, and he was glad. Chris went back to the holding area – a small space between the lobby and the squad room, closer to the Chief's office. It was empty. The on-duty officers were on patrol and the rank and detectives were all at the Harbor – although he couldn't figure why. Any decent evidence had been gathered on Sunday. He shrugged, though no one was there to see it. He was a patrol officer; they didn't include him on such things.

When the Chief walked in – unusually, he thought, through the front door – he heard him coming and stood up and stepped into the hallway. He would've stood out of respect whether he wanted to see him or not, but now he had extra motivation.

"Good morning, Chief," he said.

Tom looked at him, somewhat incredulous that he was even there. He was a hands-on chief; he knew his officers and he knew their schedules.

"Morning, Rooney," he said. "What're you doing here?"

"Just dedication, Chief," he said, and smiled. "I want to help find this guy."

"Good man," Tom said. "You need something?"

"Actually, I do, sir," Chris said. "Could I speak to you for a few minutes?"

Tom opened his office door and, without a word, indicated Chris should follow him. The officer did, and stood across from the Chief's desk while Tom picked up a stack of messages, sifted through them perfunctorily, and sat down.

"What's up?" Tom asked. "Sit down."

Chris sat across from his chief, a few sheets of paper in his hand.

"Chief," Chris said. "We have this witness. She called yesterday and walked in today. There were no dicks around so I took her statement. I hope that's OK."

Tom Richard had been chief only a few months, but he

had plenty of reason to respect his officers. He had been one of them, and had risen through the ranks over more than 20 years. He held out his hand and Rooney handed the documents across the desk.

Without a word, the chief read through Rooney's typed report, then looked up.

"Wow," he said.

"Yessir," Rooney said.

"We should call Fred," the chief said.

Chris was silently elated at Tom's use of the word "we."

Without another word, the chief picked up his phone and dialed the digits. Even from across the desk, Chris could hear the phone ring, six times, and then go to voicemail. Tom pulled the phone from his ear when the recorded voice said, "The voicemail box belonging to Fred Walder is full." The chief frowned and hung up the phone.

"That's weird," he said to Rooney. "You can always reach Fred."

Clarence was antsy. He stood at the perimeter of this crime scene wishing, as always, that he could be inside. His newspaper was "partnered" with Blair's TV station, so his conversation with colleagues from competing news outlets had to be limited. He was also bored, and he envied in some ways his chain-smoking colleagues; at least they had something to do with their hands. His notebook was in his pocket, two pens clipped to his shirt, and he had nothing to write.

Blair was just as bored. He kept an eye on her, both as a professional courtesy and as a friend. She was pretty, and little, a looming target for harassment. At the moment, she was leaning against a Crime Lab van and staring at her iPhone. She may have been texting sources and sending newsy tweets, or she may have been playing Words with Friends. From his vantage point, he couldn't see.

What he also couldn't see was the bloody crime scene,

and it was pissing him off. He hadn't seen Fred since Sunday morning and he hadn't seen Jerod Leveque, either. It was inexcusable. He had stories to write, videos to shoot, deadlines to make.

He sighed. It was only 8 a.m., or something close. He had no deadline for hours – although having something to at least tweet would be nice. Blair had done her first report in the 7 o'clock hour, and now she was free until her noon live shot. He was running out of patience.

He had walked around the house, respectful of the Crime Scene tape, and had found nothing worthy of reporting or shooting with his iPhone. This would not do. He didn't want to leave, in case Jerod showed up to brief them, but he also didn't want to waste a day standing only yards from a crime scene without anything to report. He was about to start pacing, and then realized he was ignoring a story that was at his fingertips. He walked as casually as he could to Blair, trying not to draw the attention of their competitors, and whispered as he did, "Come on."

Just as he had followed her lead yesterday at the harbor, she followed his without question. He walked ahead, towards the end of the driveway. A moment later, she followed. He found a tree – which was not difficult – and stepped behind it, out of view of the others. She met him there.

"What've you got?" he asked.

"Nada," she said. "And it's pissing me off. Where the fuck is Leveque?"

"Me, too, and good question," he said. "But we can't keep standing here waiting for an answer."

She nodded.

"Agreed."

"So let's go find a different angle," he said. "Then we'll come back and see what excuses they want to throw at us."

"I don't want to leave here," she said. "This is huge, and if it turns out to be related to the others, it's Emmy material."

"I don't want to go far," he said. "And I'll go by myself if you don't want to. But someone needs to talk to the neighbors."

She nodded.

"OK," she said. "I'll text my photographer. Let's go. You lead. People are scared of cameras."

Nick had left the crime scene in plenty of time to get home, get the kids ready and even make them breakfast. She had made sure the backseat was clear of any police-related items. She had tried to focus on her family, and had even turned the police radio off and the local music station on. She had driven slowly, intentionally trying to calm her mind.

None of it worked.

The 'O' murders hovered in her thoughts, but she was trying to focus on the Prescott family, the slaughter of three people whose bodies she had seen last night – another image that would never leave her memory, that kind of emotional impact being an occupational hazard she couldn't avoid. Whoever killed them knew what he was doing in destroying evidence – or in leaving little behind. Turning down the air conditioner to slow down decomposition might've had the desired effect. That the A/C had failed – or frozen – might've thrown off his effort, but then again, they still had no way of knowing when the machine had stopped working. They had to rely on other things.

The Crime Lab detectives had done a thorough sweep of the house and had collected what they could. Now, she had to wait for them to process it all. It could take days and for reasons she couldn't even articulate, she didn't feel like they had that much time.

Working against the killer had been the Prescott's

old-fashioned habit of having a newspaper delivered each day. Nick honestly didn't think people did that any more. Everyone she knew – herself included – got their news online and on their Smart Phones, where it was updated constantly. Thanks to their outdated choice of news delivery, however, they had that stack of newspapers on the doormat to help calculate how long they'd been dead before discovery. Nine days. Nine fucking days. How had no one noticed? How had no one reported them missing? THAT, she couldn't quite decipher.

Of course, the sense of community in this Parish had long ago evaporated. With the population boom of the last 30 years, neighbors were no longer long-known families and acquaintances, but immigrants from elsewhere in the state with little bond. The advent of the Internet and epidemic of video games also meant kids didn't play outside and people didn't form community connections like they had when she was growing up. Half the folks she knew didn't even know their neighbors' names, and no amount of Neighborhood Watch organizations or National Nights Out Against Crime block parties was going to change that. In some sense, it was anomalous that a neighbor had even noticed the Prescotts' stack of newspapers. And how had she noticed THAT, but not the weirdness of no vehicles coming or going for a full nine days. Nine. Fucking. Days. The murders were sad, but the circumstances were also indicative of a broader problem.

Nick shook her head, vigorously. She was a cop, not a social worker. "Focus," she said out loud to herself. "Just focus."

She got home in plenty time to get her kids to school, but found they were already gone. Clay had left a note on the counter: "Sweetheart, I know how busy you are so I told work I'd be in late and took the babies to school / day care. I hope everything is going well. Keep catching the bad guys! Love, Clay."

She was livid. He was being passive-aggressive again, letting her know that he could be "Mr. Mom" while she neglected their children. She crumpled the note and threw it in the trash can.

"Goddammit," she said out loud, since no one could hear her and she didn't curse in front of her kids. She took a deep breath. Maybe, just maybe, he was being sincere. Maybe he was respecting her work, not belittling it. Maybe he was being supportive. Either way – any way – she was pissed. She had left her very important job to do her even more important job as a mother, only to find she had wasted her time. Fuck him. Fuck it all. She wanted to throw something, but, as usual, Clay had cleaned the kitchen so thoroughly there was nothing left on the counter.

Roxanne left the Mandeville Police Department relatively satisfied. She had used both her clericals and her feminine wiles to make someone – no, not someone, Officer Chris Rooney – give her enough attention. No, not her. She shook her head. It wasn't about her. It was about the victims and catching the bad guy and trying to help the man who had called her. That's what she did. It's what she was about: helping.

The episode had taken a lot out of her. They didn't teach this in seminary, nor during internships, nor during her years as a hospice chaplain. She was flying blind, but leaning on prayer more heavily than ever.

She walked to her car, to the passenger side, and leaned her head on her arms against the roof, face down. "Dear God," she said aloud. "What do you need me to do?"

Before there was an answer from above, she heard footsteps on the gravel parking lot behind her. She turned. It was the woman from the dispatch room.

"Oh," she said. "Hi."

"I'm sorry," said Marlene. "I didn't mean to sneak up on you."

"It's OK. What's up?"

The older blonde woman looked around cautiously.

"There are cameras, so I need to have a reason for coming out here," she said. "Here, you left this in the lobby."

She handed Roxanne a white envelope with the Mandeville Police Department's logo and return address on it.

"But I didn't – "

"Yes, you did," said Marlene. "Take it. Thanks for coming in."

"But --."

"Please don't ask questions," Marlene said. "Rooney is new. He didn't disable the intercom system after you went back to the squad room and I heard what you said. I'm not supposed to get involved in investigations, but take it and read it."

Roxanne took the envelope, reluctantly.

"OK," she said. "Thank you. May I ask … your accent?"

"I'm French," she said. "I was a little girl when the Germans occupied my country. They seized our family home. I saw my mother raped by Nazi soldiers and my grandmother tortured to death in front of me. I've seen monsters before. We're dealing with one now. I've got to go. Read it. Be safe."

She turned and went back inside.

Roxanne got in her car and threw the envelope on the seat. She was glad the woman had told her there were cameras. She should've assumed as much, but this was all new to her. Still, she knew enough to know that she couldn't be seen on-camera reading the contents of that envelope. She put the car in reverse and accelerated more rapidly than usual, spinning in the gravel. She took a deep breath and tried again, easing out and turning right onto the highway. A short distance away was a shopping center, vacant at this hour on a Monday. She pulled in, parked, and opened the envelope.

On a plain piece of paper was written, "Go to Slidell.

Find Captain Brooks or Captain Leveque. They'll help you."

"But I'm not the one who needs help," Roxanne thought, and then put her car in drive with more force than was needed. "Come on, God!" she said aloud. "Lead me!"

Dora walked into the Coroner's private office and was surprised to see Leveque there.

"You wanted to see me, ma'am?"

"Come in and sit down, Dora," she said. "And stop with that 'ma'am' crap. You only need to call me that when I'm annoyed with you."

Dora sat in the wingback next to Leveque, her back straight, notebook in-hand.

"Jerod here has a theory and I'm hoping you can help prove it – or disprove it," Leslie said.

Jerod involuntarily cocked one eyebrow.

"Sure," Dora said. "What is it?"

Leslie gestured that Jerod should speak. She had that kind of charisma, that one simply followed her lead, waited for instructions.

"I think the victims from last night may be the family of one of the water murders," Jerod said.

Dora frowned.

"What makes you think that?"

"Timing," he said. "Nothing but timing. That, and the fact that we don't have this many murders here, so there's a better-than-average chance there's a connection."

"OK," she said quizzically, keeping her gaze on him.

Jerod reached in the evidence bag at his side – which Dora hadn't noticed before – and pulled out a handful of photographs.

"These are photographs of the missing father from the Prescott family," he said. "Could any of them possibly match one of the 'O' victims?"

Dora took them.

"I don't know," she said. "They were all a bit damaged and bloated."

"Don't just think about their faces," he said. "Look at clothes, jewelry, anything."

"OK," she said. "Give me a minute."

She took the stack of photos and went to the conference table across the room, spreading them out. Her eyes scanned them quickly and fluidly, but – Jerod could tell – thoroughly. She was a pro at this. She picked up one of them.

"Dr. Wilson," she said, still holding the photo and turning only slightly. "May I go get my file on this case?"

"Sure," Leslie said. "Just hurry, please."

Dora went out the side door, and Jerod watched as she walked swiftly through a small courtyard, swiped her entry card and went in the other door to the Inspectors' suite. He looked at Leslie.

"Who designed this crazy space?" he asked.

"My predecessor," she said. "He made this office as private as possible, so staff wouldn't even know when he was here – which he never was."

Jerod shook his head.

"Sad," he said. "And stupid."

"Both," she said. "Mostly stupid."

Dora appeared a moment later, re-entering by the door through which she had left, which surprised Jerod. He frowned, and Leslie saw it.

"Every employee has access to this office," she said. "No more secrets."

He cocked his head but said nothing, and watched as Dora returned to the conference table and opened her file over the line of photos.

"Dr. Wilson," she said, her voice in what Leslie thought of as "report mode."

"Yes?"

"This one … I mean … It's not at all conclusive… but…."

"What?"

"As you know, all three victims were found in gym clothes – sneakers, gym shorts, and T-shirts or tank tops."

"Yes."

She moved to the doctor's desk.

"Look. This brand of shorts – the logo is there," she pointed at the picture. "And the tank top, with a unique logo on it. It was an old shirt and the screen-printing had degraded in the water, but this pattern matches."

She threw another photo down next to the first.

"Look," she said.

Jerod jumped up and stood beside her. Even viewing the photos upside-down, the similarities were clear.

"Like I said, it's not conclusive."

"No," said Jerod. "But it's a hell of a coincidence."

Wilson stood also, studied the photos, and then turned. She gazed out the window at the fountain.

"So if victim number two is in those photos, and his family was killed the same day he was but just found …."

Silence loomed between them.

"Then we have two other families dead and we just haven't found them yet," Jerod said.

She swiveled back to face him and Dora, one eyebrow cocked.

"Damn this place," she said. "Just … dammit."

He didn't know what she meant and he wasn't ready to ask.

"Ma'am, I need to --."

"Go," she said. "Get back to work. Tell Nick. Find those people. Find this son of a bitch. Do it. Now."

Clarence knocked tentatively on the door of the house nearest the crime scene. It was a two-story Acadian, beautifully white with green shutters. A single Mercedes occupied the driveway. Blair and her photographer lingered at the property line on the street.

He hated doing this. He hated cold calls to average citizens. Politicians were fair game; normal folks should be off-limits. In this case, he had no choice. He heard only silence, and knocked again. A moment later, he heard footsteps. A woman answered the door. She was in her late 30s, perfectly groomed, wearing jeans and a smock stained with paint.

"Can I help you?" she said, politely but firmly.

"Yes, ma'am," he said, as submissively as his large frame allowed. "I'm with the Advocate and we're covering the incident that occurred next door."

Her gaze didn't falter. She said nothing.

"The Prescott family murder," he said, in case she didn't know.

Still, she said nothing.

"I'm wondering what your thoughts are and how you feel about a triple murder occurring so close to where you live."

"I didn't know them," she said.

"I see," he said, pen at the ready. "How long have you lived here?"

"Four years," she said.

"Do you know how long they've lived here?"

"No."

He made a mental note to check the Assessor's records online and find out.

"OK," he said. "Well, as a resident of this area, how does it make you feel to have such a horrible thing occur so close to where you live."

She didn't alter her gaze but said nothing for a moment.

"It's a terrible tragedy," she said evenly. "But I still feel safe. I have an alarm and a handgun. I'm sorry this happened, but it doesn't change my life."

Then she shut the door. Clarence turned around, descended the stairs and walked to Blair.

"Well?" she asked.

"Wow," he said, shaking his head. "Let's just try the neighbor on the other side."

They walked north, the three of them, no longer concerned with who saw. At least Clarence wasn't. He was too busy being dumbfounded at the callousness he had just witnessed.

About 50 yards away, past a pronounced tree line, they came to another driveway. This time Blair and her photographer followed him. It was a long driveway, gravel, with solar lights lining each side. It curved further to the north before ending at yet another large home, two-story, yellow. A porch lined the entire front, with steps in the center. There were no cars visible, and Clarence assumed the occupant's car was in the garage. Blair hung back a bit, but this time her photographer turned on the camera and aimed it at the front door, zooming as close as he could.

Clarence rang the bell and waited. He could hear movement inside, but it was slow. He tried to be patient. When the door finally opened, a frail woman greeted him, leaning against a walker. Her hair was short, straight and gray. He tried, but couldn't assess her age. She smiled, which he found odd.

"Good morning," he said. "I'm very sorry to bother you, but –"

"It's no problem, sweetie," she said. "Would you like to come in?"

He was taken aback. Living next door to a crime scene – and not just any crime scene, but a triple-murder – he would've expected caution. He demurred in spite of his journalistic instincts.

"Um … perhaps in a moment," he said. "I'm a reporter

with the Advocate and my friend over there" – he pointed at Blair – "is with the TV news. We're talking to folks in the area about the horrible murder that happened here to see how neighbors are reacting and what you can tell us about the Prescotts."

"Who?" she asked, waving and smiling at Blair.

"The Prescotts," he said. "The family next door. They've all been murdered."

Her face fell.

"Oh my goodness!" she said. "I had no idea! How awful."

He thought he saw tears in her eyes.

"You didn't know them?"

"No, sir," she said. "I've only lived here a short while and I don't get out much, as you can see." She indicated her walker.

"You never saw them?"

She shook her head.

"That's so sad," she said. "Do you know what happened?"

"No, ma'am, and so far we don't know if the police do, either."

She shook her head.

"Terrible," she said. "You know, I pray all the time for a better world, but I guess I need to pray even harder."

"Yes, ma'am," he said. "I pray a lot, too."

He didn't, but it was a harmless lie.

"May I get your name for my story? If you don't feel comfortable giving it, that's OK."

He was being nicer to her than he was to most witnesses he interviewed, and he realized it, deciding in an instant that it was OK to treat this lady with special care.

"Sure," she said. "I'm not afraid. My name is Hazel, but everyone calls me Zel."

"Thank you, ma'am," he said, writing it in his notebook.

"Your last name?"

"Martinez," she said.

"Thank you so much, Mrs. Martinez. Would it be OK if we come back if we have more questions?"

"Of course," she said. "I'm always happy for visitors."

He descended the stairs as Zel followed him, slowly, onto the porch.

"You be safe, young man," she said. "And keep praying."

"Yes, ma'am," he responded. "Thanks again."

He didn't turn around, and he found himself becoming strangely and atypically emotional. He shook it off.

"Holy crap," he said, as he reached Blair again.

"What?" she said.

"She didn't even know anything had happened next door," he said. "She didn't know the Prescotts. She's clearly disabled and doesn't get out much."

"Damn," Blair said. "This sidebar is a bust."

"Maybe," he said. "Maybe it is. Maybe for you."

Jerod drove faster than he should've back to the murder scene. He was cautious, as always, and he was also aware of his own level of fatigue. He was exhausted. They all were.

Another uniform lifted the tape for him and he drove closer to the house than he had before. He mostly ignored the media throng, but he noticed two interesting things: Clarence and Blair weren't there, and one of the other TV photographers was rolling and followed him as he drove past them. He didn't care. He was back in detective mode, and as much as he enjoyed his new job as PIO, he was a cop at heart. Nothing was going to change that. He jumped from his car, photos in-hand, and almost tripped as he did. He hoped the camera man hadn't caught that, but it didn't matter. Not really.

He walked fast, almost at a half-jog, to where another deputy was standing dutifully, clipboard at the ready, to log anyone who came and went.

"Where's Nick?" Jerod asked.

"Sir? Who?"

"Captain Brooks," he said. "Where is she?"

"She just got back," the deputy replied. "She's inside."

"Log me in again," Jerod directed, and bolted up the stairs and into the house. Then he froze. Instincts kicked-in again. He had to be still, slow, cautious. This was a major crime scene and he wouldn't be the one to mess up the investigation.

The bodies were gone now. Long gone, as he knew, already under DeMarco's scalpel – and maybe Leslie's, too, if she had gotten impatient. Blood – lots of it – stained the sofa and staircase. He didn't envy Sean having discovered this, nor the Coroner's Office staff who had to remove the bodies, nor even the Crime Lab detectives who were still on the scene collecting evidence. He was glad they were being so thorough, anything could matter.

His eyes adjusted to the interior light and he saw Nick across the room. There were glass doors there, opening onto a wooden deck that overlooked the river. She was on the other side of them, outside, talking to another detective. Even from this distance and through the morning glare on the glass, he could tell she was surly, in full cop mode.

For a moment, he pondered crossing the room to her, but without knowing if the floor had been swept for evidence, he wasn't going to risk it. He grabbed his phone and texted her, "Meet me in front?"

He watched her reaction as the phone vibrated in her hip pocket. She reached back without stopping her dialogue and silenced it.

Dammit, he thought. Come on, Nick. I need you.

He clutched the photos in his hand even tighter. He

dare not use his radio at this point. He squinted to see who she was talking to and realized it wasn't a detective. It was Moreau.

"What the hell is he doing here?" Jerod thought, and reached for his phone again.

This time, he dialed. Again, Nick reached into her pocket and silenced it. He dialed again. He saw frustration in her face, but she grabbed it, saw his name on the screen, and answered.

"What?" she answered. "I don't care what those vultures want, and you're just going to have to wait."

"Nick!" he said, forcefully. "I don't care what they want, either. I'm a cop, too, remember? I have something you need to see. NOW."

She sighed with annoyance.

"Where are you?" she asked.

"About 30 feet from you," he said, "in the foyer of this godforsaken mansion, afraid to walk on your crime scene."

She pivoted and saw him.

"I'll meet you on the porch," she said, and hung up.

Jerod was excited about what was in his hand. He was not excited about facing Nicole Brooks.

Roxanne was resourceful and she was smart. Marlene had said to go to Slidell, which was vague, but she had also named two people Roxanne knew could only be with the Sheriff's Office. She knew roughly where they would be, but it wasn't as if she could tell Siri to navigate to "the murder scene in Slidell."

She opened a news app on her iPhone – an app she rarely used – and pulled up the top stories. It was easy to find the link, but the media weren't reporting the exact address. She paused and thought.

"OK, God," she said aloud. "What now?"

Inspiration came, and she Googled the news room

contact number for the only station she watched. She pressed the link. "Call this number?" the phone asked her.

"Yes, dammit!" she said, and pushed the button.

A man's voice answered. He sounded young. She didn't mince words.

"I have information about the murders in Slidell, but I'll only talk to -"

Crap. What was that pretty reporter's name?

"Blair," she said. "I'll only talk to Blair."

"OK," he said. "I'll be happy to take a message and -"

"No!" Roxanne said forcefully. "I talk to her in person, now, or not at all. I'll be happy to call one of the other stations if you won't tell me where to find her!"

He paused. She knew he would not want to be responsible for losing a scoop.

"Hang on," he said.

She waited, and wasn't on hold long.

"Ma'am, she's at 71429 Middle River Road, east of Slidell," he said. "I'll send her a message and tell her to expect you if you'll give me your name."

Roxanne hung up before she could forget the address, and plugged it into her navigation system. The phone said travel time was 35 minutes. She pressed "Go" and headed east.

Jerod retreated to the front of the house and waited. It felt like she was taking her time, but she, too, was avoiding the indoor part of the crime scene and walked around the house. In a minute, he saw her turn the southwest corner and walk towards him.

"Fuck," he thought, reading her face and her gait. He had been right; she was surly.

"What?" she said when she reached him.

"I just came from the Coroner's Office," he said. "I had an idea and I wanted to check it out before I brought it to you."

Her eyes grew darker.

"What?" she said again.

He held up the photos, one in each hand.

"Look!" he said, suddenly just as surly.

She did.

"What am I looking at?" she asked.

He lowered the photos and grabbed a condescending tone he rarely used with anyone.

"This one," he said, raising his left hand, "shows the second 'O' victim. This one," he said, raising his right hand, "shows the missing man from this crime scene. See anything?"

"No," she said, this time calmly, willing to accept that she might be missing something. "The one on the left was so badly bloated and damaged by water and fish that –"

"Not the body," he said. "Not the face. Look at the clothes." He lifted both photos again.

"Oh my God," she said. "Fuck."

"Exactly," he said. "We don't have multiple killers here. We have one. 'O.' And he's a fucking serial killer psychopath on a goddamned mission, and we need to figure out what the fuck it is."

"Shit," she said. "Fuck."

"For a change, Captain, we agree. Now what the fuck are we going to do – with no chief, no major, no goddamned sheriff, a serial killer on the loose and media climbing up our ass?"

"Excuse me, captain?"

The both said "what?" at the same time, and turned. Another uniform. Behind him stood a woman in a priest outfit.

Both Jerod and Nick exhaled and involuntarily softened; it was a natural reaction to clergy.

"What is it?" Nick asked?

"This…," the deputy struggled for the right word and Roxanne guiltily enjoyed his discomfort. "This lady has some information she needs to share with someone. She said it was urgent."

Jerod and Nicole both stared at the woman. Jerod's stomach turned. Even in the morning haze and the piney shadows, he knew her. If she recognized him, she gave no indication.

"Give her to a deputy to take her statement."

"Captain Brooks," the woman said. "I know you don't know me, but I need you to trust me. I have something you both need to know."

It was hard not to trust a woman wearing a priest's collar.

Chapter Six

Headline: "Neighbors oblivious to triple murder"

Dateline: "Slidell, Louisiana

"Although crowds of deputies, detectives and Crime Lab investigators swarmed a murder scene near Slidell last night and all day Monday, neighbors seemed largely oblivious to the carnage that had unfolded only yards away and deputies seemed in no hurry to inform the public or the press.

"One neighbor who declined to give her name said she didn't know the family despite having lived next door for four years, and another was completely unaware, separated from the scene by a thick row of trees.

"In an apparent shift of effort and perspective, Sheriff George King's administration declined media interviews and had made no effort to canvass the neighborhood of a major crime scene in St. Tammany Parrish."

Margaret once again sat back in her chair.

"You misspelled 'Parish,'" she said. "Otherwise, this is really good."

"Thanks," Clarence said. "But there are no direct interviews."

"Sometimes a reporter's analysis is enough," she said, leaning forward to face her screen once again.

"Sunday night, deputies responded to a run-of-the-mill welfare check, after a neighbor called 911 with concern. The first deputy on the scene, who sources identified as Sean Baxter, found three dead bodies in the home. All had been shot, according to sources."

Margaret sat back again.

"I hate 'sources,'" she said. "Who told you this?"

"Deputies at the perimeter," he said.

"Then why not say so?"

"Because none of them is authorized to speak to us," he said. "And because some of it I just overheard."

She looked at him over the rim of her glasses.

"Really?" she said. "You overheard them?"

"Yep," he said.

"Having 'overheard' someone is not a 'source,'" she said. "I missed Eavesdropping 101 in journalism school."

He shrugged. He was calmer than yesterday, perhaps because he was – like the rest of them – exhausted and had no energy to fight.

"In that case, Margaret, I don't have much else to work with. No one is talking – not Leveque, not the Coroner, not the neighbors, no one. At least not yet."

"What about the Sheriff?"

"He's a no-show," Clarence said. "He hasn't been seen anywhere in weeks. Even Leveque's press releases have mostly quoted Major Walder instead of the Sheriff. Nobody seems to know where he is."

She raised both eyebrows.

"Then maybe that's your story," she said. "In the meantime, rework this one, and do it fast. Get it online. Unlike last time, we don't have an edge. Find it."

Nick pulled the door of the Mobile Command Center Open with more muscle than was required and stepped inside. Roxanne started to follow but Jerod grabbed her by the arm.

"Wait," he said, and pulled her gently to the side.

She looked at him, for the first time in the face. She had been focused on Nick. She frowned, finding him vaguely familiar. He read her look and shook his head.

"Not now," he said.

"But I know you," she said.

"No," he said. "No, you don't."

Understanding dawned on her and her eyes widened. She nodded.

"Got it," she said.

"Out!" they heard Nick yell inside the RV. "Everyone out." A pause. "Please. I need this room to talk to a witness."

Roxanne and Jerod stood in awkward silence as three men left the facility. When they had waited long enough – or what Jerod deemed was long enough – they entered.

He still had her by the arm, albeit with guidance instead of restraint, and steered her to the right. A small conference table with narrow, cushioned benches on either side, seemed to fill the room.

"Sit down," Nick said.

Although they were alone, Jerod closed the sliding door that separated this room from the small kitchen and bathroom area.

Roxanne sat, feeling for the first time as if she were a suspect. It hadn't been this way with Rooney.

"What do you know?" Nick asked without formality.

"I'm not sure I know anything," Roxanne said. "I can only tell you what I was told."

"Then tell me," Nick said. "Tell us."

She grabbed an old-fashioned tape recorder and placed it on the table between them, pressing the "record" button. Roxanne was unnerved.

"Am I a suspect?" she asked.

"Right now, ma'am, we're all suspects," Nick said. "Please start with your name and address."

Roxanne paused, took a deep breath, and leaned forward on the table towards the recorder.

"My name is Reverend Roxanne Clement," she began. "I'm pastor of the Metropolitan Community Church located at –"

"No, no," Nick interrupted. "Tell us where you live, not where you work."

Roxanne took a deep breath again and recited her home address in New Orleans' Garden District. Jerod was watching Nick, contrary to his training that would've had him keep his eyes on the witness. He was worried about her, and he was worried about her tone and temper.

"Thanks," Nick said, sparingly. "Now, tell us what you know."

"Once again, Captain, I don't know anything, at least not firsthand."

"Fine," Nick said. "Then tell us about this call you allegedly received yesterday, and lead into why you're here."

Roxanne heard the word "allegedly" and recoiled. So did Jerod.

"Nick," he said, a gentle reprimand.

She looked at him, bitterness in her eyes.

"Fine," she said. "Tell us about the call you did receive on Sunday."

"A man called my church yesterday," Roxanne said. "He was upset, crying. He said he and the victim from yesterday –"

"Which one?" Nick interrupted.

"The one in the Lake. He said he and that man had been secret lovers. He implied they both had wives. He sounded like he felt guilty."

"Go on," Nick said. Now, she thought, they might be

getting somewhere.

"I – I'm really not sure what you're asking me, Captain. I think I've told you everything."

Nick also sighed. Jerod was impassive.

"You know," Nick said, her tone much softer. "I believe you've told us everything you think we need to know. I don't think you're holding back on purpose. But I do think we're missing something."

"I'm here to help," she said.

"Help who?" Nick asked. "Us, or the man who called you?"

"Both," the pastor said. "All of you. Anyone who needs help, I will help."

"Wrong answer," Nick said. "Look, Pastor," she said, leaning across the table and looking Roxanne dead in the eye. "You know more than what you've said, and I know you do. You may not even know it, but there's more. Keep thinking. What did you leave out? We're dealing with a serial killer here, and I need to know everything you can remember."

Roxanne sat back as much as she could in this confined space and exhaled deeply.

"He was paranoid that we had Caller ID at the church – which we don't," Roxanne said. "He said things that made me think he's a police officer."

She hadn't intended to leave that out, but she had replayed the call so many times in her head and to Officer Rooney that she was confused.

"Like what?

"Something like, 'If I knew who had killed him I'd have arrested him already.' That sounded like something only a cop would say."

She was right about that, but Nick didn't want to probe that any more at the moment. It could lead to bad things she wasn't ready to hear.

"What else?"

"He cried a lot. And he blurted out that the victim – the one in Lake Pontchartrain – had a wife who had also been murdered and we just hadn't found her yet."

Nick's vision blurred as her blood pressure spiked. She tried to keep her cool, but it infuriated her that a preacher in New Orleans had known for almost 24 hours what Jerod had just figured out. When she had herself under control, she took another deep breath.

"Why didn't you call someone?" she asked finally.

"I did," Roxanne said. "After the 10 o'clock news."

"Why did you wait so long?"

"I'm a pastor, captain. I had to balance the confidentiality of the call with helping you catch a killer. Once I saw the news from here, from Slidell, and realized whoever called me had been telling the truth, I couldn't just sit on it anymore."

"Who did you call?"

"The Mandeville Police Department," Roxanne said. "The news said the body had been recovered there and I don't know anything about police work or – what would you call them? Jurisdictional boundaries? I left a message at Mandeville and they said they'd have a detective call me. When no one called by this morning, I went there in person and talked to an officer. Then I came here and found you."

Because of her children, Nicole had trained herself not to curse too much – especially in front of clergy – but at the moment the profanity was bouncing through her brain so fast and so hard she didn't know how much longer she could contain it. She wasn't angry at Roxanne anymore, but she wanted to find Chief Tom Richard and choke the life out of him. It was unconscionable that they'd had this information last night and hadn't shared it.

This case had taken a turn for the worse in record time, Nick thought. Half the force was out sick, the Sheriff was off God-knows-where, Fred was in the hospital, and now they had discovered that they didn't have three victims but at least eight – the 'O' bodies and their wives, and the

Prescott children. Since they had no ID on the first or third victims yet, she had no way of knowing how many of their offspring had also been slaughtered.

She didn't realize she was grinding her teeth and staring into space until Roxanne reached across the table and placed her hand gently on Nick's balled-up fist.

"Captain," the pastor said gently. "I'm here to help."

Jerod's eyes followed Roxanne's hand, and then went to Nick's face. He said nothing.

John Douglas was finally, barely starting to feel human again. He had showered, shaved – carefully, with his still-shaking hands – and put on his uniform. He went to the kitchen and found a cup of coffee under the Keurig spout, almost completely cold. He didn't remember making it, but he put it in the microwave until it was potable again. Then he stepped outside onto his deck. Behind him were acres of woods. He owned the adjacent lots, ensuring they'd never be developed, and he enjoyed the solitude. He didn't miss Donna, and it hurt him to realize it.

He pushed the thought away, and the emotions that came with it. The feelings made him want to drink, and drinking kept him from doing what had to be done. He finished his coffee and briefly pondered making another cup, but realized his stomach probably couldn't take it. He went back inside, closed the sliding glass door, and double-locked it as he always did. He glanced at the clock. It was almost 10:30. They'd be wondering where he was, but he didn't answer to anyone, not right now, not with the sheriff gone. Besides, he knew Moreau could handle whatever arose in his absences. It would all be OK.

He went into the home office, one of the kids' bedrooms they had converted when it was clear the boy – now a man – would not be coming back after college. He sat at the computer and logged-in to his personal account, the one Donna had found before she left.

There were the usual spam messages from hoax

charities, a Nigerian princess, and politicians wanting money. He deleted them all, careful to note the sender and subject line of each. Then he found the one he really was looking for but didn't want to see.

Sender: Oliver Twisted

To: MarriedShyGuy@gmail.com.

Subject: Haha!

Body: I told you I wasn't finished. How do you feel now?

It had been sent on Sunday afternoon. He had been passed out, drunk. He paled. This was his fault.

He scrolled up, seeing what else had missed in the last few days. Oliver had sent another, Friday morning.

Body: Tick-tock, Johnny boy. It's almost Sunday.

He pretended he didn't know who Oliver was. He scrolled more and found another he needed to read. Just seeing who it was from made his heart skip a beat. It was not from an alias email and had been sent 10 days earlier at 6 a.m. How had he missed it?

Sender: 'Phil Prescott'

To: MarriedShyGuy@gmail.com

Body: "Hey, John. WYD this afternoon? I'll be at the gym at 5, as usual. Hope to see you."

John wailed. Why hadn't he checked his email that morning? He couldn't remember. What had he done Friday night after work instead of going to the gym in Mandeville like usual? He didn't recall. This, he thought. Probably this. He had gotten drunk at home and had passed out. Now Phil was dead, and although he hadn't heard from Oliver again, he knew from O's previous emails that Phil's wife and kids were dead, too.

He literally ran from the room to the kitchen and opened the cabinet. There was one bottle of bourbon left, and a little bit of wine. That would do. That would be his Monday. Fuck work. Fuck the Sheriff's Office. Fuck life.

Jerod and Nick stepped out of the Command Center, leaving Roxanne to herself. Jerod had offered to have someone bring her food and she declined, so he had pointed her to the small coffee pot in the RV, told her to help herself, and they had excused themselves.

Jerod said nothing. He was still shocked – by Roxanne's appearance at the scene and by her revelation that the man who called her was a fellow cop. The caller wasn't necessarily the killer, but he clearly knew something and was holding it back. His stomach turned. Only six months ago, before his promotion and transfer, what would he have done?

"We need a meeting," Nick said. "All the rank. Everyone."

"OK," Jerod said. "I'll arrange it."

"An hour from now," she said. "Let's do it at the Coroner's Office. It's central."

"OK," he said, on autopilot.

"You, me, the Coroner, DeMarco, Dora what's-her-name, Douglas if you can find him and Moreau if you can't."

"Yes, ma'am," he said.

"And get Detectives Siwel and Silver there, too. They're the only ones who are healthy and who know what's going on. And Karly. Tell her to bring the tapes."

"Got it," Jerod said.

"Do you think we should invite Mandeville people? They're the only other agencies involved at all right now."

"I do, but it's your call."

"Do it," she said. "Please."

She paused and grabbed his wrist as he reached for his phone.

"Jerod, what's your take on the pastor?"

"She's being honest," he said. "She's telling us everything she knows."

"You were a detective," she said. "What's missing?"

"From her? I don't think anything. Why?"

"Because she knows you, that's why," Nick said. "Tell me. I won't say anything."

He took a deep breath. Now was not the time for secrets. Anything could matter.

"I've been to her church a few times with my –"

She said nothing, but her gaze didn't falter.

"With my boyfriend," he said, finally. "He's been a member there for several years."

"Good for him," she said.

"Nick ...." He started but didn't know how to finish.

"Jerod," she said, and her grip moved from his wrist to his hand. "No one cares. Be happy."

He exhaled, loudly.

"Thanks."

"You don't need to thank me for being a decent human being. Now get that meeting together. You, me, Douglas, Wilson, Karly, Dora, Siwel and Silver. Mandeville if they want to come. In one hour."

She turned to walk back away, back towards the house.

"Got it," he said. "And thank you, Nicole."

He had never called her that. No one called her that. Even her husband didn't call her that. She turned, looked at him over her shoulder, and smiled.

"You're welcome," she said. "And don't ever use that name again."

Jerod dialed Karly's direct line and waited. He was sure they were busy and he knew that like the rest of them, she had been up most of the night. She answered on the fifth ring.

"Communications, Captain -- ."

"Karly," Jerod cut her off.

"Hi, Jerod," she replied. "What's up?"

"I need you to send a group page and I need it ASAP."

"You got it. To who and what do I say?"

"Douglas, Moreau, Siwel, Silver. Me and Brooks. And do you have Mandeville P.D. in your system?"

"Yessir," she said.

"Coroner and Dr. DeMarco?"

"Affirmative."

"Include them. Meeting at the Coroner's Office at 1000 hours. Urgent."

"Consider it done," she said. "Anything else?"

"Yeah," he said. "Include the sheriff and Fred on it, too. Just in case."

"Done," she said, and he could hear her typing on her keyboard already.

"Brooks wants you there, too. Bring the tapes."

"OK," she said, and he could tell she was multi-tasking. He hoped she had heard him.

"Bye," he said.

He heard only silence. She had already hung up.

Jerod walked into the Coroner's Office like he owned it. He was in that kind of mood. He had called Leslie on the way. She was expecting him, and so was the receptionist, who walked him to her door and swiped it open with her access card.

He went in without introduction and sat down without waiting for an invitation. He slouched back on the sofa. He felt like they were friends. He felt like, given the circumstances, most protocols were out the window.

"Doc, this is a mess."

She was standing behind her desk, looking at the fountain again. Maybe that water feature hadn't been such a bad idea, she thought.

"I told you to call me by my name when we're alone," she said.

"OK," he said. "Leslie, this is a fucking mess."

She turned around.

"Elaborate," she said.

He paused, a bit stunned. She knew very well what kind of mess it was. At least he hoped she did.

"We have six victims now and at least two others we haven't found yet," he said. "That makes it a fucking mess."

"I know that," she said. "What else."

"We also have a pastor – a pastor who leads a gay church – who got a call from someone we think was a cop who said he knows who the victims are and that he knows their wives have been killed, too."

"Interesting," she said.

He paused again, stunned at her impassiveness. This was more than "interesting." It was alarming.

"How can you be so calm?" he asked.

"Two reasons," she said. "First, someone has to be. Second, I'm a scientist. I look at data, not feelings."

Jerod said nothing.

"OK," he said. "Then let's talk about 'data.' Six dead bodies. Four IDs. Zero suspects. How's that?"

"That sucks," she said. "It fucking sucks. But that's not what we do here, Jerod. That's not the kind of data I need."

"Then what do you fucking need?" he asked, leaning forward. "What would make you care about these people?"

"I do care," she said. "I care so much I keep my feelings locked away and I deal with it at church on Sundays and on my knees every day. Sometimes I let my feelings out when I'm at home. But here, we need to focus on facts to reach solutions."

He shut up. She was right. He took a deep breath.

"OK," he said. "What do we need?"

"Cause of death and manner of death are a great start," she said. "Shall we review?"

He said nothing.

"Manner of death on all six victims is homicide," she said. "One human killed another. Homicide. You knew that. Cause of death on the three original 'O' victims is blunt force trauma to the head. Their bodies being disposed of in the water is incidental. Cause of death on the Prescotts – not counting Phillip – was gunshot wounds and, on the children, exsanguination secondary to gunshot wounds. As for the spouses and possibly children of the other 'O' victims, I can't say yet, and neither can you."

He was silent, seething, staring at his boots.

"You think I'm cold, Jerod, but what we do here is take the details of death and hand them over to professionals like you, like Nick, who connect the dots. We help you do that. And here's a news flash for you, Jerod: You're not supposed to care, either. Not about the people. Not now. Not until you're finished. When you care about the people you start letting your emotions guide you. The facts of the case need to guide you. Anything else is nothing but fucking bullshit."

He was used to her foul language, so what caught him up short was the reality of what she said. This was not about the human beings who had been killed, at least it couldn't be right now, not to him. At least, it shouldn't be, not if they were going to catch this madman. They needed to use science, facts, data, to figure out who and what this killer was. He took a deep breath again.

"You're right, doctor."

"I told you not to fucking call me that," she said. "Go take a seat at the table. The others will be here soon."

By 10 a.m., Leslie's office was full. The table seated six and there were two sofas and three wingbacks for the others. All who had been invited were there, except Major Douglas, Nick noted. At the moment, she didn't care about his absence but she was mildly concerned for his well-being. That had to wait.

She was not the highest-ranking person in the room – the Coroner was – but as acting chief detective on a serial case, she was in charge by force of circumstance, if not will.

"Leveque," she said. "For now, you're not PIO. You're a detective again.   Report, please."

"Thank you, ma'am," he said. Then, to the group, "We all know what we have here, although no one has yet said it publicly. We have a serial killer in our Parish."

"Is that actually what we're dealing with?" It was the Mandeville Police Chief who spoke. "It doesn't seem like he's that prolific."

"Yes. Respectfully, Chief, you've only had one of the victims," Jerod said. "All three victims were found in the water. Just today, we learned that 'O' is killing his victims' families, too."

That pronouncement seemed to suck the air out of the room.

"How do we know that?" It was Michael Siwel who spoke. He was an experienced cop, in both patrol and investigations, but his background was in property crimes. He wasn't flying blind, but he wasn't fully familiar with homicide cases, either.

Jerod and Nick exchanged glances. Leslie and Dora remained impassive; accustomed to dealing with the families of the dead, they had perfect poker faces.

"Someone made a call," Jerod said.

"To a pastor," Nick added.

"Was it the killer?" Robbie Silver chimed in. He was in the same boat as Siwel. This was not his comfort zone, either.

"We don't know," Nick said.

"Probably not," said Jerod. "We can't say for sure, but it seems unlikely."

Siwel and Silver shifted uneasily.

"Um ... could you be more specific, Captain?" Silver asked.

Jerod looked at Nick.

"We've only got one witness in this case so far," he said. "And she's entirely trustworthy and disconnected from this community. Why not just bring her in?"

Nick looked at him with daggers, but softened in seconds as she processed the suggestion. She cocked one eyebrow.

"That may not be a bad idea," she said. "Where is she?"

"I'll get her here," he said, and stepped from the room.

"While we're waiting, let's move on," Nick said. "We're in a bad situation here. Major Walder is out, Major Douglas is out, the Sheriff is out, and half our force is out sick. We need to go over this case and we need to do it together."

She stood, walking to the white board on the Coroner's Office wall.

Across the top she wrote, "Victim 1," "Phil Prescott," "Victim 3."

"Now," she said. "Talk."

There was silence. Her eyes darted the room and she suddenly realized there was a uniform behind Chief Richard that she didn't recognize.

"Excuse me," she said, "but who are you?

He stood out of respect.

"Chris Rooney, ma'am," he said. "Mandeville P.D."

"Chris took the witness statement this morning," Chief Richard said. "I asked him to come."

"Good," she said. "We're going to need you. Thank you, Chief. OK... so back to this. Victims 1, 2 and 3. We have ID on 2, and his family. Now ... let's talk through this."

There was silence for a moment.

"Victim 1 was found in the Middle Pearl River," Dr.

Wilson said, breaking the silence. It was a pedestrian comment that Nick knew was designed to get people talking. Wilson was smart, and not just medically.

"Victim 2 – Prescott – was found in Bayou Lacombe," Siwel said, "nowhere near his home."

"Victim 3 was in Lake Pontchartrain," said Moreau.

These were elementary observations, but Nick jotted them on the board in appropriate columns.

"OK," she said. "What else?"

"All three 'O' victims died of blunt force trauma to the head," Dr. DeMarco said.

"The killer called us on Sunday morning each week to tell us where to find the body," Karly added.

"He wants to be caught," Chief Richard said.

"Maybe," Nick said. "Or maybe he just wants the attention of the media while he kills. I think he calls them, too."

"Probably," Jerod said, "but I haven't been able to confirm that. I haven't had time to confirm that."

"He's on a mission?" Silver asked.

"I'm starting to think so," Nick said. "I didn't until this morning when our witness came forward, but yes. I think he is."

"What was it about the witness statement that makes you think that," Moreau asked. It was uncharacteristic of him; Special Operations deputies did water-related incidents and rescues, not investigations, but she had invited him here and she valued any insight.

"Leveque is tracking down the witness," she said. "We'll let her answer that directly. Good question, though. Standby. What else?"

She was almost dancing, bouncing back and forth on her feet. This was energizing, but not in a good way. It just had to be done, and she had to keep herself alert. There was no one to lean on.

"He clearly has a fixation with water," Siwel said. "But water is not how he kills."

She jotted on the white board again.

"Good point," she said. "Really good. So what does that mean? How does that help us find him?"

"Maybe it won't," Silver said. "Maybe it's just a good way to dispose of bodies – or evidence."

"I might buy that, Silver, if he didn't call to tell us where they are," Nick said. "He might be disposing of evidence but he wouldn't let us know when he kills if he didn't want the bodies found."

Robbie shrugged and nodded. She was right.

"So why water?" Richard asked.

"Why not?" asked Leslie.

All eyes turned to her. She was in front of her desk, close to them, but the window behind her gave her an almost-holy glow.

"What?" Nick said.

"Why not water? Maybe you're asking the wrong question. Maybe you're not. I'm just throwing out a perspective."

"What do you mean?" Nick asked.

"Well, there are enough isolated areas in this Parish that he could dispose of bodies. He could choose a dead end in Hickory or a dairy farm in Sun," she said. "He chooses water."

"You know there are almost 900 miles of waterways in St. Tammany," Moreau said.

There was silence again.

"You're saying there may be other victims we haven't found?" Nick asked.

"No," Siwel said. "I don't think so, Captain. He craves attention. He'd let us know."

"I agree," Leslie said. "He has shown his desire to have his victims discovered – two days after he kills them. He doesn't care about the families. They are incidental."

There was silence.

"What do you mean?" Nick asked.

"Whatever reason he has for killing the wives and children is secondary," Leslie said. "I don't know the reason. But the men are his primary targets. The water is symbolic. So are the families. He doesn't kill the secondary victims for attention, or he'd tell us. He does it because it means something to him."

Jerod reentered the room.

"She'll be here in 5 minutes," he said.

"Who?" Silver asked.

"Roxanne Clement," he said. "Reverend Roxanne Clement."

"Reverend?"

So many of them said it, Nick wasn't sure who to respond to.

"Maybe you should explain that, Rooney," she said, a modicum of venom in her tone.

"Yes, ma'am," he said. "Rev. Clement called our office last night to report receiving a phone call. Then she came to our office this morning to give a statement."

"Yes, we know," Nick said. "Why weren't we informed of this when she called? Why did she have to tell us herself?"

"I don't know, ma'am," he said. "Maybe Chief Richard can address that. I'm a patrol officer. I just took the call, wrote down her information and passed it along."

"We were flooded with calls last night," Richard said. "They probably just didn't get to hers yet."

"Yeah," Nick said. "Well, fortunately, she came to us. I took her statement myself this morning."

The tension in the room was suddenly palpable. Nick looked awful, exhausted. Richard said nothing.

"Unfortunately, we had already figured out what she had told your detectives last night," Nick said. "That 'O' is killing his primary victims' families."

"Nick," Jerod said. She hadn't realized he had come back, and he stood in the shadows by the door. "Roxanne is on her way. But the real question might be why is he killing the families? Working this in reverse may help us figure out why he's killing to begin with."

Leslie smiled at him. She wasn't sure if he saw. This is what she wanted: Take out the emotion.

"OK, fine," Siwel said. "So let's profile who he IS killing. Who are his primary targets?"

Leslie's phone beeped on her desk and she pressed a button.

"Dr. Wilson," the woman said. "There's a Reverend Clement here to see you?"

"Send her back," Leslie said. "I'll meet her at the door."

Jedediah Cone ran his hands over his military haircut and leaned back on his sofa. He was proud to be a cop and a veteran, but as a result he was often confounded by silence. He hated it. Give him the sounds of bombs in Baghdad any day over the silence of Mandeville. He was losing his mind.

It was frustrating enough to see the case unfold on the news. It was worse to know how incomplete the coverage was. And it was worse, still, to have been there and have to keep silent. He didn't know much, but he knew more than Leveque was releasing. It was frustrating.

"What's up?" his wife asked. She came up behind him as he sat on the sofa and rubbed his shoulders. "Why are you awake?

"Can't sleep," he said, his eyes not leaving the TV. "This is awful."

"It's sad," she said. "I'm glad you're a part of solving it. I'm proud."

He smiled, half-heartedly. He wasn't part of it enough. He was part of it too much, too, but he didn't know it.

"Thanks, baby," he said, touching her hand. "Your support means everything."

"I knew I married a cop," she said. "I knew what I was in for."

Maybe she did, he thought. Maybe not.

"Do you need anything?" she asked.

"No, ma'am," he said, affectionately, and he kissed her hand.

"OK," she said. "If you don't mind, I'm going to get some sleep now."

She was a nurse, and they both worked night shifts.

"Go ahead, baby," he said. "Thank you. I'll see you later."

The noon news was coming on. He wasn't going to miss it.

"Love you," she said, kissing him on his forehead from behind.

"Love you back," he said, and he meant it.

She vanished into the back of the house. The news started with the usual fanfare, music and graphics.

"I'm Frank Jordan.

"And I'm Blair Francingues.

"You're watching Louisiana's News Station, live at noon."

Then, the teasers, videos with voiceovers.

"Northshore residents are reacting to a series of murders that have gripped a community," in Frank's voice.

"While in Kenner, citizens react to revelations of a local politician's alleged dalliances with a teenaged boy," Blair read.

There was a dramatic musical conclusion, as he wondered why Blair was in-studio instead of in St. Tammany.

"Our top story today is from Slidell, where an entire family has apparently been killed in their home. Blair,

126

what can you tell us?"

"Well, Frank, it's been a dramatic 24 hours in St. Tammany, as detectives have handled not one but four murders – three of them in the same home," she said. "I was on both scenes yesterday, and police are being very guarded with releasing information."

Her package was heavy with B-roll, shots from both the Mandeville Harbor and the Middle Road crime scene.

Jedediah watched half-mindedly. He saw himself in some of the Mandeville shots, but he wasn't impressed with himself. He never had been.

When he was sure his wife was asleep, he picked up his laptop from the end table and opened it. It was about time he checked his private email; it had been a few days. There were a few unread, the one that interested him from this morning.

"From: MarriedShyGuy@gmail.com

"To: Conehead

"Subject: Miss you.

"Body: Hey, baby. Haven't seen you in a while. Does your wife never leave you alone?"

He hit "reply."

"She goes to work at 6 tonight and I have 12 hours to myself. You free? You know where to find me."

He hit "send." He didn't expect a response, but he knew where he'd be in six hours, just in case.

Chapter Seven

Headline: "Public frightened by recent murder spree

Dateline: "Mandeville, LA

"Two days after a body was pulled from Lake Pontchartrain near Mandeville and three more were discovered in a Slidell-area home, authorities have refused to provide any update to the public.

"Reporters received a statement from Sheriff's Office spokesman Jerod Leveque on Sunday morning, but law enforcement agencies in St. Tammany Parish have maintained mostly silence for the last two days, only feeding public fear and speculation.

"At the Port Marigny shopping center in Mandeville, consumers expressed grave concern.

"'It's really frightening that we might have a serial killer on the loose in St. Tammany Parish,' said a woman who would only give her first name, Debbie. 'My husband and I were already afraid for ourselves and our children, but with a whole family being wiped out in Slidell last weekend, it makes us even more scared.'

"In Slidell, the reaction was similar. Outside a coffee shop just three miles from the triple-murder scene, Yousef Mahour said he is guarding his children – and himself.

"'This person who is annihilating families, he is a grave menace,' Mahour said. 'We already have fear because we are of the Muslim faith, but now we fear for our lives just because we are alive.'

"Calls to officials at virtually all local agencies went unanswered."

Margaret leaned back in her chair and looked at Clarence.

"It's good," she said. "It's short. It's not hard-hitting journalism, but given what you have to work with, it's good. Post it. Print it. But find me something with some meat to it."

Roxanne was surprised to be greeted by the Coroner herself. She was surprised the Coroner was a woman, but her ignorance of that fact was reasonable given how little she consumed the news. In her mind, she laughed; her surprise at seeing a female physician in a position of power was similar to the surprise some felt when meeting a female pastor. Despite progress, people were still stuck in some antiquated notions – including, she realized, herself.

Dr. Wilson introduced herself and escorted Roxanne to her office and the large conference room. Walking in, she was surprised by the number of people in the room.

"Oh!" she said aloud before she could catch herself. She glanced around and recognized Captains Brooks and Leveque – and no one else. Jerod stood.

"Roxanne," he said. "Please take a seat. We need your help."

He indicated a wingback chair on the far end of the room, which faced what she assumed was Dr. Wilson's desk. Without a word, Leslie turned the chair around for her and patted it – a gesture Roxanne initially took as condescending but quickly realized was an awkward graciousness. She walked around the sofa and seated herself.

"Rev. Clement, if you don't mind I'd like to finish the thread we were on when you arrived," Nick said. "We appreciate you coming, and I'm trusting that anything you hear in this room will remain confidential."

"You've got that promise," Roxanne said.

"Good," Nick said. The others seemed uneasy with a civilian in the room – not just a woman but a clergy person. Nick sensed it, but didn't have time to deal with it. For now, this was her investigation and she was making these decisions. Too few people had been involved until now.

"Jerod," she said. "You had just asked an important question: Why is he killing the families? So ...why?"

There was, again, stony silence.

"What if he's killing them to delay a missing persons report or identification of the body?" Siwel asked.

Nick jotted it on the white board, which was quickly filling up.

"Good thought," she said. "Other theories?"

"Family annihilators kill their own families because they feel like they're saving them from something," Silver said. "What if this is similar? Not killing his own family but killing someone else's because he identifies with them somehow?"

Nick raised one eyebrow.

"That's a very interesting theory," she said. "It's unusual. Let's pull that thread for a minute. What could he be saving them from?"

"Most family annihilators are saving their families from financial ruin or public embarrassment, aren't they?" Richard asked.

There was a moment of silence again, then Nick sighed.

"None of us are trained profilers, but we all have good sense, education, training, and instincts," she said. "I've asked the feds for help but there's a weird policy that only the chief law enforcement officer can make that request, and the Sheriff himself is ... unavailable. We're on our own for now, so let's just do our best. It might not get us where we need to be, but it will help. Hell, it might not get us anywhere, but it's our best shot at this very moment. So ... can anyone answer Chief Richard's question? My answer would be 'yes,' but if anyone has more experience in the area ..."

"Ma'am?" It was Rooney.

"Yeah?" she asked.

"I'm pretty sure the chief is correct," he said. "When I worked for NYPD, I worked one of those cases. The father was about to be arrested for embezzling from his employer, and he wanted to save his wife and kids from the humiliation – and the financial ruin."

"OK," Nick said. "Thank you. So let's talk through how that works vicariously. Killer targets Victim X because he – the victim – has done something criminal, morally wrong or embarrassing. After he kills X, he kills X's family to save them from the shame?"

"That would mean whatever it was that motivated the killing of X was going to become public anyway, right?" asked Silver.

"Maybe," said Jerod. "Or maybe the killer only thinks it is. Maybe the killing itself is what would make his wrongdoing public. And whatever the victim has done 'wrong' in the killer's mind, the killer has taken it very, very personally. Maybe the killer is walking in a circle here."

"Can we agree that we're not dealing with a stable and sane person here?" Siwel asked. "Is he even predictable?"

"So far he is," Karly said. "He's called my dispatchers every Sunday morning for the last three weeks and told us exactly where to find a body. He's dumped them all in the water."

"I think his sanity is my field, folks," Dr. Wilson said. "Yes, we should be able to agree that he's unstable. But that doesn't mean he's insane – in either the legal or medical sense. He may well believe that what he's doing is the right thing to do. He's clearly very organized. The murders are well thought-out. The evidence is minimal.

So, yes, he's unstable but intelligent. But if you're asking if the motive makes sense ... it does to him, even if it doesn't to us or to other rational people."

"So, if Silver's theory holds water – that the killer targets men who have done something wrong and then kills their families as an act of mercy – how does it play out next?" Siwel asked. "How can we possibly figure out who the next target is?"

"With what we know now, we can't," Nick said. "We need to dig into these men's backgrounds. Ignore their families for now. Find out everything we can about each of them – finances, work life, military records, even their sex lives."

"There's only one problem with that, Captain," Siwel said. "We only know who one of them is. If we find the other two sets of family victims, we can figure out who victims 1 and 3 are."

"Well how the fuck do we do that?" Nick blurted. Her eyes then moved instinctively to Roxanne. "Sorry, Reverend," she said.

They all turned to look at her, suddenly remembering she was there. Roxanne wanted to shrink down to nothing and hide under Dr. Wilson's desk.

Terry peeled off his scrubs as he entered through the garage and threw them in the wash. Monday was his short day, so he was home already and it was only 1 o'clock. There was no need to worry about walking in the house in his underwear; Jerod clearly wasn't home. Actually, there'd have been no need to be bashful even if Jerod were home. It's not like they hadn't interacted in their underwear, and less.

When they had first started dating, Jerod was fresh from a divorce, newly exploring this side of himself. Unlike others Terry had known in the same situation, Jerod wasn't shy. He was cautious, but never timid. In fact, he's the one who had asked Terry out – discreetly, at Terry's dental practice. Terry had accepted immediately, and quietly, but only on the condition that Jerod find a new dentist. It had been better than a fair exchange.

Their first public date had been in New Orleans. Jerod didn't want to be seen out with a man here, where he worked, where he was a cop. All their subsequent dates had been in New Orleans or Gulfport, too. Even now, two years into the relationship and cohabitating for months, they didn't even grocery shop together.

At first, Jerod had been very leery, not of Terry in particular but of dating anyone at all. He had lost his wife not because of his emerging sexuality, but because she couldn't handle his work schedule. Terry had assured him it wouldn't be a problem, had dared him to test it, even. Jerod had. Terry had held up his end of the bargain. It had worked.

Now, however, Terry was having issues with it. It wasn't that Jerod was working long hours tracking a killer concerned him. It was that Jerod seemed obsessed with this case. Terry had seen him work about 25 murder cases – and dozens of other types – in the last two years. There had never been a case like this. Jerod tried not to discuss his work at home, in part because he couldn't, but Terry wasn't stupid. He had seen the news and had rather easily inferred that his boyfriend was dealing with a serial killer, although he had yet to hear those words from any "official" source.

He threw on some shorts and a tank top, cleaned up the morning's dishes, and went back into the garage to their home gym. It was hot, but that was fine. He turned on the radio. He usually listened to music, but Jerod liked talk radio. In the absence of his lover, he put on Jerod's brand of audio entertainment and climbed on the treadmill, listening as he walked faster and faster until he was at a full run.

Unsurprisingly, the top story was about the New Orleans Saints and the run-up to the fall season. He chuckled. Only in the South would a serial killer fall down in the newscast because of a football team. It wasn't until the third or fourth minute into the top of the hour newscast that the St. Tammany Serial Killer – he was surprised the media hadn't come up with a more catchy moniker – was mentioned. The story was an overview of what had already been reported; there was nothing new. But the reporter ended the broadcast with, "In our drive time newscast we'll have an update on the St. Tammany story."

Terry finished his run, moved his work clothes into the dryer, and headed for the shower. He had an afternoon to kill – and probably an evening, too, since he didn't expect Jerod home – and he wasn't going to do it in sweaty clothes. On his way to the bathroom the doorbell rang, and he diverted in the direction of the front of the house. He opened the door to someone holding a large bouquet of flowers.

"I have a delivery for Dr. Mozingo."

"That's me," Terry said, reaching for the vase. "Thank you so much, I –"

The blow to his chin came so fast and hard that he fell backwards, water and flowers falling onto his chest and face. Despite his fitness and tall frame, he was undone. He struggled to regain his senses, anticipating another blow and steeling himself. It never came. Instead, he heard an engine start, and then he was alone, drifting into darkness as the room spun around him.

"Jerod, I can only think of one way to accelerate finding the victim families," Nick said.

"Yeah," he said. "Me, too. I don't like it, but I don't see a choice."

"I don't like it a lot," she said.

"Do it," Leslie said. She had been quite for a while. "Do it here. I'll stand with you."

"Do you have a computer I can use, Doctor?" he asked.

"Use mine," she said, moving behind her desk to enter

135

her password. "Do what you have to do."

Roxanne's anxiety had risen to an impossible level.

"Excuse me," she said, and they all turned. "I'm sorry to interrupt, but I'm still not sure why I'm here. I want to help. Tell me what to do."

Jerod spun around, looking over the pastor at Nick.

"I have an idea," he said. "Roxanne, please tell everyone about the call you received yesterday. Include all the details you can remember. Everyone, try not to interrupt. Listen to her. I've got a press release to write."

Leslie listened as Roxanne talked, but her eyes were over Jerod's shoulder looking at her own screen.

Any time Jerod called a press conference, he wrote two things: a media advisory with minimal information but enough to get them there, and a press release to be issued while the press conference was ongoing, giving prefabricated and preapproved quotes for media to use, photos if any were available, and a lot more facts than the advisory.

For Immediate Release

Monday, Aug. 8

SHERIFF REQUESTS HELP IN FINDING SERIAL KILLER VICTIMS

St. Tammany Parish Sheriff George Stewart King is asking for the public's help in locating at least two victims of a serial killer who authorities know have been victimized but have yet to discover.

"In the last 15 days, a serial killer who calls himself 'O' has killed three men and disposed of their remains in waterways," Sheriff King said. "In the last 24 hours, our detectives and Mandeville Police officers have discovered that 'O' is not only killing the initial victims but their families, as well."

"The body discovered in Lake Pontchartrain yesterday has yet to be identified, but our inspectors are working diligently to ascertain his identity and the identity of the man found in the Middle River 15 days ago," said St. Tammany Parish Coroner Dr. Leslie Wilson. "Finding other victims who are related to these two unidentified bodies will help law enforcement immeasurably."

"It's an unusual request, but we need the public's help more than ever," King said. "We need everyone – everyone – to go check on their neighbors. Even if you're in the rural part of the Parish and your neighbor is half a mile away, go check on them. If anything is unusual, call 911 immediately."

"Unusual circumstances might include dying plants that were previously well kept, a stack of newspapers on the front porch, cars that haven't moved in days or weeks, or any other change in lifestyle patterns," said Captain Nick Brooks. "This is extremely serious, and we are working hard to identify these victims not only to bring closure to their families but to find this monster. Please, please help us."

-30-

When he had finished typing, he turned to Leslie.

"Good by you?"

"Sure," she said. "But won't they miss the sheriff at the press conference you're about to call?"

"They'll miss him less if they have quotes to use," he whispered, and pressed "print" four times. He passed the copies around for everyone to read.

"I need to get back to the Radio Room," Karly said. "Once this hits, our phones are going to blow up."

"Siwel, go with her," Nick said. "You can vet the calls as they come in and assign follow-ups appropriately."

"But Captain—" he started.

"I know this is not your field, but trust your instincts," she said. "Use your discretion, but save every damn one of those messages. Go! Silver, go the Slidell office and let everyone know what's about to happen. Take a copy of the press release with you. Rally the troops. This is priority for everyone."

"Yes, ma'am," he said, and headed for the door. Karly and Siwel were behind him. They all got in their vehicles quickly and drove off.

"Chief," Nick said. "I certainly can't tell you what to do, but if you would also spread the word to your people in Mandeville. Since the news has covered our agencies specifically, any of us could be getting the calls."

"Agreed," said Tom, and stood to go.

"And, please," Nick said. "Please, don't let tips fall through the cracks. He may not kill again for another four days, or he may alter his schedule, but we've got to be on the same page."

Clay honestly didn't mind his wife's work. He was actually very proud of what she did and how far she had come. A woman in law enforcement was still a rarity. For her to have achieved the rank she had in the time she had was remarkable, and he was happy to be the primary caregiver to their children when necessary. At six-foot-four he was a significantly taller than Nicole. According to stereotypes, he should've been macho, in-charge, and always in control of their family. He didn't care about that. He cared about her being safe and happy.

He had finished work early and had picked up the children from the daycare at church. He didn't want or need "alone time." He wanted time with the kids.

As two of them played on the floor, the other two were glued to the television and the Veggie Tales video he had selected for them. They did not let the kids watch adult TV, and never news. He stood in the kitchen, watching them through the Dutch window, marveling at how wonderful they were and how they completed his life. He was lost in thought when the doorbell rang.

He walked through the living room, around the kids, to the front door. Visitors were rare in the country, and he half expected it to be his mother with a pot of red beans and rice. They all knew how hard Nick was working, if only by watching the news, and it wouldn't be unusual for her to just show up unannounced with food.

He opened the door and was face-to-face with a bundle of balloons.

"I have a delivery for Clay Brooks," the voice behind the balloons said. His heart swelled and he reached for the bundle.

He heard more than felt the gunshot. It knocked him down in the foyer and the bouquet of balloons rose, separated by the doorframe, half indoors and half out. Not in front of the kids, he thought, as he faded. His assailant slammed the door, not quite severing the ribbons; the balloons floated upwards on both sides of the portal. He vaguely heard an engine start, and then he was out.

Jerod and Leslie stood in the Training Room at the Coroner's Office, multiple microphones on the podium. A room full of journalists had awaited them. It was Jerod's job to know who they were, and he counted five TV cameras, each with a reporter, and at least four newspaper writers.

"Thank you all for coming," Jerod began. "As you all know by, St. Tammany Parish is dealing with a serial killer."

He had expected some rumblings at the first use of the phrase. Instead, they were silent, listening intently.

"We know this killer has struck at least three primary victims, one a week for the last three weeks, but we didn't know until yesterday that he is also targeting the victims' families," Jerod continued. "We know that now, but there's still a lot missing.

"To advance this investigation more quickly, we need to find the families of the first and third victims," he said. "The problem is – and this is where we need your help – we have not yet identified those victims.

"Since we discovered the bodies of the second victim's family yesterday – the Prescotts – we now believe there are two other families who have probably been murdered, one as recently as this past weekend and one as long as 17 days ago. We need everyone in this Parish – everyone – to check on their neighbors. Anything unusual should be reported to 911 immediately. Any questions?"

There was silence for a moment, and then Clarence spoke.

"Captain, are you saying there are two families in St. Tammany Parish who have already been murdered and are literally rotting in their own homes right now?" he asked.

Jerod didn't like his choice of words and hoped the TV and radio reporters wouldn't use that sound bite, but he couldn't dispute its accuracy.

"That is our belief," Jerod said simply. "And we need help to find them."

"What about the men you call his 'primary' victims?" Blair asked from the other side of the room. "Can you tell us more about them?"

Dr. Wilson stepped forward.

"The first victim, the one found in the Middle River, was a white male, approximately 40 years old," she said. "He was in good physical condition, about 5'10" and we estimate about 185 pounds. The third victim was also a white male, found in Lake Pontchartrain yesterday morning. He was approximately 6'1" and 200 pounds. We believe he had three tattoos on his body, two on the arms and one on the lower leg, that were non-surgically excised post-mortem."

"You mean the killer cut off chunks of flesh to remove identifiers?" Clarence asked, again mincing no words.

"Yes," Leslie said impassively.

"What other identifiers are there?" he asked.

She hated his clinical language. She talked that way, but when appealing to the public she preferred less coarse language.

"All three were wearing gym clothes," she said. "Shorts

and T-shirts."

"Why did you wait so long to notify the public about this?" Blair asked, pointedly.

Jerod returned to the podium.

"We weren't sure what we were dealing with until yesterday," he said. "Now that we know, we're pulling out all the stops, including requesting your assistance."

"Do you have any advice for citizens to avoid becoming victims?" asked another newspaper reporter, a new one in the market who he didn't quite know yet.

"Well," he said, "we don't believe these are random killings. Once we have a profile of the victims – which can happen only after we identify them – we can better answer that question."

"Excuse me, but where is the sheriff?" Clarence asked.

Jerod had expected the question, but he hadn't expected the rush of blood to his face that he currently felt.

"The Sheriff is being kept informed about this Investigation but is unavailable to see to it personally," Jerod said. "I'm afraid I can't say any more about that at this time, but we really appreciate your help in getting this word out as quickly as possible."

He motioned to Leslie and they left the stage through a door directly into her office. Nick met them there.

"That went as well as could be expected," Leslie said.

"Yes," said Nick. "But now the three of us need to talk. Just us. There's a lot more to go over that the rest of the team doesn't need to know yet."

Roxanne was still sitting in the wingback.

"Um… do you still need me here?" she asked.

"No," Jerod said. "Thank you."

"Actually, yes," Nick said. "I think you might be able to add some insights, if you don't mind."

"Well …," Roxanne hesitated and stood up.

Nick smiled, the first time Roxanne had seen that happen.

"You said you wanted to help," she said.

Clarence and Blair sat silently at their respective computers, their fingers moving frantically across the keyboards. Margaret paced behind them.

They had both sent tweets to their followers after the press conference while driving back to the office.

"Sheriff admits there's a serial killer, but doesn't show at press conference," Blair tweeted.

"Sheriff & Coroner seeking murdered families that may have been undiscovered for weeks," Clarence posted.

The social media flurry was instant and frenetic, but neither of them had time to follow it right now, let alone respond. They had deadlines.

Margaret got on the phone behind them.

"We need a satellite truck over here ASAP," Blair heard her say, and swiveled in her chair. "No, not the Coroner's Office. That's too far from the bridges." She looked at Blair and widened her eyes in question.

"Mandeville," Blair said back to her. "The Harbor."

"Mandeville Harbor," Margaret said into the phone. "Blair needs to go live at 5 and 6, and get someone else over here for 10."

"No!" Blair said, turning again. "I'll do that one, too. This is mine and I'll see it through."

"Never mind on another reporter," Margaret said without hesitating. "Blair will take all three." She paused. "Fuck the overtime. Blair will handle it….. What do you mean you don't have anyone to send with a sat truck until 10? Oh, holy hell!" She hung up and looked back at the young reporter. "Write!" she said. Then, to Clarence, "How soon 'til I have something from you?"

His fingers didn't stop flying across the keyboard as he responded, "30 minutes."

She wanted to go back to her desk and sit down but she couldn't. Margaret continued to pace.

"Listen up!" Karly said. "The phones are about to start ringing off the hook with tips about a serial killer. Most of them will be garbage but put them all into CAD."

Computer Aided Dispatching had been the best thing to come along ever, Karly thought. No longer was there a literal "paper trail." It was all electronic, including not just audio recordings but dispatcher's notes, times, everything.

"Detective Siwel will be screening them. I'm setting him up on the backup station. Log all of them as being dispatched to him so they'll appear on his screen. Do not – I repeat, do NOT – put any of them out over the air until Siwel has reviewed them and authorizes it. Everybody 10-4?"

"10-4, Captain," they all said, almost in unison.

This was the kind of well-oiled machine she had been wanting to run. It sucked that it took six murders to get it to that point. She went into her office and started calling other staff. Although they had a limited number of dispatch stations and computers, they did have extra phones. She figured she needed at least two extra hands. She kept dialing until she found some dispatchers willing to work overtime. No one in upper management was going to question personnel costs right now, and she didn't care if they did.

The first afternoon newscast started at 4 p.m. The phones started lighting up at 4:02.

"There are some things we didn't talk about yet," Nick said.

The others said nothing.

"One, transporting the bodies. It's easy enough to get someone into the Middle River and Bayou Lacombe, but how did this motherfucker get someone nine miles out

143

into the Lake without using the Causeway?" She paused. "Sorry for the profanity, Pastor."

Roxanne was unbothered, but said nothing.

"We can come back to that one later, I guess," Nick said. "But let's talk about the mutilation."

Roxanne felt herself stiffen. She did not like violence, even in movies, and she certainly didn't like it in real life. She wasn't sure what she was about to hear and she pressed her body backwards into the chair to steel herself. Surprisingly, the chair went backwards with her and a footrest popped up beneath her. Wingback recliners were a great invention, she thought. She leaned back and closed her eyes.

"Wait a minute," Nick said. "We need Dora and DeMarco, if he's here."

Dr. Wilson, who had not yet taken a seat, pressed a button on her phone and summoned her Pathologist and Chief Inspector. Dora was there in 30 seconds, entering through the private door adjacent the patio again. Jerod once again shook his head at the odd layout of this facility, but at the moment he didn't care about that or any other distractions.

"Sit down, please, Dora," Leslie said. "We're about to get to the juicy stuff."

DeMarco followed a minute later, entering through the interior door. Leslie said nothing, but indicated with a jerk of her head that he was to sit.

"We need to talk about the mutilations," Nick said again.

"Oh, God," Roxanne said quietly.

DeMarco wondered why a priest was in the room but didn't care enough to ask.

"Dr. DeMarco," Leslie said. "Could you go over those details again, starting with yesterday's victim?"

"Sure," he said. He closed his eyes for a moment, accessing his memory. What he lacked in charm he made up for in intellect, Leslie thought as she watched his jaw muscles clench.

"Victim number 3 was a white male, approximately 6'1" and 200 pounds. Like the other two, he was in excellent physical condition. There was no sign of coronary artery disease or pulmonary dysfunction of any kind. All internal organs were within normal size and weight and therefore, presumably, functionality."

This kind of clinical talk, Roxanne thought, was fine. But he hadn't yet mentioned "mutilations" and she continued to keep her eyes closed and lean back in the chair.

"Victim three had undergone three dermal excisions, non-surgical and imprecise," he said. "The killer or killers had effectively removed up to 10 layers of skin, roughly 3 to 4 inches square. In consult with detectives, it's not unreasonable to conclude this was done to remove tattoos or other identifiers.

"Like the other victims, number 3 had had his genitals excised, as well. This wound was also imprecise. It included both penis and scrotum, and was administered postmortem. The excised portions were not recovered in any of the cases."

Roxanne moaned, louder than she thought.

"Are you OK?" Nick asked.

"Yes," she said, unconvincingly. "This is just all new to me."

"Go on, Dr. DeMarco," Nick said.

"Cause of death was blunt force trauma to the head and neck, probably administered with a hollow pipe or similar object, based on the bone-shattering and pattern of breakage," he said. "Submersion in water was apparently a means of disposal, but was not contributory to cause of death. Manner of death, clearly, was homicide."

They were all silent. Roxanne opened her eyes.

"Are you done?" she asked.

"With that victim, yes," DeMarco said. "By the way, who are you?"

"She can answer that in a minute," Nick said. "Right now, I need to see the bodies. I think we all do."

Chapter Eight

The phones at the 911 Call Center wouldn't stop ringing. God forbid there was a real emergency, Karly thought. No one would ever get through the mass chaos caused by the press conference. Still, she couldn't blame Jerod or Dr. Wilson or Nick. They had to do something.

Most of the calls were pedestrian, even stupid. "My neighbor's dog has been barking more than usual lately, but I did see her this morning." "The dude next door usually has three or four people on Saturday night and loud music, but he only had two people this weekend and they weren't loud." "I think my neighbor is the killer! I had a vision while I was napping this afternoon!"

It wasn't unusual for lunatics to see danger at every turn when there was a high-profile crime. It was unusual to have this volume of calls. Then again, Karly thought, it was also unusual to have a serial killer striking here. Nothing close had happened, in fact, since Robert Lee Willie's killing spree nearly 40 years ago.

She was answering calls, too, as the overload forwarded to her desk and she used her painfully arthritic hands to enter data into the CAD fields. She couldn't wait to retire.

"911, where is your emergency?" she asked as she answered the phone.

"This is 'O,'" the voice said.

She hadn't expected this one, as she had the previous day – a day that already seemed like it had happened long ago.

"Good evening, sir," she said.

"Your voice sounds familiar," he said.

"I spoke to you yesterday," she said.

Caller ID screens only worked in the other room, not when a call was forwarded. She cursed to herself, silently. Still, if she could keep him on the line long enough there might the possibility of a trace.

"I see," he said. "You were very polite then, as well."

"I'm polite to everyone," she said, although it was a lie.

He chuckled, as if he knew she was fibbing. The voice was altered somehow, as she had heard before. She wasn't an expert in such things by any means, but after enough words were spoken almost anyone could tell a real voice from a computer-affected one.

"What can I do for you this evening?" she said.

"It's kind of you to ask," he said. "Several things, actually. First, tell Captain Leveque his press conference today may cause me to accelerate my schedule."

Karly tried not to gasp. He heard her anyway, and chuckled.

"Second, I have some messages for you to deliver."

"OK," she said. "What are those?"

"Tell Captain Brooks she has beautiful children."

This time Karly couldn't even begin to keep her intake of breath quiet. He chuckled again, and hung up.

Karly ran to her office door and flung it open.

"Brandi!" she said. "The call I just took! I need the tapes NOW!"

Then she ran back to her desk and pulled up the personnel file she had compiled. It contained vital information about every employee – address, spouse, children, allergies, blood types – just in case anything happened. Something had just happened.

She opened her file on Nicole Brooks and entered Brooks' home address into the CAD with a signal 21 – a welfare check. In the notes, she typed, "Do not broadcast this part, but this is a 26's home and the family may be in danger. Send a unit and then post a unit at the house. Have whoever you send call and transfer to me." She clicked "send." It would appear on the dispatcher's screen in seconds.

Then she opened Leveque's file. He had no emergency contact, and his home address had changed fairly recently. She entered it into CAD with almost identical verbiage. Then she ran to the door again.

"Whoever is on Channel 2, I just entered two items of traffic for you," she yelled over the din. "They're top priority. Dispatch them 10-18. Do the one to Pearl River first. NOW!"

Siwel looked up from his computer, where he was going through volumes of bullshit.

"Anything I can do, Captain?" he asked, calmly.

"Negative," she said. "Thanks."

Mail delivery in the Oak Harbor subdivision was usually last on the Postal Service's rounds for the 70461 ZIP code. The carrier didn't like this area much. There weren't mailboxes on the street, so he had to walk the route. Neither rain, nor hail, nor whatever was all fine, but whoever wrote that motto worked in a city where most of the walking was between apartments, he figured, not suburban subdivisions.

Clyde had worked this route for years. He knew the names and addresses pretty much by memory, and he even knew some of the residents. As he approached Dr. Mozingo's house, he noticed the front door was open. As he neared the door and the mail slot he called out.

"Doctor? Doctor Mozingo?"

There was no response, but as he got to the door itself he looked through the broad crack and saw what he assumed was a pool of blood. He retreated quickly, realizing he had left his cell phone in his truck. He hesitated briefly as he considered entering the house but decided against it and broke into a full run. The phone was nearly a block away, but he reached it in what felt like two seconds. Still, he was panting as he dialed 911. He swore it rang 15 times before someone answered.

"911, where is your emergency?"

He rattled off the address from the mail still in his hand.

"I just got to this house and ... the door is open ... I can see a pool of blood."

"Did you go in the house, sir?" she asked.

"No!" he said. "I ran back to my car and called you!"

"What's your name, sir?"

"What the fuck does that matter?" he asked. "Just send help. I'm going back to the house now."

He hung up and raced back. This was no time to worry about details.

Sean was still tired. He had worked Sunday night and his mind and body were still recovering from the discovery of the Prescott family. He was not happy to be called in to work on Monday night when he was supposed to be off until Wednesday, but given the circumstances he didn't want to complain. What was happening was serious.

He was in a different zone tonight, although in the same district. Instead of East Slidell he was in the northern part of District 2, in and around the town of Pearl River. Nothing ever happened here, but he was filling the gap so extra units could be in place elsewhere. It wouldn't help him reach his goal of being a detective, except inasmuch as he was pulling extra duty. His superiors had probably put him here tonight to try and make his workload lighter.

His radio chirped.

"Central, 2317."

"10-71," he replied. He was more than ready to do something, even if turned out to be an alarm going off at the local taco stand or a cow in the road.

"Welfare check, 12571 Franklin Road, Pearl River. Per 4401, signal 25 for more, 10-18."

Call Central per the captain? ASAP? This was weird. What couldn't be put out over the radio?

He turned his vehicle in the direction of the call and grabbed his cell and dialed the non-emergency number available only to employees.

"Radio Room," a female voice answered.

"This is 2317," he said. "What's up?"

"Standby, sir."

In a moment, the Captain answered.

"Sean," she said. "This is Karly."

Rank had no meaning in times of stress – or distress.

"That call we just gave you is Captain Brooks' house."

"10-4, ma'am. On my way."

"You don't understand," she said. "The killer, the serial killer just called. He said, 'Tell Captain Brooks she has beautiful children.' I'm trying to reach her now but this can't wait."

Sean reached for his console, switching on his overhead lights and siren.

"Send backup," he said. Then he hung up so he could put both hands on the wheel. He hoped there was backup to send.

Karly ran back to her office and slammed the door. She reached for the phone and dialed Nick Brooks' cell number from memory. There was no answer.

Sean pulled into the Brooks' driveway, shut off his siren and ran towards the house. Before he got to the door it was clear something was wrong: Half a dozen balloons were flying from the top of the door clearly caught above the portal itself. He slowed and drew his weapon, approaching cautiously. He tried the knob and found it unlocked, then twisted it and shoved the door open as fast as he could, leveling his weapon as he did.

He saw the bloody figure on the floor but his eyes darted back to the room and he pivoted quickly, scanning the room, weapon at the ready. He absorbed it all in an instant. One of the older children – maybe 9 or 10, he thought – was standing 10 feet from his father, frozen. The middle two were crying. The youngest also seemed catatonic.

He re-holstered his weapon and got down on one knee.

"It's OK," he said to the children, holding up one hand to signal they should stay back. He didn't know them or how obedient they were, but he hoped it would be enough. He bent over Clay and tried to visually assess the injury. From a pouch on his belt he withdrew two latex gloves.

"Mr. Brooks," he said, leaning over and staring the semi-conscious victim in the face. There was no response. "Mr. Brooks!" he said, louder. Clay moved slightly and moaned. Sean could hear sirens but wanted to have a full assessment to give paramedics.

There was a good bit of blood, but he couldn't clearly see the source. He opened Clay's shirt, forcefully ripping it apart and popping the buttons off. Blood. Lots of blood. But it wasn't surging, squirting or pumping. This was not a chest wound.

He felt his way through the red puddle, searching for a wound. He found none.

"Mr. Brooks!" he said.

Clay moaned.

Dammit, he thought. I need you to tell me what happened.

His fingers moved to Clay's neck, again palpating for any sign of injury. Just below the chin, he found it, a deep incision all the way to the bone. No, not an incision; it was a split, not a cut, as if he had been struck, hard. His jaw was probably broken.

"He shot me," Clay said, badly slurring his speech and moaning still.

"No," Sean said. "No, he didn't. I'm Deputy Baxter. More help is on the way. You'll be fine. Your kids are fine."

"Nick...," Clay muttered.

"We're tracking her down," Sean said. "It'll be OK."

He heard the sound of tires on the gravel driveway outside and peeled off his gloves, grabbing his radio.

"2317, Central," he said.

"Go ahead, 2317."

"If you can find –" he paused, Nick's call number on the tip of his tongue, and thought better of it. "If you can't find the mother, you may need to call Social Services or a Juvenile Division detective," he said over the air. "Victim will be fine, but the kids have suffered some trauma."

"10-4, sir. Juvenile victims are code 4?"

"That's affirmative, Central. All are unharmed, just shaken. Ambulance has just arrived so I'll have to stay with the minors while the victim is transported."

"10-4, sir. Trying to find the mother now. Any other units needed?"

"Affirmative, Central," he said. "Supervisor, a detective and the Lab. And get a unit to the hospital 10-18."

"CO?" she asked tentatively. It was a subtle way of asking if Clay was still alive.

"Negative, Central," he said into his mic, and then "thank God," to himself off the air. "Victim will be code 4 once he reaches the ER."

"10-4, sir," she said, and he would've sworn he heard cheering behind her in the Radio Room.

Sean stepped aside as paramedics came through the

door and went about tending to their patient.

"Hey, kids," Sean said, still stooping to their level. "How about we go to your rooms and get ready for a little trip to see your mommy?"

He had expected them to be relieved. Instead, all four of them burst into tears. He was glad he was not yet a parent.

Nick and Leslie stood to the side as DeMarco wheeled in a gurney holding the first "O" victim. He closed the door, passed around a vial of Vick's, and each of them smeared some under their nostrils. Then he opened the bag's zipper, slowly, to avoid filling the room too quickly with the smell of death.

DeMarco peeled back the thick covering and stepped back. Leslie moved to the head of the gurney.

"His face and dentition are badly damaged," she said.

"Yes," DeMarco said.

She leaned over to see more.

"His jaw is shattered." She pointed with a gloved finger so Nick would see. "Right here," she said, pointing to the very base of his chin. "This is where it started."

"A blow he didn't expect," Nick said. "An uppercut. With what?"

"My best guess is a hollow pipe or similar instrument," DeMarco said. "That would've knocked him out, not only from the blow but from pain and shock. After that, it didn't matter how strong he was."

"Fuck," Nick said. "This was a total ambush."

"An ambush, yes, but not 'total,'" Leslie said. "Wherever he was, he went willingly."

"Why do you say that?" Nick asked.

"Because there are no ligature marks," Leslie said. "Look at his wrists and ankles. He wasn't restrained. The killer cold-cocked him, yes, but he didn't have to forcibly abduct him. And look," she said, tilting the victim's head sideways. "No marks to the head anywhere. A man this strong wouldn't have submitted to an assailant with a knife or gun who didn't actually use the weapon, at least to subdue him – pistol-whipping or actually poking him with the knife, which would've left marks."

"So he was lured to his death," Nick said.

"Exactly."

"How could someone do that?" Nick asked. "What would compel someone like this to go into a dangerous situation where he could be caught so off-guard?"

"I think the answer is in what's not here," Leslie said. She let that sink in for a moment. "What motivates men?"

"Money. Status. Power. Sex."

"And what's missing from this man?" Leslie asked.

Nick paused.

"His sex organs."

Leslie just nodded.

"So he was lured by a woman, a lover, and was caught by surprise," Nick said. "Maybe by her husband or boyfriend, or –"

"Maybe by her," Leslie said.

Nick paused.

"She'd have to be very strong to inflict this much damage."

She thought back to her own days as a patrol deputy, when she'd had to fight with suspects. No matter how much she trained, she was still not as strong as most men. She had to use her wits as much as her strength.

"I'm not buying that theory, Doctor," she said. "Even with the kind of weapon Dr. DeMarco describes, it would take significant strength to throw a blow with enough force to break a jaw this brutally. Then to cause this other damage to the head...."

Leslie shrugged.

155

"It's just a thought," she said. "But whoever did this had some sort of sexual motivation. Fortunately for the victims, the killer didn't see fit to remove the genitals until after they were dead."

"Central, 2412."

Ben was on edge, as all of them were, but he wasn't complaining. He always told himself that when cops were working this hard it was because other people were having far worse days.

"10-71," he said.

"Signal 21, welfare check, 13 Eden View Court. Signal 25 10-18 for further."

Like Sean a few minutes ago, he wondered why he had to call for more information and why it was "10-18" – urgent. It was not his place to wonder, so he grabbed his phone and dialed. A dispatcher answered and immediately transferred him.

"Ben, Karly here. That 21 is to Captain Leveque's house. I just got a call from the serial killer and he made a reference to Jerod that made me uneasy. I just want you to check on the house. I don't even know if anyone is there."

"10-4," ma'am. "On it."

"Thanks," she said. "I'll notify your supervisor."

They had just hung up when his radio chirped again.

"Central, 2412. I have additional information on that traffic. 911 caller advised he just found a subject bleeding and unresponsive in the doorway of the home."

"10-4," he responded, and hit his lights and siren. He was only a mile away.

Brandi opened Karly's door without knocking.

"Captain, we just had a 911 call from Captain Leveque's home. Mailman found someone bleeding and unconscious in the foyer. Thought you should know."

"Shit," Karly said. "Thank you." She reached for her

desk phone and dialed Jerod's number from memory. There was no answer.

"God almighty fucking dammit!" she yelled to no one. "Does nobody answer their goddamned fucking phones anymore?"

Jerod sat in the Coroner's Office grieving room with Roxanne. It was the most private place in the building and they wouldn't be interrupted. Chaplains regularly met in these rooms with the families of the departed, and no one even wanted to come in here. Like DeMarco's autopsy suites on the other side of the building had the smell of death, this room had an aura of grief.

Roxanne was silent as her eyes studied the room. Although the walls contained a crucifix – not a bare cross, she noted, reminded that the area was heavily Catholic – they also held a Star of David and a Crescent Moon, the symbol of Islam. She admired Dr. Wilson for being so broad-minded. That wouldn't happen in a lot of places.

"You've probably seen a lot," she finally said, breaking the silence.

"Yeah," he said. "So have you."

She half-smiled.

"I thought I had seen a lot until today," she said. "Actually, until yesterday when the phone rang at my office. How do you deal with this?"

He paused.

"Could you be more specific?" he asked gently. He wasn't being snarky, and she could tell.

"How do you deal with violence and death? How do you deal with grieving families? How do you tolerate gore – or even talking about it?" And, then, the question she really wanted to ask: "How do you manage being a closeted gay cop?"

He was fully prepared to answer the first three. The last one caught him off-guard, but in this private setting he didn't mind. Not really. Not from her.

"Well ... around here we don't have to be so closeted," he said. "Sheriff King is open-minded. He knows I'm bisexual."

Roxanne raised her eyebrows, questioningly but without judgment.

"He knows I'm gay," he said. "He knows my partner. I don't run around telling people about it, but some know and no one seems to give a damn."

On his belt, Jerod felt his phone vibrate. He knew it was another reporter wanting follow-up from the press conference and he was in no mood to give any. In this rare moment, his work was intersecting with both his personal and spiritual lives, and he wasn't going to interrupt it.

"Terry," Roxanne said.

"Yes," Jerod said, and he involuntarily smiled. "Yeah, Terry."

"I didn't get to speak to him at church yesterday. How is he?"

"I've barely spoken to him myself since this all started," Jerod said. "But I saw him early this morning. He's fine."

"Good," she said.

"So Jerod...," she began, and then wasn't sure where to go.

He frowned.

"Yes?"

"What can I do for you?"

He smiled again.

"Pastor, at the moment, I'm more concerned about you," he said. "Like you said, this is all new to you."

"It's not new to you?"

"Well, a serial killer is. But I'm used to the violence."

"That's too bad," she said. "No one should ever have to get used to that."

Ben pulled up to Jerod's house and turned off his siren, but not his light bar. He approached cautiously, weapon in-hand. A figure was bent over the victim, halfway in the house. His clothes looked familiar, and as he approached he realized it was a Post Office uniform. He leveled his weapon.

"Sheriff's Office!" he yelled. "Stand up and turn around! Keep your hands where I can see them!"

The mail carrier froze for a moment and then did as instructed.

"You'd better get an ambulance here," he said. "This man is badly hurt."

"They're on the way," Ben said. "Now who the hell are you?"

"Clyde Francingues," he said. "I'm the mail carrier for this neighborhood. Dr. Mozingo is really hurt bad."

"Keep your hands where I can see them," Ben said, and approached cautiously. "Turn around." Clyde did, and Ben awkwardly patted him down with one hand. He grabbed the postman's pepper spray from his belt and tossed it into the yard as far as he could, then holstered his own weapon and quickly handcuffed the witness.

"Hey!" Clyde said. "What are you doing? I'm the good guy here."

"That's probably true," Ben said. "And once I have some backup here I'll be happy to un-cuff you. For now, you're going to sit in my car."

He led Clyde forcefully but not abusively to his vehicle and put him carefully in the back seat.

"2412, Central."

"Go ahead, 2412."

"There was a civilian on-scene. He is 10-15 for his own safety. I'm going in now."

"10-4. Backup is en route."

Ben scoffed. With half the damn force out sick and more than a few on their way to Pearl River, he didn't expect any help very soon. He walked quickly to the door and grabbed his weapon again. This entire scene was unstable and unsafe, but he didn't have much choice in how to handle it.

He nudged the door fully open with his foot and scanned the house, as much of it as he could see. The victim was priority, but paramedics were on the way and he would be of no use if the assailant was still in the house and cold-cocked him from behind. He reached down carefully, still holding his weapon and trying to scan the place for movement with both his eyes and ears. He felt for a pulse on the victim and found one. It was stronger than he'd have expected based on the blood loss. Suddenly, Terry moved and moaned and Ben startled.

"You're going to be OK," he said. "Help is on the way."

Terry just moaned again. Ben hated to leave him as much as he had hated to stall while he corralled the mailman, but there was a natural order of things and that order was designed to keep everyone safe.

He stood erect and kept his weapon drawn as he moved carefully and as quietly as he could through the house. When he was confident they were alone he re-holstered his weapon and went back to the bloody patient. He heard the sound of fire trucks and ambulance sirens and breathed a sigh of relief. This wouldn't be his scene any more, at least not for long.

John Douglas stirred and struggled to consciousness. He could see light through the windows, around the blinds, but that didn't help him discern the time. It was summer. It could be 10 a.m. or 7 p.m. He wondered why he cared.

As he struggled to drunken half-consciousness he realized two things: He was still in his uniform and he was on the floor in his home office. His last memory had been in the kitchen. How many hours ago? He didn't know. He didn't know anything, in fact. He rolled over and jerked, suddenly wider awake, as his collar brass poked him in the neck. He would've shouted if he'd had the energy.

He forced himself to a sitting upright position, still on the floor, and blinked hard. He had no clocks in the house and had long ago stopped wearing a watch, so he used the desk to pull himself up and look at the computer screen. It should've been blank, automatically sleeping for lack of use. Instead, his personal email was open and the screen was lit. He looked at the bottom-right corner for the clock. 6 p.m. Where had the day gone?

He laid down on the floor again and began to snore.

DeMarco was silent, as he wheeled in body number two, Phil Prescott, the only one with a name. That made it harder somehow, knowing the cadaver on the table was a person and not just a piece of science. He opened the bag and began his report without being prompted.

"White male, early 40s, in excellent physical condition. Heart, liver and lung size and weight all within normal range. Cause of death was multiple blunt force trauma to the head and neck   Manner of death was homicide."

Both Leslie and Nick leaned over the corpse.

"Genitals also removed," Leslie said.

"Correct," DeMarco said.

"Dentition heavily damaged?"

"Yes," DeMarco said, "which makes ID by dental records almost impossible – although for this victim it doesn't matter since we know who he is."

"Any signs of sexual trauma or activity?" Nick asked. "On him or victim one?"

"Negative," DeMarco said, "other than removal of the genitals. But it's really hard to discern sexual activity after two days in the water. A body bloats from decomposition and gas builds up.   It only has two escape routes. Meanwhile, microbes in the water are doing their thing."

"Understood," Nick said. "It would be helpful to know, since this is apparently a sexually motivated crime."

"Agreed," DeMarco said. "But science has its limits."

Nick nodded, solemnly.

"That's enough," Leslie said. "Bring in number three. He's the most interesting."

Nick looked at the Coroner curiously.

"The excisions," Leslie said. "The probable tattoos."

In a few minutes, DeMarco was back, unzipping the case and pulling back the flaps.

"The excisions were here and here," he said, pointing to the arms. "And another on the right ankle."

"Were these postmortem also?" Nick asked.

"Yes," he said. "The killer didn't make them suffer. He just wanted them dead and unidentifiable – and sexless."

"And there's no way to tell what the tats were?"

"Negative," he said. "He was thorough and deep. Most tattoos go seven or eight skin layers deep. He took 10 to 12 layers."

She nodded.

"That's enough," she said.

"Is it?" Leslie asked.

"What's missing?"

"The blows to the head. Are they all the same, Simon?"

DeMarco paused.

"Yes," he said. "Initial blow to the chin, shattering the bone and rendering the victim unconscious. Subsequent wounds were to the face and neck, completing the kill while the victim was unconscious. Then, the excision of the genitals and, in the case of victim three, removal of the tattoos."

"Thank you," Leslie said. "Nick, let's get back. We need to feed Jerod some of this information."

"Not yet," Nick said. "I need to see their clothes."

DeMarco raised his eyebrows and withdrew, taking the body with him. He returned a few minutes later with three brown paper bags, each bearing the date and time of discovery. From the first bag he withdrew a pair of gym shorts and a t-shirt. From the second, shorts and a tank top. From the third, shorts and another t-shirt. He laid them out sequentially on the autopsy table. Nick and Leslie both leaned over to examine them.

"They were wearing these when the bodies were recovered?" she asked.

"Yes," DeMarco said.

She leaned in, looking closer. Then Nick reached upwards and adjusted the overhead light.

"The shirts are cheap," she said.

"We're not here to critique their fashion sense," Leslie said.

Nick looked at her sharply.

"Look," she said. "They're mass-produced, inexpensive material and even cheaper screening."

Leslie looked but saw nothing.

"Look closer," Nick said. "They all have markings on them that faded quickly in the water. Cheap."

Leslie leaned over and, this time, so did DeMarco.

"I see what you're saying," DeMarco said.

"I don't," Leslie said.

"Look at the shorts," Nick said.

All three had a brand on the left leg, screen-printing that had faded from use, laundry, and submersion. All three looked the same.

"This is a brand label," Nick said. "But it's a local one. It looks like ..." she struggled to make out the words.

DeMarco leaned forward.

"Pisces Fitness," he said, excitedly.

Both women looked at him curiously.

"It's a local chain, 24-hour," he said. "I work out there, and they give you a pair of shorts and a shirt with your membership. You can buy more. I have three."

"What?" Leslie asked.

"What didn't you get? All the shorts have the label 'Pisces Fitness,'" he said. "It's a local chain. They have gyms in Slidell, Lacombe and Mandeville. I have a membership there."

Leslie and Nick looked at each other. It was a meaningful clue.

"You didn't notice this before?" Leslie asked.

"My job is bodies, not clothes," he said. "So no, I didn't."

"Fuck," Nick said. "Fuck fuck fuck."

"Just a suggestion: Don't work out there for a while," Leslie said.

With Mr. Brooks gone, Sean was left to deal with the children until a Juvenile Division detective arrived. He didn't like children. He didn't hate them, but he much preferred adult company. He had pondered putting his weapon in his car, but that would've left him defenseless – and unable to defend the children – had any threat returned to the house. He had, instead, put it back in his holster while remaining acutely conscious of it. He would be sure none of the four children would come close to his right hip, and he positioned himself appropriately as he sat with difficulty in what his teachers had called "Indian style" when he was in school (but which was politically incorrect now).

"Hey," he said to them. Two of them still wept, albeit more quietly than before. "My name is Sean. What's yours?"

There was only silence in reply.

"What's your favorite game?"

More of the same.

"Your favorite toy?"

He hated this. He reached out and grabbed one of the toys on the floor. He didn't know what it was, but he figured it belonged to one of them.

"Whose is this?" he asked.

The younger one reached for it without hesitation. He handed it over.

"Well there you go, sweetheart," he said. "What's your name?"

She said nothing, but took the toy and retreated to a corner.

Dear God, he thought. Let someone get here soon.

Leslie knocked on the door of the Grieving Room gently.

"Come in," Jerod said.

She opened the door to find him seated across the desk from the pastor.

"Jerod, we need you."

He rose.

"What about me, doctor?" Roxanne asked.

"Yes. Please come," Leslie said.

Roxanne rose, too.

"I'm here to help," she said.

The four of them relocated to Leslie's office. Roxanne and Jerod both headed for the conference table.

"No, no," Leslie said. "On the couches. We need to just talk."

The cop and the preacher followed and sat.

Leslie leaned forward, elbows on her knees, hands on her cheeks.

"Pastor," she said. "We need your insights. Jerod, we have more information for you, but sit tight."

Nick's phone buzzed on her hip. She silenced it without looking down.

"Roxanne," Leslie said. "You're familiar with sexual diversity."

She nodded, not sure where this was going.

"All three of our primary victims had their genitals removed. Why?"

She was taken aback.

"I'm not a profiler," she said.

"Neither are we," Nick said. "So speculate."

Roxanne paused and closed her eyes.

"The killer is angry," she said. "He's angry about … wait … she's angry. She's very angry."

Leslie looked at Nick. The detective's eyebrows rose.

"Why is she angry?" Nick asked.

"Her husband was unfaithful," Roxanne said.

"Lots of husbands are unfaithful," Leslie said. "So are wives."

"He was unfaithful with another man, just like the man who called me."

The others were silent.

"All three of them?" Nick asked, almost incredulous.

"Yes," Roxanne said, opening her eyes and looking at Nick. "It's more common than you think. In many cultures, bisexuality is accepted. Here, it's frowned upon. Men who are bi are assumed to be gay but unwilling to admit it."

They were silent.

"I'm not saying I approve at all, but many men who are married to women have secret male lovers on the side," she said. "If they don't have one, they have many, finding whoever they can."

"What the fuck?" Nick said.

"I know," Roxanne said. "It's hard to understand. But sexuality is fluid. It's on a spectrum."

"The Kinsey Scale," Leslie said.

"That's one," Roxanne said. "But even without the science behind it, like Kinsey did 60 years ago, it's real."

Nick thought of Clay with another man and felt both

confusion and anger. Her face showed it.

"I get it, Captain," Roxanne said. "But it's real. It's common."

"Agreed," Leslie said. "So… that's why the killer cutting off the victims' genitals?"

"A woman scorned," Nick said.

"Yes," Roxanne said. "And in one of the most hurtful ways possible."

Chapter Nine

Robbie Silver had done as his captain instructed, making his rounds of the Sheriff's Office facility in the eastern end of the parish and briefing his fellow detectives – the ones who weren't out sick or in the field. There were only about five of them in the office's Property and Personal Crimes sections. He rounded the corner to go to the Domestic Violence and Juvenile offices, and found the door locked. He went back to Property, to his own desk, and looked around. There was no one there.

He sat down at his desk and dialed the Radio Room. He was surprised to hear Karly's voice answer.

"Radio Room, Captain Devereaux," she answered, and he could tell she was frazzled.

"Captain, this is Silver," Robbie said.

She sighed.

"Thank God," she said. "I need you to find Brooks and Leveque."

"Find them?"

"Yes," she said forcefully. "Find them. Neither of them is answering their goddamned cell phones and I have emergency traffic for both of them."

"Have you tried the radio?" he asked. It was an innocent question.

"No, I have not tried the fucking radio!" she said. "Media are crawling up our ass right now, so nobody is checking in when they arrive anywhere! No detectives anyway, and certainly not Leveque. So please just fucking find them and have them call me immediately!"

"Yes, ma'am," he said.

Karly disconnected and pulled off her headset. She felt like the whole world was spinning, or even crumbling around her.

"Fuck," she said to no one, and she whispered it this time.

Silver stared at the receiver in his hand. This was really, really odd. Everything was odd. Without radio logs showing where people were, the job was getting ridiculously hard – harder than it needed to be. With this severe stomach flu – or whatever it was – afflicting damn near everyone, nobody had the resources they needed. It wasn't just frustrating. It was very, very dangerous.

He didn't think it was wise to spend time driving to random locations trying to find the missing captains, so he put on his detective hat and started with their last known location, as he would've for any missing person. He picked up the phone again and dialed the Coroner's Office. The receptionist answered on the first ring.

"This is Detective Silver with the S.O.," he said abruptly. "Are Captain Leveque and Captain Brooks still there?"

"Yes, sir," she said. "They're in Dr. Wilson's office."

"Ma'am, I hate to do this, but I need you to interrupt them. Tell both of them to call Captain Devereaux 10-18."

"Call him what?" she asked, confused.

"Tell them to call Karly ASAP," he said. "Please."

He disconnected and called Karly back, this time on her direct line.

"I found them," he said. "They're still at the Coroner's Office. I told the receptionist to interrupt them and have them call you."

"Thanks," she said, sighing in relief and giving herself a mental reprimand for not thinking of that herself. "Dammit."

"What?" he said.

"Nothing," she replied. "Look, now I need you to do something else. Go to Captain Brooks' house. I'll text you the address."

"OK," he said. "Why?"

"Because you're the closest detective I have there, the whole fucking juvenile division is out sick, and shit has gone down."

She didn't have time to give him details, and she had to clear the line for when Nick and Jerod called.

"Sean is there," she said. "He'll be glad to see you. Trust me."

She hung up and texted him Nick's home address. Then she put her face in her hands again. This time, she cried.

Clarence was pacing, which made Margaret nervous. Pacing through the joint TV-newspaper newsroom was usually her job. She and Blair sat on opposite sides of the room, watching him like a tennis match as the three of them talked. Clarence occasionally stopped pacing long enough to write something on the big white board on the wall. So far, all it said was, "Where is the sheriff?"

"Wondering where the great George Stewart King has been hiding is dandy," Clarence said, "but with nobody talking it's hard to speculate. Plus, no one but us seems to be missing him, so we'd be manufacturing news."

"Wouldn't be the first time we did that," Blair said.

The both looked at her quizzically.

"Well, seriously," Blair said. "We just did it the other day. That iPhone video wasn't news. It was click bait and we all knew it."

"So you're suggesting we do a 'Where is Sheriff King?'

story without any quotes but ours?" Margaret asked.

Blair shrugged.

"I'm not suggesting anything," she said. "We could easily drum-up some MOTS quotes simply by posing the question."

"Man on the streets quotes aren't good enough," Margaret said. "Not for this one."

They all sighed.

"OK," Clarence said. "So we back-burner that one for now – but I think we should come back to it sooner than later."

"Agreed," Margaret said. "But for now ... what?"

Clarence puffed out his cheeks and looked at the ceiling. This was his "thoughtful" pose, Margaret had learned. His complex mind was working on it and she just waited.

"Blair," he said, suddenly snapping out of it.

"Huh?"

"Who called in the Prescott murder?"

"I don't know."

"Exactly," he said. "The deputies on the scene said a neighbor called it in after noticing the stack of newspapers."

"So?" Blair asked. "There's nothing unusual about that."

"Not usually," he said. "But we were there. We talked to the neighbors."

Her eyes flickered as she started to see what he was saying.

"The one on the left couldn't be bothered and really didn't give a rat's ass," he said. "The one on the right – the old lady – couldn't even see their yard from hers, let alone their front porch. And she's in such bad health it's not like she's strolling around dropping off cookies."

"So who called it in?" Blair asked.

"I don't know," he said. "And maybe they don't, either."

"Then we need to find out," Margaret said. "Clarence, do you have a contact in Central Dispatch?"

"Yeah," he said. "I think so. My tennis partner's wife works there."

"Work your magic," she said. "Blair, why don't you head back out to the scene and see what you can find out."

"On it," she said, and then her cell phone rang.

She looked at the caller ID and pulled her head back in confusion. Her brother was usually at work at this hour.

"Hey, Clyde," she said. "What's wrong?"

"With me, nothing," he said. "But something happened on my route today that you need to know about."

The horrible choice Nick had to make was between her traumatized children and her injured husband. It was an easy decision, and it was the same one she'd have wanted him to make: Go to the kids.

She hit her lights and siren – far outside of protocol but entirely excusable, as if she even had anyone to answer to at the moment. She hadn't waited to see what Jerod's news had been, but he peeled out of the parking lot in the same manner and at top speed.

Pearl River seemed like it was 100 miles away, and she drove as fast as she could maneuver through traffic. She reached her driveway in 10 minutes, and was dismayed to see only one unit – a marked one – there. She threw herself at the door, barely turning the knob, and rushed into the house.

Deputy Baxter was there, crouched on the floor, trying to engage the children and keep them calm. Her abrupt entrance startled them all, and Sean pivoted on the floor and reached for his weapon, stopping short of drawing it. It took him half a second to de-escalate, and he quietly stepped aside. Nick took his exact spot without saying a word, still panting, and the children – all four of them – rushed to her. Sean had never seen a single person, especially a relatively small woman such as Nick, wrap her arms around four people at once, but she managed it, consoling them all, kissing their foreheads, stroking their hair, telling them it would be all right and that Daddy would be fine.

As discreetly as he could, Sean slipped out the front door. Nick didn't even notice.

When he was relatively sure he was far enough that they wouldn't hear anything remotely like a police-related sound, he keyed-up his radio.

"2317, Central."

"Go ahead, 2317."

"The victim's wife has arrived. Any ETA on a juvenile detective?"

"Negative on Juvenile, but a 7000 unit is 10-8 to your location."

He had turned his radio volume down to nothing while he dealt with the children, and he realized now, in retrospect, what a bad idea that had been. He had put the comfort of the victims – and the kids were victims, too – over their safety and his own, not to mention the safety of his fellow deputies. He hoped no one had called him during that brief time, but he couldn't worry about it now. He had acted on parental instincts he didn't even know he had, and that thought struck him. He put it away, compartmentalizing it as cops learn to do.

In the distance, he heard the siren of a single police car and grabbed his radio mic.

"Central, make sure that 7000 unit is not Code 3!"

Lights and sirens would only further traumatize the children.

"10-4, sir."

Seconds later, the sound stopped, and shortly an unmarked unit pulled up in front of the house, stopping on the street. Sean watched and was surprised to see Silver climb out. Robbie walked towards him fast, his tie loose, collar unbuttoned and sleeves rolled up. Detectives could do that; uniforms couldn't.

"Hey, pal," Silver said.

"What're you doing here?"

"Good to see you, too," Robbie replied.

"Sorry. I was just expecting a Juvenile detective."

"Believe it or not, that whole fucking division is out sick. So run this down for me. It's Captain Brooks so I'll make time, but we've got another battery victim at the same hospital and a real shortage of detectives."

Sean gave him the narrative, sequentially, starting with the call from Central and his arrival – and the balloons.

"So the balloon delivery gave the doer entrée," Robbie said.

"That would be my guess. And then a surprise attack before the victim even knew he was in danger."

"Brooks was a specific target?"

"I'd suggest you get the tapes from Central, but from the call Karly made to me, there's no doubt," Sean said. "The caller told Karly to tell Brooks she has beautiful children. Karly freaked out and did what needed to be done, and she kept it off the air."

"Fuck," Robbie said.

"Yeah," Sean said. "This whole thing is fucked."

Karly was running out of majors and captains. With Walder hospitalized, Douglas MIA, Brooks and Leveque understandably occupied with family issues, she was it. That's not where she wanted to be – or how she wanted things to be. She was an expert in law enforcement communications and she had command rank, but detectives and patrol – not to mention a serial killer – were seriously out of her comfort zone. She needed help. No, she wanted help. Whether she needed it would be something they could deal with post-mortem, when the case was solved. And she had no doubt they would solve it.

For now, she had to assume command, and she hadn't yet realized that she already had.

She picked up the phone and dialed Moreau's number.

"Lieutenant Moreau," he answered.

"Captain Devereaux here," she said. "What's your 20?"

"Covington office, ma'am."

"I need you here," she said. "Can you get to the Radio Room in the next 10 minutes?"

"On my way," he said.

She stepped from behind her desk and opened her door.

"Siwel," she called above the din.

He looked up from the computer where he was reading probably scores of calls with mostly bogus tips about 'O.' He had yet to find anything worth pursuing.

"Ma'am?" he said.

"Come here, please."

She stepped back and left the door open. He followed and closed it behind him.

"Ma'am?" he said again.

"Sit down, please," she said, as she poured herself back into her desk chair and put her head in her hands.

"Are you OK, Captain?"

She paused.

"I'm as OK as any of us are right now," she said. "Please just give me a minute. Moreau is on his way."

Moreau's 10 minutes was more like 5, and when he knocked Karly lifted her head and called him in, gesturing to a seat.

"I need to speak to you both in confidence, for now, and as peers."

"Yes, ma'am," Siwel said. Moreau said nothing.

"Michael ... Dan... we're in a bad situation. Rank in the

Criminal Division are all out of pocket. How soon we get them back is anyone's guess."

They said nothing. She ran down the list of the sick, missing and otherwise-occupied.

"I'm the only captain in the Criminal Division who is on duty," she said.

Again, they were silent.

"So I'm it," she said. "And I need you both. I can't be in charge by myself."

"Yes, ma'am," they both said at once.

"I don't know everything Nick and Jerod know, but here's what I do know: Captain Brooks' husband was attacked this afternoon, in front of their children. So was someone at Captain Leveque's house."

They both got wide-eyed.

"I didn't hear any traffic on that," Moreau said.

"I kept it off the air," Karly said. "Media scan us, remember? That's why they were all over the Prescott house last night. That's why they were all over Mandeville Harbor yesterday morning. We have to be more careful."

"10-4," Siwel said. "What do we need to do?"

"Moreau, go to the hospital in Slidell. The victims from Leveque and Brooks' houses are there. Baxter and Silver are at the Brooks house and … I actually don't know at the moment who the hell is at Leveque's house. We're short on detectives and Lab units, too. But someone is there. We need victim statements."

She looked at Siwel.

"Right?" she asked.

"Yes, ma'am."

"Moreau, I know you're used to working on the water, but right now I need you working on blood," she said. "Got it?"

"Yes, ma'am," he said. "I'll do my best."

"Siwel … please tell me what I need you to do."

Jerod rushed into the ER faster than he had ever done for a crime victim. He had his badge around his neck on a lanyard and the reception desk saw him coming. He stood.

"Which victim do you want to see first?" he asked.

"The male," Jerod said.

"Room 2," he said, and Jerod knew where that was from previous visits, both as a detective and as public information officer.

He pulled back the curtain and rushed in, not bothering to close it behind him. Terry lay on a gurney, his face heavily bandaged. Jerod slowed and approached cautiously, assessing the injuries as thoroughly as he could, both as a detective but as a spouse.

Terry's chin was bandaged and taped. His eyes were bruised but Jerod saw no evidence of bone breaks or other damage. His cheek bones were the same. His lower lip was split.

Jerod walked to the gurney and placed his hand gently on Terry's arm. The patient stirred, and Jerod moved his hand to hold Terry's. In all the times he had been in these rooms, he had never before touched a crime victim. It wasn't appropriate, wasn't his place. Today, it was. It was his only place. He had left his radio and cell phone in the car, even, and he never did that; Terry was going to get his undivided attention.

The bandaged figure on the bed stirred, and Jerod gripped his hand tighter.

"Hey, baby," Terry said, without opening his eyes.

Jerod smiled, and realized his eyes had teared. He blinked, hard.

"How'd you know it was me?" Jerod asked. "You haven't opened your eyes."

"Because I knew you'd come," Terry said.

Jerod squeezed his hand tighter and said nothing.

Nick emerged from her house holding Charley, the youngest, and left the door open. Sean and Robbie both turned to face her, silently.

"My mother is coming to get the kids," she said. "Then I'm going to the hospital. Then I'm going back to work."

"Yes, ma'am," Silver said.

Nick turned to Sean.

"Thank you, Baxter," she said.

"Just doing my job, ma'am," he said. "Anything you need, just let us know."

"I need us to catch this bastard," she said, remembering as she did that there was a growing possibility the killer was a woman.

"We will," Robbie said.

"Yeah," she said, calmly. "We will. Soon. We have to."

When Jedediah's wife left for work, he was still on the sofa, ESPN on the television and his mind elsewhere. She leaned over and kissed him goodnight, he smiled sweetly, and she left for the hospital. He waited to get up until he heard both the engine and the sound of her driving away.

He took a quick shower and then changed into his gym clothes. It was odd to bathe before a run, but he had his reasons.

The lakefront was only a few blocks away, and he walked that part. Then he turned left, jogging at a low speed to the Harbor, the east end, before turning 180 degrees without even pausing. The fact that he had just passed the same crime scene he had worked yesterday didn't even register. His mind was elsewhere. His military training, his police work and his own fitness regimen kept not only his muscles in shape but his lungs at full capacity; he didn't need to pause to catch his breath.

He ran back westward, passing his starting intersection, and continued. The Mandeville Lakefront was essentially a three-mile long park, with mansions on the north side of the street and Lake Pontchartrain on the south. To the southwest, the Lake Pontchartrain Causeway – the world's longest over-water bridge – was clearly visible. He kept his pace until he neared the western end, where Lakeshore Drive reached a dead end. There, he slowed, stopped, leaning over with his hands on his knees, and waited.

It seemed like both a moment and an hour before he saw the headlights. It was still daylight, barely, approaching dusk. The SUV pulled up and stopped, and the headlights went off. The driver waited, not bothering to roll down the windows. The silence turned him on, and Jedediah hesitated, savoring the moment. He knew what to do.

He walked to the back of the vehicle, opened the handle between the decals that read "Sheriff's" and "Office," and climbed in. There was already a blanket laid out. He got on his back, as he had done so many times before, and waited. It seemed like he was there in silence for a while, but it was probably only moments. He felt the engine come alive again and the vehicle began to move. He wondered where he was being taken tonight, but he trusted from experience, enjoyed the suspense, and kept his eyes closed. It didn't matter. No one was going to question a marked police vehicle no matter where the driver chose to park. It had been too long, and the anticipation was building.

He felt the vehicle turn left, in a short distance felt another left, and only a minute later, another. The ride stopped in two minutes, the engine went off, and Jedediah let out a breath. Based on the distance and direction, he knew where they were: the pier at Sunset Point. He smiled. It had a great view, although he wouldn't see it tonight.

The back door opened and he flinched a little, the moment getting close. He felt a hand on his thigh, leaning with only a bit of weight, for balance. It wasn't his usual posture, but Jedediah was open to whatever lay ahead. He had all night and it had been a while, so he wanted it to last. As usual, he said nothing. It was more pleasurable, more secretive, more naughty this way.

The hand moved up his thigh and his manhood throbbed. He squirmed a bit, moaned quietly, but did not speak. His breathing increased. He sensed movement, abrupt, and barely even felt it when the pipe hit him square on the chin.

Roxanne paced in the Coroner's private office; Leslie stood behind her desk, her eyes fixed on the fountain outside.

"What are you thinking?" Leslie asked her.

Roxanne was no longer in pastor mode. She was angry, tired, stressed, and utterly frenetic.

"I'm thinking this is all very, very fucked up, and I don't know how you live in this world."

"Death is a part of life," Leslie said. "Didn't you learn that in seminary?"

Roxanne scoffed.

"Death, yes. Murder, no."

"Hmm," Leslie said, still not turning from the view of the sunset light on the water behind her. "I suppose not. Except that sometimes, it is. I've read the Old Testament."

"That's not OK," Roxanne said. "Not now. I'm not OK with that."

"Sweetheart, none of us is OK with that," Leslie said. "That's why we do what we do."

Roxanne turned, stopped, let out a deep breath.

"Are you going to catch this woman?" Roxanne asked.

"Of course," Leslie said. "In time. But I can't promise you we'll find her before she kills again."

"How can you be so calm?"

Leslie turned to face her.

"What choice do I have?" she asked, harshly. "How can you not be calm? Do you think feelings will catch this person? No. Facts will. Data. Science. Tenacity. That's what will catch him. Her. Whoever. Being upset only slows us down."

"I'm not part of that 'us,'" Roxanne said.

Leslie rocked her head from side to side, smirking.

"As of today, yes, you are," the doctor said.

"Fuck that," Roxanne said, dropping all pretense of her pastoral collar as her stress and disgust boiled over. "I will not be cold."

"I'm not cold," Leslie said. "I'm methodical. I want this bastard – this bitch – as much as you do. More, even. I can't get there by being emotionally involved."

They were both silent for a moment.

"I need to go," Roxanne said.

"Yes," Leslie said. "Yes, you do. You need to go to the hospital and tend to the living. You're very well equipped to do that. I'll handle the dead."

Blair and her photographer arrived at the scene in Oak Harbor quickly. Having a van with the station logo on it pretty much meant that no cop would stop them, and speed limits were even more ignored today than usual.

"Spray the scene," she said. "Get as much as you can. On this one, B-roll is more important than interviews."

He nodded, hopped out, and grabbed the camera from the back. Blair had no intention of trying to interview anyone here. Everyone with any authority to speak or any rank at all was missing in action, and she wasn't going to waste her time with people she knew without a doubt would clam up.

From the passenger seat of the van, she looked around. There was one marked unit, roof lights still on. That was all. Maybe this wasn't such a big deal as her brother the mail carrier had made it out to be.

She grabbed her iPhone and pulled up the Assessor's website. It would be a starting point to know who owned the house. She got to the right page, entered the address with difficulty on the small screen, and waited. It took two seconds for the page to tell her the house belonged to a Terry Mozingo. She had no idea who that was, and only because of her brother knew the victim was male, but she was going to find out.

She toggled to Google and searched the name. Terry was a he, a dentist here in Slidell. She called the office phone number. A machine answered, and she hung up. Next stop, the Clerk of Court's website, where land records were stored. Because the Clerk's Office also handled criminal and civil court issues, as well as land records, there were more buttons to push. She searched criminal records first, as those were always the most salacious; there were none that matched the name or the address. Then she searched civil records; Dr. Mozingo had no lawsuits pending. She settled on land records and searched again, hitting pay dirt. Six months ago Dr. Terry Mozingo had filed papers with the Clerk giving half-ownership of the home to Jerod C. Leveque.

She smiled a bit, but shook her head. This explained a lot, including, at least in part, why Jerod had been inaccessible. She rolled down the window and called her photographer.

"That's enough," she said. "We need to go to the hospital."

The breezeway behind the Emergency Operations Center in Covington was quiet and dark, as usual. It was also where 911 operators and other emergency personnel took their smoke breaks. Clarence sat on a bench across the street, watching. He knew she'd come along sooner or later. Her husband was an athlete, but she had a sedentary job and a tobacco habit.

He couldn't call her. They'd only met a few times and, besides, he couldn't be on a computer-recorded police line asking for her to step outside. He was patient.

A little after 7 p.m., he saw her walk out through

the back door and find a place in the shadows. It was August, still very hot, and even though the sun was setting sweat still dripped from the face of anyone brave enough to venture outdoors. There was a slight breeze tonight, and that helped, but it wasn't enough to make things comfortable. He approached slowly, mostly for his own comfort, and crossed New Hampshire Street to where she stood, cigarette in her right hand and the whole pack in her left.

"Hey, Brandi," he said.

She was startled.

"Hey," she said, cautiously.

"It's me," he said. "Clarence."

He didn't much like his name, but its uniqueness made him memorable. Most people had never known anyone named Clarence.

"Oh, hey!" she said. "How're you."

"Not bad," he said, lying, because he was utterly exhausted. "You?"

"The same," she said, also lying.

"Cool," he said. "I need to find your husband soon and hit some tennis balls. It's been a while."

She chuckled politely.

"I hear you," she said. "I need to see my husband soon, too! It's been too long for me, also."

He laughed politely.

"So, Brandi," he said. "I need some help."

She stiffened, but she didn't bristle, he observed. She was leery but interested.

"Yeah?" she said.

"Yeah," he replied. "It's a simple thing, really, and it's a public record. I'd just really appreciate it if you could save me some time and cut out the middle man."

"OK," she said. "What is it?"

He was direct this time.

"Who called in the Prescott murders last night?"

She paused.

"A neighbor."

"Can I get a name?"

"I wasn't here so I'd have to look it up, but I can. Want me to text it to you?"

"That would be great!" he said, more effusively than he felt. "Any contact info would be super, too."

She threw her cigarette into the gutter.

"I'll see what I can do," she said, and walked off.

Given her demeanor, he didn't know if she was going to help or not. It had been worth a shot.

Rooney was vexed. He was also tired. He had worked all weekend and now all day on Monday, but he couldn't stop. He felt like he was the only one so dedicated, but he knew it wasn't true. The Chief was here, too, and had also worked God-knows how many hours on Sunday. They had a killer to catch, and they were all sure that killer would strike again.

In some ways, he was blessed: At his job as an NYPD cop, he'd never have gotten this close to such an important investigation. But he also mourned. His adopted city was battling a serial killer, multiple deaths, and at least two victims who hadn't been found yet. His jurisdiction was limited. His rank was limiting. He didn't know what to do.

Marlene's voice sounded on the intercom.

"Officer Rooney, please report to the Chief's office," she said with her unmistakable lilt.

Under any other circumstances, he'd have thought he was in trouble. Today, he hoped he was being asked for input and assistance.

He walked past Marlene's empty desk – her usual post – and into Chief Richard's office.

"Sir?" he said. "You wanted to see me?"

He looked to his right and realized Marlene was there, too, notebook and pen in-hand.

"Yes," Tom said. "Sit down."

Rooney sat, feeling suddenly nervous.

"Relax," the chief said. "Nothing's wrong. Well – lots of things are wrong, but none of them are your fault."

"Yes, sir," Rooney said.

"Some really awful things have happened since we finished our meeting at the Coroner's Office," Chief said. "People at both Brooks' and Leveque's homes have been attacked. The killer called in one of them himself."

Rooney was taken aback but tried to remain stoic.

"That's horrible," he said.

"Yes," Tom said. "They're going to need even more help. Can I detail you to the Sheriff's Office Serial Killer Task Force?"

Rooney was flattered.

"Sure, Chief, but I didn't know there was a task force."

"Well, that's just what I'm calling it," he said. "The whole group of us that was at the meeting today. We need to start working together. Everyone is exhausted and something is going to fall through the cracks if we're not careful. I just want you to organize it. I'll lead it, if they need me."

"Chief, I'll do whatever I can."

"Great," he said. "I think your experience and obvious dedication will be helpful in catching 'O.'"

Marlene looked up and spoke for the first time.

"O?" she said.

"Yeah," Chief said. "That's what the killer calls himself. But I shouldn't have let that slip, so keep it to yourself."

"O?" she said again, this time mostly to herself. Rooney and the chief exchanged a glance. Marlene looked at them.

"Chief," she said, "I'm not trying to get in your business, but what if it's not 'O' but 'eau'?"

"Sorry," Tom said, but I don't hear the difference.

"J'oublie les Américains ne parlent qu'une seule langue," she said almost under her breath. They didn't understand but the tone was one of disgust.

"What?" Chief asked.

"Sorry," she said. "Eau. E. A. U. It's French. It means 'water.'"

They both stared at her again.

"Water!" she said again. "Wa-ter. As in 'eau de parfume,' what Americans just call 'perfume.' 'Eau de parfum' means 'scented water.'"

"Marlene," Chief said, "I'm not sure I'm following this."

She sighed.

"Chief, he keeps calling himself 'O,' you said. But what if he's really saying 'eau'?"

"Marlene," he said, getting frustrated, "I can't hear the difference."

"Exactly!" she said. "All the bodies were found in the water, right?"

"Right," Rooney said.

"So what if his name actually means 'water'? What if that's significant somehow?"

"She may be onto something, Chief," Rooney said. "If you don't mind, I'll run it past Captain Brooks... or, whoever."

Chief shrugged.

"Sure," he said. "Can't hurt."

Chapter Ten

Clarence had just gotten back to the bureau when his cell phone rang. It was Brandi.

"Hey there," he said, trying not to sound as excited as he felt. He climbed out of his car and slammed the door.

"Hey," she said. "I've got to be quick."

"OK," he said, fumbling for his keys. Margaret always locked the door when she was there alone. "Let me get to my desk."

"You won't need to write this down," she said. "There's nothing."

"What do you mean, 'nothing'?"

"I mean the dispatcher who took the call didn't get the caller's name. All I know is it came in from at 1950 hours yesterday. The caller was a woman. I listened to the tape. She said what you already know, I think. Newspapers stacked up, hadn't seen them in nine days."

"OK," Clarence said, hiding his frustration this time. "What about a Caller ID number?"

"I thought you might ask that. It was a pay phone on Fremaux Avenue."

"Payphones still exist?" he asked.

She chuckled.

"Apparently," she said. "This one's at a convenience

store just west of I-10."

That was about four miles from the scene, Clarence thought. And it was weird.

"OK," he said. "Thanks. Any chance I can get my hands on that recording?"

"Now you're pushing it," she said.

He laughed it off.

"OK," he said. "Thanks so much. Owe you one."

"Yeah," she said. "Just let my husband win the next time you play tennis."

"Ha! Thanks again, Brandi. See you soon."

He hung up and shook his head.

"What's up?" Margaret asked.

He ran down the conversation.

"So what now?" he asked.

"Seems obvious to me," she said, surprised he wasn't thinking of the next step. "Go to that convenience store. Talk to the clerk or manager. See if they have surveillance video."

He perked-up.

"Good idea," he said. "I'll let you know what I come up with."

And he was back out the door. Margaret got up and locked it behind him, then sat back down and texted Blair, "What've you got?" She did not expect a prompt answer, and she was not disappointed.

John awakened again, this time to the sound of his garage door opening. If he had been more lucid, he might've been alarmed. Instead, he was merely startled. He tried to get his bearings. He was still on the floor of the home office and it was getting dark fast. He heard the sound of an engine. It sounded like his own. Then the garage door slowly closed.

"What the hell?" he said aloud, struggling to a seated

position on the floor.

He heard the door from the garage to the house open and footsteps down the hall. Whoever it was didn't turn on any lights. His police instincts told him to take a defensive position, grab his weapon and wait. Instead, he called out.

"Who's there?"

There was no response as she walked down the hall into the kitchen.

Unlike at Jerod's house, Blair jumped out of the van and headed for the ER door, calling back to her photographer, "Set up over there, but standby," she said. "Let me see what I can do in there."

She walked in as if she owned the place, her charismatic 4-foot-11-inch frame and pretty face capturing as much attention as Jerod had when he walked in wearing his badge. She marched to the desk.

"I need to see Jerod Leveque," she said.

The receptionist flipped through the papers on his desk.

"We don't have a patient by that name, ma'am," he said.

"I know," she said. "But I also know you know who he is and who he's here to see, so don't play dumb."

His face flushed.

"I can't release that information," he said.

She glanced over his head to the white board every ER had, listing patient names, room numbers and doctor assigned. She saw "Mozingo" and got what she needed.

"Thanks," she said. "I'll be in Room 2." She walked off down the hall as he called after her. She ignored him and kept going. Even if security came after her, they weren't going to make a scene – and she gambled on Jerod vouching for her.

She reached the "room" – really just a curtained-off

area. She was surprised the cloth barrier was pulled back, and it caused her to hesitate. Story or not, she was still dealing with real people here. She brought herself back to a calm demeanor and stepped into the entryway. Jerod's back was to her. The patient, looking badly injured but clearly not dead, had his eyes half-open. Jerod held his hand, tears coming slowly down his face.

Blair was momentarily caught up short. Cops didn't cry. Jerod Leveque certainly didn't. Not in front of anyone.

"I'm so sorry," she heard Jerod say, almost in a whisper. "I'm so sorry. When this is over I'm going to get a new job. No more long hours, no more danger."

"Baby," the patient said back. "I don't want you to do that. This is not your fault. And by the way, I think you have a visitor."

Jerod spun abruptly. His face flushed, whether with rage or embarrassment – or a combination of the two – Blair wasn't sure.

"I'm sorry," she said, instinctively. She said those words as rarely as cops cried.

Jerod said nothing, wiping his eyes with his sleeve.

"I'm sorry," she said again.

"It's OK," Jerod said, surprisingly gently. "What do you want?"

"A story," she said. "I don't have to name anyone. I'll respect your privacy. But I need to know what's going on with this killer. The public needs to know. And all of you have vanished all day."

"I don't have much to tell you," he said, and wiped his eyes again. "The killer is still at-large. We have two more victims, both alive and without critical injuries. This is one of them." He indicated Terry.

Blair stepped forward, politely yet still assertively.

"Hi," she said, holding out her hand. "I'm Blair Francingues. My brother is the one who found you and called 911."

"Terry Mozingo," he said raising his hand to hers. "Nice to meet you. Please tell him thank you for me."

"I will," she said, then looked at Jerod. "Has anyone taken his statement yet?"

Jerod shook his head.

"We're short on –" he stopped himself.

"I know," Blair said. "You're short on manpower, especially detectives. We're short on photographers and technicians, which is why I'm not doing a live shot right now outside this hospital. Every damn body is sick."

They were all silent.

"I'll make you a deal," she said.

"I hate deals with reporters," Jerod said.

"I know. I don't blame you. But this will work out for both our benefits. You're a trained detective, but you can't take his statement for obvious reasons. It could be hours before anyone is here. How about *I* take it. On-camera."

"That's insane," Jerod said.

"No, no. Not really," she said. "I'll take his statement with you present. Then I'll hand you the tape – literally the only copy. Then you tell me what parts of his statement I can use in my 10 o'clock live shot. I won't use the address of the house, or Dr. Mozingo's name – or yours."

He thought for a moment. He was tired. He was more tired than he had ever been in his life. He needed help, but this wasn't exactly what he had been praying for.

"I think it's a great idea," Terry said.

Blair and Jerod looked at him simultaneously.

"Are you sure?" Jerod asked.

"Absolutely," he said. "It'll help the investigation, it'll help her, and it'll get us home faster."

Jerod hadn't thought of that last part, of putting Terry in his own bed – in their own bed – to recover.

"OK," he said. "Go get your camera. I'll smooth it with

hospital security."

Brooks might have his balls for breakfast, but at this point he didn't give a damn.

"Who's there?" John called again, still sitting on the floor.

The light in the hallway came on and Donna came down the hall. He hadn't seen his wife in months, but even in his hazy frame of mind and half-drunken vision, he knew her by her movement even if not her face. Her hair was pulled back in a ponytail, a baseball cap was on her head, and she wore a blue coverall.

"Baby," he said, almost falling over. "You came back."

"I've been back lots of times," she said.

He was confused.

"I haven't seen you," he said.

"That's because every time I've been here you've been gone or passed-out drunk," she replied. "Usually drunk."

He didn't doubt her words. He never had.

Roxanne had an easier time with the ER receptionist than Blair had. The clerical collar helped, and she was glad she had made the wardrobe decision she had that morning – and she was glad she had selected her black smock, which concealed the sweat she was feeling all over her body.

Now, she was standing at the entry to the curtained room where Nick Brooks' husband was being treated. As a pastor, she had made more than a few trips to emergency rooms, but this was different. She had met Nick Brooks that morning and didn't know her husband at all. Deep breaths and a quick prayer steeled her nerves and she pulled the curtain back only partway.

"Mr. Brooks," she said, softly.

"Hi," he said in the half-lit room, eyes still closed.

"I'm Pastor Roxanne," she said.

He opened his eyes and lifted his head a bit.

"Hi," he said again. "You're the hospital chaplain?"

"No," she said. "I'm a friend of your wife's."

He frowned.

"She's never mentioned you," he said.

She ignored the comment.

"May I come in?" she asked.

He should've been wary since being attacked a few hours earlier, but he wasn't. Fear of people wasn't in his nature.

"Sure," he said, and started to struggle to sit up.

"You don't need to get up," she said.

"It's OK," he said. "I actually want to."

She helped him put some pillows behind him and found the button to move the bed to a more upright position.

"Thanks," he said. "Would you mind turning on a light?"

Roxanne found the switch on the wall and flipped it. The fluorescents above flickered and came on.

Despite his injuries, Clay had a very handsome face, Roxanne thought. His chin was bandaged but he otherwise looked OK. His eyes were a steel blue that women loved, although she was immune.

"How're you feeling?" she asked.

"Hurts like hell," he said impassively.

"I'm sorry," she said. "Can I get you anything?"

He thought for a moment and then shook his head.

"Where's Nick?"

"She's on her way," Roxanne lied. She honestly had no idea where Nick was or how soon she'd be here. "I just thought you could use a visitor and a friendly face."

"I really appreciate it," he said. "So how do you know my wife?"

She should've anticipated that question but hadn't.

195

Oh, well, she thought. Nothing works like the truth.

"We're working together on a case," she said, finally.

He frowned.

"This serial killer?"

"Yes," she said.

He assessed her for a moment.

"You're not one of those crazy psychic pagan priestesses, are you?"

She laughed, and he chuckled for a second, then winced in pain.

"Sorry," she said. "No, I'm a garden variety protestant minister."

"That's great," he said. "You know, I like seeing women do jobs people used to say they couldn't do. I'm so proud of Nick being a cop and coming so far."

Roxanne smiled.

"I'm sure you are," she said. "She's a really good person and a really dedicated worker. She really has the heart of a servant."

Rooney went to his car and headed towards Lacombe, dialing the Coroner's Office on the way. He confirmed Dr. Wilson was still there with whoever answered the phone, left a message asking her to wait for him, and drove quickly east. It was well after closing time for administrative offices, but in times like this people worked around the clock. They had to.

Dr. Wilson met him at the door and let him in.

"Doctor, Chief Richard has asked me to help organize a Task Force to find 'O,'" he said. "I told him I would, but everyone seems to have disappeared. I can't find Captain Leveque or Captain Brooks, and I really need to know what's going on. Can we operate out of here since it's in the middle of the parish?"

Leslie looked at him warily.

"You could've asked me all of that on the phone, Rooney," she said, and turned towards her office. "Come on."

He followed her sheepishly.

"Sorry, Doctor," he said. "I guess I could've. I get a little eager sometimes. It's the New Yorker in me."

"It's OK," she said. "I'm not leaving anyway. Let's talk. Want some coffee?"

"Yes, ma'am, that would be great. It's been a long day."

She changed paths on the way to her office and went to the break room. Dora was there, pouring herself a cup of what Leslie's nose told her was a fresh pot.

"Hey, Dora," she said. "Anything new?"

Dora nodded at Rooney, then faced the Coroner.

"Nothing new, Doc, but something occurred to me and I can't stop thinking about it and whether it might mean anything."

"Well, then, let's all have some coffee and sit down in my office," she said. "At this point, anything could matter – and there's a shrinking number of us to even care."

She poured coffee for herself and Rooney and headed back to her office. They followed and she led them to the comfortable seats in the center of the room.

"OK, Dora, what are you thinking?"

"Yesterday morning when we got here with the third victim, there was a photographer standing outside," she said. "I called Jerod and he said to ignore her."

"OK," Leslie said. "I agree with Jerod."

"Yeah," Dora said. "Me, too, I guess, but the more I think about it the more odd it was."

"Why?" Rooney asked. "Media have been crawling all over the Parish the last two days."

"Not alone, they haven't," Dora said. "They seem to travel in packs. I mean, right?"

"True enough," Rooney said. "And yesterday almost all of them were at the Harbor."

"Right," Dora said. "So why wasn't she?"

"Maybe her station thought they'd get some kind of exclusive by sending someone here?" Leslie said.

"I guess," Dora said. "Media isn't my specialty. But she was so far away – I assumed being careful not to be on public property, although she had every right to in the parking lot as long as she didn't get in the way. And then I watched the news last night and this morning, and there was no footage from here. It was all from the Mandeville Harbor and the Prescott crime scene in Slidell."

Rooney and the doctor digested this for a moment.

"So you think it wasn't a news photographer," Rooney said.

"No," Dora said. "I think it was the killer."

The phone lines at Central Dispatch had finally slowed to a dull roar, and Karly had sent two dispatchers home. Siwel was headed to the hospital to take statements from Clay Brooks and whoever it was from Jerod's house. She had sent Moreau to the Crime Lab with instructions to do whatever had to be done, commandeer resources, personnel or anything needed to collect evidence from those scenes. Then she had sat down again in her office, this time on the small couch against the wall, and had leaned over until she was laying down, one foot still on the floor.

Like all of them, she was spent. Like all of them, she couldn't stop until this killer was caught. That he had suggested "accelerating" his timetable deeply disturbed her. On the other hand, it indicated there would be an end-point when he was just finished killing and life could get back to normal. If they didn't catch him, though, things would never actually feel normal again.

She was lost in thought and starting to doze when

someone knocked on her office door. She sat up abruptly.

"Yeah?" she yelled. "Come in!"

Her booming voice was legendary. Brandi opened the door.

"Sorry to bother you, Captain, but Dr. Wilson just called."

"Shit," Karly said. "What's up?"

"She didn't say, but she asked that you go back to her office."

"Shit," Karly said again. "OK. Thank you. Please call her back and tell her I'm on the way."

Dan Moreau knew about as much of working the Crime Lab as he did about performing brain surgery, but he also knew he had to get it done. At the moment, there was only one Lab investigator working, and he was handling another fatal accident; as much as they needed all available people on the 'O' case, they couldn't leave a dead body in a car on the interstate, either. Fortunately, that detective had left the door unlocked.

Moreau let himself into the small structure at the rear of the Sheriff's Office western complex. There were three marked Crime Lab vans in the parking lot, which meant there were also three sets of keys in here somewhere. He went from desk to desk, searching in drawers, until he found a set and hoped they worked on one of those vans.

The vehicles were old and somewhat outdated; there was no keyless entry or alarm system on them. He tried the keys on the first one and had no luck. He moved to the next and inserted the key. Again, no luck.

"OK, Jesus," he prayed. "Give a good cop a break."

The door of the third one opened with ease and he climbed in, realizing that in 20 years of police work he had never been inside one of these things. He looked in the back and saw rows of shelving lined with equipment, chemicals, goggles, masks. A lockable cage covered each shelf, securing the supplies when in transit. It was a good thing, he thought; he didn't want to be responsible for breaking or spilling anything, especially since he didn't know what half of it was.

He pulled out onto the highway and headed south towards the interstate. This vehicle was almost as noisy as one of the boats he usually piloted. He grabbed his cell phone from a holster on his hip and dialed Mandeville Police. When the dispatcher answered he identified himself and asked for the chief.

"Richard," the Chief answered when the call transferred.

"Chief, Lt. Moreau here from the S.O. I need some help."

"Name it, brother," he said.

"Yesterday morning at the harbor, you had an officer who had prior experience in the Crime Lab. Major Walder got him to help with the body."

"Cone," Richard said. "Jedediah Cone. What about him?"

"We're so short-handed right now that I've gotten assigned to Crime Lab duty. We've got two active scenes in Slidell, two victims at the hospital, and only me to process them. Do you think I could borrow Cone for the night?"

"He's not on duty tonight, but if I can reach him, you can have him. I'll pay the overtime."

"Thanks, Chief. Please let me know."

"10-4, Moreau. I'll reach you through Central."

They hung up and Richard grabbed his cell and dialed Cone's cell number from his contacts. No answer. He tried his home phone with the same result.

"Shit," he said. "This is no time to disappear, Jedediah. Damn near everyone else has."

He grabbed his keys and walked to his dispatcher's station.

"Can you look up Cone's home address for me, please?" he asked. "I know he's not far from here and I can't reach

200

him by phone."

"Yes, sir," she said, and in about five mouse clicks had it on her screen. She jotted it down on a Post-It note and handed it to him.

"Thanks," he said, and headed for the back door.

Rooney and Dora walked out the back door of the Coroner's Office, into the bay.

"I had backed in when I saw her," Dora said. "I had started to get out of the truck when I saw the camera, and I got back in until I talked to Jerod."

"Do you remember which direction?"

It was dark now, so Dora took a moment to reorient herself. The bay was clear now, so she eyeballed the space and stood roughly where she would've been when sitting in the vehicle.

"That way," she said, and pointed to the perimeter of the property on its eastern edge. "It's nothing but woods back there. No road connects us to that space, but I didn't see any suspicious vehicles. I don't know why this didn't occur to me before."

"What vehicles did you see?"

"The usual. Ours. Some unmarked sedans. A Sheriff's Office SUV. But I always see those."

"OK," said Rooney. "Let's go."

"Go where?" she asked.

"Over there," he said, pointing towards where she had seen the female photographer.

"Why?"

"To look for evidence," he said. "Marks from a tripod, footprints, cigarette butts, candy bar wrappers, whatever."

"But it's dark," she said.

"Yeah, I kind of noticed that," he said wryly. "You're wearing boots. I've got a flashlight on my belt. Do you have one?"

"In my kit," she said.

"Well go get it and let's go."

She was too tired to argue.

Clarence pulled his Toyota into the parking lot of the Quik-n-Easy on Fremaux, scanning in the beam of his headlights for a payphone. He slowly turned the car in a circle. Sometimes at places like this, the phone was on a post in the parking lot. At least that's how he remembered life back when payphones had been common. Seeing nothing, he pulled into the lot. There was no phone outside, either.

"Dammit," he said, getting out of the car and slamming the door. He wondered if he was at the wrong convenience store, but this was the only one he could think of in the area and he was in no mood to go exploring. He had to pee anyway, and needed some caffeine.

He walked in, waved politely at the cashier, and headed for the restroom. At the end of the narrow hall, he saw a payphone mounted to the wall. He was relieved, but he had to relieve himself first. When he finished in the restroom, he came back out, listened to the squeak of the metal hinges, and walked not towards the store but to the phone. He didn't touch it. As rare as these things were any more, it wasn't impossible that fingerprints from a call 24 hours ago still remained. He stood on his toes and looked at the top of the phone, just in case there was something there of interest. An empty trail mix bag. He sighed, pulled out his phone, and snapped pictures of the phone; they would probably be useless, but it wouldn't hurt to have them.

He turned around to head back into the store and found the clerk standing at the end of the hall, arms folded, staring at him.

"What the hell are you doing back here?" he asked.

"Um ... nothing," Clarence said. "Haven't seen a payphone in years. Just reminiscing."

"Uh-huh. You gonna buy something?"

"Yes!" Clarence said. "I need coffee."

"Well come on and get it, then."

Clarence said nothing, but walked past the clerk, sucking in his gut as he slid through the narrow opening that had been left for him between the corpulent clerk and the door frame. He got his coffee and went to the counter. He needed to ask some questions but he was obviously on thin ice with this surly fellow.

He pulled out some money and handed it over for the coffee.

"You own this place?" Clarence asked, thinking it might open the door for conversation regardless of the answer

"Yup," he said, handing Clarence his change without breaking eye contact. "Bought it a few years ago. Why?"

"Just wondering," Clarence said. "So many chains these days, it's nice to see a local business doing well."

"Uh-huh."

"Were you working last night?"

The store owner – not just a clerk – stared at him, hard. "Why?"

Clarence paused. It was time to prevaricate.

"Look, I'll tell you the truth," he said. "I'm a private investigator. My client thinks his wife is cheating on him and hired me to look into it. I think she made a phone call from that payphone last night, maybe calling her boyfriend."

"That ugly thing?" he said. "If she has a boyfriend, he must be blind."

Clarence chuckled insincerely.

"That bad, huh?"

The owner shrugged.

"I've seen uglier," he said. "Hell, I've probably done uglier."

Clarence laughed legitimately at that, and the owner

seemed to relax.

"Just to make sure we're talking about the same woman, could you describe her? And do you remember what time it was?"

"Right before 8," he said. "I was starting to clean up since I close early on Sundays."

"And what did she look like?" Clarence asked, scribbling notes in his always-handy reporter's notebook.

"I dunno. White lady. Blonde, I think, but probably out of a bottle."

"Anything else you remember? Glasses? Clothes?"

"No glasses. Blue coverall, which is weird for a lady, you know?"

"You mean like what a mechanic wears?"

"Yeah, kinda," he said. "Or someone in the Navy."

Donna stepped over her husband more than she walked around him, and nudged him aside with her foot. He backed up as she pulled out the desk chair and sat down at the computer. She minimized the email window that was open and with a few clicks had pulled up a document she had secured on the hard drive.

Password-protecting it hadn't been necessary; she had known for months that her husband only used this computer for one purpose, and that was his secret email communication with his boyfriends. When she had first found out, she had been devastated. Then she had put her laser-sharp mind to work. She had combed through months of emails and found four men with whom he regularly communicated and, apparently, regularly met.

She had considered searching back farther but was honestly afraid of what she'd find. Then she became worried that if she found more, the duty she'd need to carry out would be more than she could handle. These four would be enough. It would send a message. It would save their families. It would cleanse them all. She would redeem them.

It had been easier than she had thought to arrange assignations. It had been easy enough to find out all she needed to know without ever speaking to them except by email, and with the use of simple search engines. Once she knew their names, the Assessor's Office website told her where they lived and what their wives names were. She had done it all right here, sometimes while her husband was at work, sometimes while he was passed out in the other room or, as he was right now, a pickled mess on the floor right behind her.

She didn't bother to delete any of her emails with the men. At this point, it didn't matter. What was annoying her was that she couldn't get to Jedediah's wife as easily as she had needed to in order to complete her mission. The schedule had to change.

"How did you find out?" John asked from behind her, his drunken self still on the floor.

"What did I do when I was in the Coast Guard, John?" she asked, not looking away from the computer as she used a ballpoint pen to write on her hand.

"Huh?"

"You asked a question and you should already know the answer," she said. "What did I do in the Coast Guard?"

"You made training videos," he said.

"Right," she said. "With cameras. And computers. When you started spending too much time in here, I set up a program so any time you logged on, whatever you did on this machine appeared on my screen, too. That camera mounted on the ceiling over there helped, too. That, I can see from my iPhone."

He started to cry.

"Don't tell me you didn't know," she said. "I know you knew. You knew good and well what I've been doing."

"But why?" he said through tears.

"Because they deserved it," she said. "The men did.

The families deserved better, just like I do. I couldn't give them better, but I could end the deception and prevent their shame. So I did."

"But you just killed them and threw them in the water like they were nothing," he said. His hysteria was rising and it was only making him weaker. He curled up into a fetal position on the floor.

"They were not nothing!" she said. "You treated them like they were nothing! I didn't discard them like you discarded me and they discarded their own families. I cleaned them up. I gave them three days in the water to be cleansed and brought them forth on the Lord's day."

Even in his current state, John knew she had completely lost her mind. He just wept and said nothing.

"Don't cry, John," she said. "It's almost over."

Roxanne was still sitting with Clay when Nick walked in, and the detective was startled, stopping in the entry.

Clay looked up and smiled as best he could and Roxanne spun around.

"Hey, baby!" Clay said.

"Hello, Captain," Roxanne said.

"Hey," Nick said, returning to herself and walking quickly to her husband. She leaned over the hugged him as best she could, given the angle and the IV tube that hung from his arm. She kissed him gently on the lips and hugged him again, then pulled back and just looked at his face.

"Where are the kids?" he asked, and Roxanne easily discerned that his question wasn't asked out of worry; he was fully confident his wife had them well-secured somewhere.

"My mom has them," she said.

"Good old Sara," he said. "Don't know what we'd do without her."

Nick chuckled through choked-backed tears.

"I won't tell her you called her old," she said.

They both laughed gently, and he moaned a bit with the pain of it.

"Your friend the pastor has been great company while we were waiting for you," Clay said, and Nick turned around as if just remembering Roxanne was still there.

Nick looked at her gently and wiped her nose and eyes. She gazed at Roxanne gently, unsure what to say at first.

"Thank you," she said.

"You're welcome," Roxanne said. "I told you I was here to help."

"You did," Nick said. "You have. A whole lot. Unfortunately, we're not done yet."

She turned back to Clay.

"Has anyone come to take your statement yet? Has the Crime Lab been here?"

Clay shook his head.

"I'm sorry," she said. "We're so short-handed right now."

Clay shrugged.

"It's OK," he said. "I can wait. Not like I have anywhere to be at this hour, and it goes without saying that I won't be going to work in the morning."

She chuckled again through tears.

"OK," she said. "I want to get you home to our own bed but the Lab hasn't been there yet, either, and I don't want to leave you alone."

He shrugged again.

"Go," he said non-chalantly. "I'll just have a little nap while I'm waiting. I'm sure you and Roxanne have some work to do to catch this guy."

"Yeah," she said. "Yeah, we do."

He took her hand and squeezed it.

"Go get the SOB," he said. "I'm fine."

She reluctantly let go, and her glance at Roxanne let the pastor know she was needed, as well. The women reached the entryway when Clay interrupted.

"Hey, Nick," he said. She turned back to him. "I'm proud of you."

"Hey, you wouldn't happen to have surveillance video in here, do you?" Clarence asked.

"Yeah," said the store owner. "Why?"

"Well, my client is really trying to catch his wife with her boyfriend, but I haven't had any luck yet. But if I can get pictures of her using your payphone that will be a step closer. Do you think you could share that with me? Please?"

The man held out his hand. Clarence reached to shake it, and he pulled back.

"No, dude," he said. "I'm not trying to make friends. You pay, the tape is yours."

"How much?"

The man thought.

"Fifty dollars."

"Aw, come on, man," Clarence said. "If this was your old lady cheating on you, you'd want some help, wouldn't you?"

The owner pondered that for a moment.

"Forty dollars," he said.

Clarence reached for his wallet.

"What about a 20?" he asked.

"Done," the man said. Then he shook hands. "I'll be right back."

"That was great," Blair said, handing Jerod the tape from her photographer's camera. "Thank you. Now, what parts can I use?"

Terry was sitting in the car, the engine running and the air conditioning on. Jerod sighed and thought for a minute.

He had heard Terry's statement for the first time as he gave it to Blair, so he was trying to compartmentalize, to separate the emotional impact of an attack on his partner from his instincts and responsibilities as a detective.

"Report the assailant used the guise of making a delivery to ambush the victim," he said. "Please don't say it was flowers. I don't want every florist in the Parish falling under suspicion."

Blair smiled.

"OK."

"You can say the victim didn't see the attacker's face. You can say it doesn't appear the attacker wanted to kill him, or he could've."

"Is this connected to the serial killer?"

Jerod looked her in the eye.

"Off the record for a minute?" he asked.

She nodded.

"Probably," he said. "I think so. But officially, no – not because we're withholding information but because I honestly can't say for sure. I don't want to make a statement that's unintentionally false and that may not pan out to be true."

"Fair enough," she said. "I won't use his name, like I said, but can I say a 'prominent local doctor' and say it was in an area 'south of Slidell'?"

Jerod chuckled.

"Sure," he said. "Terry will like that 'prominent' part."

She smiled.

"OK," she said. "I'll make it work. Thanks for trusting me."

He nodded.

"Hey," he said. "How'd you connect this crime and Terry to me? How did you even know there was a crime?"

She smiled.

"Reporter skillz," she said, emphasizing the "z."

"Come on," he said. "Seriously."

"It was relatively easy," she said. "And coincidental. My brother is a mail carrier. He's the one who found Terry and called 911. After Barney Fife uncuffed him –"

"Hey, Ben is a good cop," Jerod said.

"I'm sure," she said, dismissively. "Anyway, after that deputy let him go, Clyde called me, like a good brother. We went to the scene. I used my phone and entered the address in the Assessor's Office website, and it came back to Terry Mozingo. Then I googled his name and found out he was a dentist. Then I went to the Clerk of Court's website and searched land records. There was a filing a few months ago changing ownership of the property, giving half-ownership to Jerod Leveque. Then we came to the hospital and instead of asking for him I asked for you."

Jerod said nothing for a moment.

"He did what?"

"Who?" Blair said. "Who did what? The killer?"

"No," he said. "Terry. He did what with the property?"

"He filed legal paperwork making you his partner in that investment," she said. "You own half that house."

His face told the tale.

"You didn't know that?"

"No," he said. "I didn't."

"Well!" she said. "Congratulations! Nothing says love like a mortgage. Gotta run now. I'm way past deadline. God knows what they've put on the air to fill time."

She turned and walked back to the van, jumped into the passenger seat, and left.

Jerod took a deep breath. He felt like he'd been hit in the head with something, and realized as he thought it that it was an inappropriate metaphor at the moment. He also felt like a real jackass.

Chapter Eleven

Margaret continued to pace the newsroom, frustrated with her team, with the situation, with her bosses, with the fucking 24-hour news cycle in general. She could not manufacture news just to make editors happy. She wouldn't. She thought she should go ahead and retire rather than work in the "new journalism" that made even good reporters put crap on the air and on the web.

She heard a key in the door and Clarence burst in, holding a videotape in one hand and a large Walmart bag in the other.

"Woo-hoo!" he said, holding the tape aloft.

Margaret sighed at his childishness. It was near 8 p.m. on Monday and she was as exhausted as the rest of them.

"What's that?" she asked, hoping she already knew the answer.

"Surveillance video, baby!" he said. "Video of the tipster making the call from a payphone on Fremaux!"

He spun around, still holding the tape up, dancing like a fool.

"And what's in the bag?" she asked.

"A VCR and some coaxial cables," he said.

"What? Why?"

"Because nobody uses VHS tapes any more except,

apparently, the Quik-N-Easy on Fremaux, and because Blair's video equipment isn't compatible. And the cables are so we can watch this thing and feed the video into the computer to put it online fast!"

"Great, good, but not so fast," Margaret said.

He stopped spinning.

"What?" he said.

"We can't just go throwing someone's picture online or on TV without something more substantial," she said. "What if that's not the woman who called? What if we defame someone or create a new potential victim in the process?"

"Well, sure," he said. "I had thought about all that."

He hadn't. Not really.

"And?" she said.

"I have more," he answered.

She raised her eyebrows, listening.

"Um …. This will go better if I write it instead of saying it out loud," he said.

"OK," she said. "There's your desk. Get busy. I'll get this thing wired up and take a look."

Donna reached into the pocket of her BDUs and pulled out a small bottle of whiskey, the size one could buy at any gas station around here. She threw it on the floor.

"Drink up," she said.

"What?" he said, still weeping on the floor.

"Have a drink," she said. "Drink the whole damn bottle if you want. You need it. I'll be back in a few."

She left, and he heard her walk down the hall, the door to the garage open, and then the door to his SUV slam. He had no idea what was next. Timidly, he grabbed the bottle, twisted off the cap, and took a long swig.

Chief Richard pulled into Cone's driveway behind the

officer's marked car. The garage was open, which wasn't uncommon in Mandeville, and a motorcycle occupied the space in front of the police car. Crime was rare here, and he was sure Jedediah had an alarm system. All cops did.

The porch light was on and through the window he saw the flicker of a television screen inside the house. He went to the front door and rang the bell. There was no response, and he listened for footsteps and the shifting of floorboards. Nothing. Maybe he was asleep, Tom thought.

He went back to his own vehicle and turned on the headlights, illuminating the garage as much as he could. It wasn't enough, and he grabbed his flashlight from the console and entered. It smelled like a typical garage – the faint odor of gasoline and fumes, as if someone had started a car before opening the door, or where a lawnmower was stored. He looked around. Nothing was unusual, except that he couldn't reach one of his best officers.

He went to the door from the garage to the house and knocked. He waited. Nothing.

In any other circumstance, he wouldn't have worried. In any other circumstance he wouldn't even have been here. But with what was going on, he was terrified – not for himself, but for what might be inside, for Jedediah's safety, for all of them. Not only was a serial killer on the loose, but the families of two prominent cops had been attacked today. Jedediah had been on the scene yesterday, his image on the evening news. Not knowing more about this killer, anyone could now be a target.

He knocked again and called his officer's name. Nothing.

He sighed. He had no probable cause to make entry but, then again, he wasn't investigating Cone, just trying to ensure his well-being. He tried the knob and found it unlocked. There was either something amiss or Jedediah had exercised pure carelessness. He turned the knob and pushed the door abruptly open, his right hand on his sidearm as a precaution and his left holding the flashlight as it beamed into the house. His breathing was steady but he could feel his heart accelerating.

"Jedediah!" he called again into the darkness, his deep voice resonating in the nothingness. Only the hum of the refrigerator broke the silence.

He reached for the wall and found a light switch, flipping it to illuminate the hall. Nothing was out of place.

"Jedediah!" he called again as he stepped in.

Still, silence. He moved more swiftly now, relatively confident Jedediah was gone. He moved ahead.

In the living room, he flipped another switch. The large flat-screen TV was on the wall, a ball game on and the volume turned almost all the way down. Everything was in perfect order – sofa, cushions, even the remote control on the arm of the sofa. A laptop was on the sofa, though, to the left of the seat by the remote.

Tom tried to balance his respect for Jedediah's privacy with his need to make sure his officer was safe. It was very unlike the man to disappear.

"Fuck it," he said out loud, then he crouched down and clicked the touchpad of the laptop. A password screen popped up. His years of police work told him this was usually an easy problem to get past. Cone's wife's name was Collette, but Tom couldn't remember if she spelled it with one "L" or two. He guessed and got it right. The screen opened to an email platform.

Tom scanned the last message, left open on the screen.

"Fuck," he said.

With both Jedediah's police unit and his motorcycle here, whatever rendezvous point he had must've been close, Tom thought. He grabbed his radio.

"MPD-1 to Dispatch," he said.

"Go ahead, chief," the voice responded.

"Get all available units to the lakefront, the trailhead and Sunset Point," he said. "242 is MIA."

Before the dispatcher could respond, other officers

started responding. He listened with pride and satisfaction. A fellow officer was missing and they were going to go, regardless of all else.

"320 to MPD-1," one of them said over the air.

"Go ahead," Tom said.

"Any more information, sir?"

"Nothing suitable for air," Tom said. "Just consider 242 an unreported M/P. Consider all vehicles suspicious in those areas. Stop anyone and everyone. Lock down Old Mandeville."

"10-4, chief," he responded, then he heard the clicking of radio transmission buttons as the others acknowledged his order without words.

"Dispatch, see if the S.O. has an available Crime Lab unit to send this way," he said. "And call in the morning shift. Call in everybody."

Karly pulled into the Coroner's Office parking lot at warp speed. She was tired and she was tired of this case. It had to end. She parked in the employee lot behind the building, exited her car, and remembered the building was secured; she'd have to walk around it to the front door and call for someone to open it. She started to head that way when she heard voices behind her and turned. The beam of two flashlights approached.

She didn't carry a sidearm but she had a revolver in her car; she took three steps to the Taurus and pulled it from the console. She didn't aim it at the approaching lights, but held it at her side resolutely. If necessary, she wouldn't hesitate.

"Who's there?" she shouted.

The motion of the lights stopped.

"It's Rooney and Dora," the man shouted. She put the gun away in her hip pocket.

"OK," she said back. "Just checking. Now come let me in."

The voices went silent and the lights grew closer until she could see them and they turned off the beams. Dora swiped her card on the back door and she followed them inside.

"What's going on?" Karly asked.

"Lots," Rooney said. "A whole lot."

"That's remarkably non-specific," she said. "So let me rephrase. What the fuck is going on?"

"Come on, Captain," he said, leading the way into Dr. Wilson's office. "There's a lot."

She acquiesced, but she was annoyed.

"Yeah," she said. "You mentioned that."

They filed into the Coroner's private conference room. The doctor was already there, standing behind her desk with her back to them. They all sat.

"Thanks for coming, Karly," Leslie said without turning around. "Jerod and Nick are on the way. I've been trying to reach Chief Richard."

"I'll try, too," Rooney said, reaching for his phone and typing a text message.

A few minutes later, Nick and Jerod walked in together, both looking exhausted, their eyes swollen and Nick's nose red, as if she had a cold. Roxanne was with them.

"OK, everybody," Leslie said. "In the last 12 hours this investigation has devolved into too many separate elements and groups."

"Ma'am?" Rooney said.

"Karly has been at Central with Siwel, you've been at MPD with the chief, Silver has been at the Pearl River scene, and Leveque and Brooks have been at their own personal crime scenes," she said, her tone calm and level. "Do I need to be more clear?"

"No, ma'am," he said.

"Walder is still in the hospital, Douglas is MIA, and the sheriff is … out of town," she said. "So far I've let

Brooks and Leveque lead this as ranking Sheriff's Office personnel, but they've got their own issues now so I'm taking control."

"Ma'am," Jerod said, "with all due respect –"

"Your respect is noted, Captain," Leslie said, "but shut the fuck up and relax. I'm not going to tell you how to be a cop. What I'm going to do is make sure we're all on the same page."

There was silence.

"While you all have been out doing your jobs, here's what I've managed to gather here: The killer is a woman. The victims are closeted gay or bisexual men with wives, and probably children. The killer is probably a jilted wife whose husband prefers the company of men."

"But Doctor," Karly said, "the callers have sounded male."

"Do you have the tapes?"

"Brandi does," she said. "We don't have the resources of the FBI to run voice analyses, and I know what you're going to ask."

Leslie cocked one eyebrow.

"Clearly, you do," she said. "But even without Quantico's resources, we can have a listen. Can she email them to us here if you don't have the recordings with you?"

"Yes," Karly said.

"Please make that happen."

Karly reached for her phone.

"Before you do that," Leslie said. "You took two of his calls. Two of his five calls. Please relate the last one as best you can."

Karly thought for a moment.

"He said to tell Captain Brooks she had beautiful children. He said to tell Jerod that because of the press conference he would be accelerating his schedule."

"That's helpful," Leslie said. "But why is he having to

accelerate things?"

Karly shook her head and returned to her phone, texting her lieutenant.

"Something Jerod said – or you said – struck a nerve," Nick said.

"Or maybe he just didn't like being called out," Jerod said.

"She," Leslie said. "The killer is a female."

"You're sure about that?" he asked.

"As sure as I can be," she said.

Roxanne spoke for the first time.

"She's a jilted woman," Roxanne said. "Probably thrown over for a male lover. She's lashing out."

"Against who?" Rooney asked.

"Against other gay or bisexual men who are cheating on their wives with men," Roxanne said.

There was silence for a moment.

"There's more," Leslie said. "Dora?"

"Yesterday when I got here with the body from the Harbor, there was a woman across the yard with a video camera," she said. "I assumed she was a news person. I even called Jerod about it. But there was nothing on the news from here. Rooney and I just walked to where she had been a bit ago; there are imprints from a tripod, shoe prints, a snack food package – trail mix or something – but nothing else."

"Did you call the Crime Lab?" Nick asked.

Jerod looked at her.

"And who would that be, exactly?" he asked.

"I sent Moreau to take that over," Karly said.

"What?" Nick said. "Why?"

"What choice did I have?" Karly asked. "There was no one else. There is no one else. We're fucked."

"No," Leslie said. "No, we're not. We know at least

one other thing. Karly, you said the caller said she'd be accelerating the schedule. That means there's an end-point. This won't go on forever. She's got a mission and she's almost done."

"Small comfort to the next victim and his family," Roxanne said.

Leslie looked at her pointedly.

"I think the next primary victim has already been taken," she said. "We should worry about the wife and children – if we can identify them."

"Dateline: Slidell, Louisiana.

"While investigators pored over the crime scene of a triple murder Sunday night, they apparently failed to probe who notified them of the crime.

"Deputies on the scene of the murder of the Prescott family east of the suburban New Orleans city said a neighbor had called 911 to report the crime, but there was no witness on the scene and neighbors interviewed the next day were oblivious that a crime had even occurred.

"One neighbor said she didn't even know the Prescotts and the other's home was separated by a thick row of trees that would've prevented her from even seeing the stack of newspapers on the porch that allegedly precipitated the call to law enforcement. That neighbor is also disabled and does not drive.

"Sheriff's Office Public information Officer Jerod Leveque did not return phone calls Monday evening and has, in fact, been unseen by reporters since a noon press conference at the Coroner's Office asking residents for information.

"Police and Coroner's Office inspectors seem to believe the mysterious serial killer has struck at least two other families, but they have failed to identify or locate those victims.

"Sources at the Sheriff's Office say the caller who

reported the Prescott family murders called 911 from a cell phone at a convenience store a few miles from the crime scene, but the 911 operator did not record the caller's name or any other identifiers.

"Advocate reporters visited that convenience store Monday night and were able to acquire video of a blond woman in a Navy or Coast Guard uniform using the payphone in the building. Click HERE to view that video."

Margaret read the copy and looked at Clarence. She sighed.

"This is good," she said. "A real scoop, getting information before the cops do. But does it help solve the murders?"

"Is that our job?" he asked.

"No," she said. "But we do have a responsibility not only to inform the public but to protect public safety – or at least not to make it worse."

"Since when?" he asked.

She looked at the iPad in front of her and said nothing for a moment.

"Since forever," she said. "We just tend to forget it."

"Look," he said. "The last thing I want to do is endanger anyone. I live here, too. I have a family – a family I've barely seen in the last few days. But if we have information that might help solve this case, don't we have an obligation to share it?"

"We do," she said. "With the police first. Then, with the public."

Donna came back down the hall and John watched her shadowy figure approach, made more ominous by the light behind her. She was in no hurry. He had a hard time focusing, but he could see that in her left hand was a large object shaped like a milk jug; in her right was a cylindrical object. She finally reached the door to the office, set down the jug, and turned on the light.

She picked up the flask she had handed him and held it up.

"Half-empty," she said. "Or is it half-full? Are you an optimist or a pessimist?"

He sobbed.

"What are you doing?" he asked.

"I can't put you in the water," she said. "You're beyond cleansing, and I have other work to do. So I brought the water here."

She picked up the gallon jug and popped off the top, throwing the plastic disc at him. Then she stepped towards him and upended it, emptying its contents over his head.

"Do you feel clean?" she asked. "Baptized? Born anew?"

He sobbed.

"No."

"I didn't think so. You're irredeemable."

Then he realized the object in her right hand wasn't just a pipe, but a cross, the horizontal piece bound so high on the other that it looked more like a sword.

"This needs to happen," she said.

She held the pipe above the crosspiece with both hands, raised it up, and brought it down squarely across the top of his head. He collapsed onto his side, then rolled onto his back, twitching.

Donna stood over her husband until she was sure he was finished. Then she calmly walked to the far side of the room, reached upwards, and smashed the camera lens she had long ago mounted on the ceiling.

"Sorry to leave again," she said. "One more thing to take care of."

She walked back towards the door, stepping over John, and left the same way she had arrived.

Moreau was so confused he wasn't sure where to go. It seemed like crime scenes were popping up all over the

Parish, and he was only one guy with one van, and he wasn't even trained for this. He wasn't even sure who to ask for direction.

His best bet was the hospital, he thought. Both victims had to be there. The alternatives were Leveque's house in south Slidell or Brooks' house in Pearl River – 15 miles apart in opposite directions from the interstate. At least the ER was in the middle and easier to access.

He pulled into the Emergency Room entrance, careful not to block ambulance access. He turned around and looked into the back of the van. He saw something that seemed like what they called a "kit" – a large plastic box with a handle on top that looked, to him, like a large box of fishing tackle. He popped it open, scanned the contents quickly, and grabbed it. He wasn't exactly sure how to use it all, but he knew he was supposed to have it.

Inside the ER, the receptionist pointed him to Brooks' room and he headed down the hall. He walked in and found Clay asleep, looking peaceful. He was used to dealing with missing hunters and drowning victims. Waking a battery victim wasn't his forte.

"Excuse me, Mr. Brooks?" he said. Clay stirred, barely. "Mr. Brooks," Moreau said, a little louder.

Moreau's radio suddenly chirped.

"Central, 9102."

He quickly retreated to the hallway.

"9102," he said. "Go ahead."

"9102, 7102 is requesting you 10-19 the Coroner's Office."

He sighed. Nick Brooks was calling him away from her own husband to go back the way he had just come. To explain this over the radio or to simply obey? He didn't have to decide before another request came out.

"9102, MPD is reporting a 26 missing from their agency and are requesting your help."

A missing cop took precedence over just about

anything.

"10-4, Central," he said. "Advise MPD I'm en route from Slidell. Send location to my phone."

He ran back to the Crime Lab van he had commandeered, jumped behind the wheel and headed west as fast as the aging vehicle would go.

Jerod's cell phone vibrated. He didn't want to interrupt the discussion in Dr. Wilson's office but he had learned earlier today not to ignore his phone. He looked down and recognized the phone number of the Advocate's office. He had also learned never to ignore reporters.

"Excuse me," he said, and stepped to the back of the room.

"Leveque," he answered.

"Jerod, it's Margaret at the Advocate."

"What's up?" he said. "I'm in a briefing."

"We have something you need to see, and even before you do, you need to know: The killer is probably a woman."

"We know," he said. "How do you know?"

"Where are you?" she asked.

"Coroner's Office," he said. He wouldn't have usually been so forthcoming – and she wouldn't normally have been so forward – but times were different. "What do you have?"

"Video," she said. "Video of the woman who called in the Prescott murders."

He felt a chill run up his spine. Margaret and her staff had figured out what he already knew, that the caller was not a neighbor but more likely the perp.

"Can you email it?" he asked.

"It's VHS," she said. "I'm trying to convert it to electronic format right now. I could probably bring it to you more quickly."

"Standby," he said, then put the phone to his chest.

"Doc," he said. "Do you have a VCR here?"

She nodded.

"Yes. We use it for old training videos."

He picked up the phone again.

"Bring it," he said. "Call when you get here and I'll let you in."

Every police car in Mandeville was patrolling Cone's neighborhood. They all knew him. They all knew he was a fitness freak and ran along the Lakefront every night he wasn't working. They fanned out not only along Lakeshore Drive but through the streets in the old part of town. Even the chief had left Cone's residence and was driving the streets. Sheriff's Office units – what few there were – were also in the city or on the way. So far, there was no sign of Jedediah.

Chief Tom Richard felt like he was driving in circles – and he was. Mandeville had about 10,000 residents, half of them in the east part of town, a two-mile long swath of suburbia with streets lined in a near-perfect grid. Cone's house in what was officially deemed "Old Mandeville" was a one-story cottage, perfect for a starter home for small families or couples with no children yet. Cone and his wife fit the latter category.

On what felt like his fourth pass in front of the Cone residence, he saw a Sheriff's Office unit, one of the larger ones, down the block. He was relieved to see there was relief and backup, and made a mental note that he didn't need to pass this way again.

Donna watched him through the window. The Chief's F150 pickup truck was black and unmarked, but she wasn't stupid. She had been married to a cop for three decades; she knew the patterns and the habits, and that was clearly a police maneuver – and a police vehicle.

Mandeville was swarming with cops and it pissed her off. They needed to leave her alone. It was aggravating enough that they'd released the tidbit about gym clothes at their press conference. She couldn't lose that edge. Besides, she was almost done. She wouldn't let them ruin it.

She walked away from the window to the back of Cone's house and pulled out her husband's cell. Cell signals automatically routed to the nearest police tower, but she didn't want to talk to Mandeville P.D. She wanted to talk to the Sheriff's Office.

She dialed the non-emergency line, the same one she used to dial when she wanted to reach her husband. At this hour, she knew it automatically forwarded to Central Dispatch.

"911, what's your emergency?" the dispatcher answered.

"It's not my emergency," she said, no longer bothering to disguise her voice. "It's yours. 1402 Sumner Street, Covington. I left the garage open. Go in that way and you'll find him in the second room on the left."

The dispatcher paused.

"OK, ma'am," she said. "What's your name?"

"This is Eau," she said. "And I'm almost done. I'm almost finished cleansing them."

Then she hung up.

She walked onto Jedediah's patio and listened. In the distance, in a moment, she heard sirens heading to her husband's body, to her house, eight miles north of here. She had bought some time.

Next, she called the hospital.

"This is Sergeant Morris," she said, making up a name. "I need to speak to Nurse Collette Cone immediately."

Hang on, please."

A moment later, the phone rang on the ICU floor. When the nurse answered she repeated the same line.

"Hold on," the voice said, and a moment later someone else picked up.

225

"This is Nurse Cone," the woman said.

"This is Sergeant Morris at the Sheriff's Office," she said. "There's an emergency at your house. You need to go home immediately, please."

"Oh my God," Collette said. "What's wrong?"

"I can't discuss it on the phone, ma'am," Donna said. "Please just go home. We'll explain there."

Then she hung up and waited in the dark.

Jerod met Margaret at the door and let her into the Coroner's Office.

"Thanks," she said. She held up the tape in her hand. "Where can we watch it?"

"This way," he said.

In the Coroner's Office Training Room, Dora had lowered the giant projection screen and hauled in a cart with a VCR and projector. To the rest of them Margaret said nothing, but handed over the cassette. Dora popped it into the player.

The others on the Task Force sat in the rows. Only Dr. Wilson turned to look at Margaret.

"One of our reporters got this from a convenience store clerk on Fremaux earlier tonight."

She pressed "play" and the screen lit up with faint and somewhat grainy pictures. At first, the only image was the empty aisles of the Quick-N-Easy. Seconds later, a woman walked in, waved to the man behind the counter, and headed to the bathroom down a hall at the top of the frame.

"What does this show us?" Nick asked. "It's a woman going to the bathroom."

"At the end of the hall to the bathroom is a payphone," Margaret said. "It's not visible on the tape but it fits the time signature and your own records of where the call came from."

"How could you possibly know that?" Jerod said.

"We have many sources," Margaret said. "When authorized personnel won't talk to us, we have ways of finding things out."

No one said anything. They knew what had and hadn't happened, and what they'd been able and unable to do in the last 48 hours. They had done their best, and Margaret knew it. They all did.

"Now," Margaret said, "watch. When she comes out of the bathroom hall, there's a clear picture of her face.... There!"

Dora pressed pause and the still image filled the screen. The woman was in her 50s with shoulder-length blonde hair. She wore navy blue BDUs and a hat.

"I wouldn't let our people put this online yet," she said. "I won't risk casting suspicion on an innocent person. I brought it to you first."

"Thank you for that," Nick said.

"You're welcome. Anyone know her? Does she look familiar to anyone?"

Jerod got up and approached the screen, his body briefly blocking the projection as he approached.

"Yeah, I know her," he said. "That's Major Douglas' wife, Donna. Nick, come see."

His fellow captain stood and approached.

"I'll be damned," she said. "Yeah. That's who it is. Now where is she? And where is he?"

"That, I don't know," Margaret said. "But I'd like your permission to name her as a suspect and to post the video online – and give it to Blair for TV."

"I don't know," Jerod said.

"Do it," Nick said. She looked at Jerod. "We don't have any time to waste. This is our biggest lead."

"9102, Central," Moreau said into his mic. "Where

does MPD need me?"

"Standby, sir," the dispatcher said. She hated that she couldn't directly link Mandeville to her own channel, but while the technology was there, the risk was too great at the moment – and linking channels was so rare she wasn't sure she remembered how to do it. She grabbed the phone and called MPD Dispatch.

"9102, MPD advises you're needed at Sunset Point," she said.

"10-4," he said. "Just getting off the interstate. ETA 10 minutes."

Sunset Point was a narrow park that ran between the upscale Hermitage subdivision and the new commercial-residential development called Port Marigny, named after Bernard de Mandeville de Marigny, the founder of the city more than 200 years earlier. The Point had a narrow road for entry that spread into a wider parking and picnic area along the lakefront, separated from both Old Mandeville and Port Marigny by waterways. It was a dark and quiet place.

As he turned the corner from the narrow street into the park area, his vision was overtaken by flashing lights – police cars, fire trucks and at least one ambulance. It was literally stunning.

He pulled to the side of the crowded field and jumped out. Until he knew what they were dealing with, he wasn't worrying about the kit. Siwel came towards him.

"Lieutenant," Michael said. "Detectives have still been told to maintain radio silence but I heard this call and decided I'd come help. I hope that's OK."

Moreau sighed.

"It's more than OK," he said. "I'm really glad to see you, Brother. What's going on?"

"Officer Cone turned up," Siwel said. "On the rocks in the canal."

"Holy crap," Moreau said. "10-7?"

"Negative, he's still alive. Bad head injuries, and some superficial cuts to his junk, though. Looks like she didn't finish the job. Maybe got startled by something. Who knows with this nut job. We're speculating the killer tried to throw him in the water – like the others – but didn't push hard enough and he landed on the rocks."

"And the killer didn't hear that?" Moreau said.

"She probably heard his big feet hit the water and splash, and thought he was in or figured he was going to bleed out anyway."

"She?" Moreau said.

"Yeah," Siwel said. "That's the going theory."

"OK." Moreau shrugged. "A murderer is a murderer. Don't care who or how. So how can I help?"

"Beats the fuck out of me, Brother," Siwel said, and shrugged. "Cone's in an ambulance and the crime scene is mostly water. There might be some evidence to recover on the rocks."

"Where's Mrs. Cone?" Moreau asked.

Siwel looked at him sharply and then the penny dropped.

"Fuck," he said.

Sean was dropping off a drunk driver at the jail when he heard the call come out to Douglas' house. It wasn't his district, but he had his radio set to scan all channels.

"2317, Central," he said. "I'm about two miles from that location. I'm 10-8 en route."

"10-4," she said. "Other units?"

The radio blew up with answers.

"3201, en route," said the shift lieutenant.

Others followed suit. Sean was still the closest. He ran from the jail, jetted out of the sally port, and took off in the direction of Douglas' house as he hit his lights and siren. It took him a little more than a minute.

"2317, Central, I'm 10-97."

"10-4, sir," she said. "Be careful."

Dispatchers weren't supposed to say things like that, but she knew he was alone and he appreciated the comfort. He was always careful.

The caller said the garage door had been left open, and that's how he found it. He put his flashlight in his left hand, his weapon in his right, and proceeded cautiously towards the interior door. He kept his back to the wall, facing the side of the garage that was closed, fearing an ambush from behind. He reached the door and turned the knob, finding it unlocked as promised.

Sean opened the door quickly and shone his flashlight beam directly down the hall. There was nothing to see and he heard no movement.

"Sheriff's Office!" he yelled.

There was no response. He made entry, flipping the light switch and illuminating the hall. The caller said Major Douglas was in the second room on the left, so he moved in that direction as quickly as possible without disregarding his own safety, closing other doors on his way. When he reached the second door, he reached inside and hit the switch.

John was on the floor, a significant wound to his head and a pool of blood beneath him. Sean leaned over.

"Major?" he said. "John?"

Douglas tried to speak but only gurgled. He was alive.

"2317, Central. Get me an ambulance 10-18. Victim is still alive."

He scanned the room. There was no weapon, no signs of a struggle, but fragments of plastic and glass on the floor a few feet away.

Collette drove home as fast as she could. She cursed at every stoplight and at everyone who got in her way. The sergeant said something was wrong at home, and that could only mean Jedediah. On the upside, she thought, they hadn't told her to go a hospital. But maybe that meant he was already dead and they didn't want to tell her in a clinical setting. Whatever it was, she was in a hurry to find out.

She pulled off the interstate onto the highway to Mandeville. She tried not to speed, but she also figured any cop on duty tonight would be working this serial killer case, not chasing bad drivers. Her concern wasn't getting a ticket, but being delayed. She wouldn't risk that.

In a few minutes, she pulled up to her house and into the driveway. There was no one there. No cars, no ambulances, not even a fire truck. She didn't understand. An "officer down" call would've drawn everyone. The garage door was open, so she went in that way, parking behind her husband's marked police car.

Chapter Twelve

"What's the meaning of the water?" Dr. Wilson asked.

"What?" Nick asked. "She's just disposing of the bodies."

"No," Roxanne said resolutely. "There's a spiritual element to what she's doing. It's a baptism of sorts."

"Ma'am," Rooney said.

All of them looked at him.

"One of our officers suggested this afternoon that 'O' is actually 'eau,'" he said.

"What?" Nick said.

"Eau," Rooney said. "E A U. The French word for water. It seems to make sense."

"What do you mean?" Jerod asked.

"I think he means that water isn't just a way to get rid of bodies," Roxanne said. "It's symbolic. She's trying to cleanse the victims of their sins – or what she perceives as sins."

"Well, damn," Leslie said.

Siwel parked a block from Cone's house and turned off his headlights. There wasn't much to see. This part of Mandeville was dark on purpose. People here liked it that way. He started walking, slowly, as intentionally as the darkness allowed. As he neared the house, he spotted the Sheriff's Office SUV parked a block further on. It wasn't a coincidence, he decided, but he wasn't completely sure what it meant.

"C'mon, Grand Architect of the Universe," he said aloud. "Guide me, please."

In the driveway were Cone's marked unit and a white Honda he assumed belonged to Cone's wife. He felt the hood; it was still hot. She hadn't been home for long. He hoped she was still alive.

Siwel walked into the garage and found the interior door partially ajar – not fully open, but not latched. He pushed it inward and followed with his flashlight. He didn't announce himself, despite his training; sometimes instincts were more important than protocol. He inched down the hallway, finally flipping on a switch. The living room burst into light. On the far side of it was a fireplace, beyond that a counter that separated the room from a modest kitchen. To the left, a set of French doors led to a darkened back yard.

The wind blew and one of the doors rattled. Siwel jumped, pivoted, reached for his weapon.

"That's not necessary," said a woman's voice.

He spun again, this time in the opposite direction. The noise from the door had been only the wind; the killer was behind him. He leveled his weapon at her and announced himself.

"Sheriff's Office!" he said. "Drop your weapon!"

"I know who you are," she said, calmly, "and I have no weapon."

He regarded her, his gaze acute. She did not hold any traditional weapon, but a large crucifix in her right hand was foreboding enough.

"OK," he said. "Drop the cross."

She did the opposite, raising it to her own eye level.

"This?" she said. "I will never drop this. It's what drives

and powers me."

"I understand," he said, placating her. "I'm a believer, too."

She looked at him askance, her eyes visible over the crossbeam of the cross.

"A believer in what?"

"Jesus. God. The law," he said. "All of it."

"Marriage?" she asked. "Are you married?"

"No, ma'am," he said. "I'm engaged. Where is Mrs. Cone?"

"Engaged," she said simply, ignoring the question. "Are you faithful?"

"Always," he said, and he meant it.

She scoffed.

"No men are faithful," she said. "The worst of the offenders are unfaithful with other men."

He paused.

"I wouldn't know about that," he said. "Where's Mrs. Cone?"

She turned and walked back towards the garage.

"Look in the yard," she said. "Or follow me. You can't do both."

She flipped the light switch and walked off, leaving them both in darkness.

"Fuck!" Siwel said, louder than he intended. He pondered his options for a millisecond; he had no choice.

Quickly, he turned to the back door and ran. He pulled the French doors open and rushed into the yard, the August heat hitting him in the face.

"Mrs. Cone!" he yelled, racking his brain to remember her first name. "Hello?" he yelled again. There was silence, nothing but the slight breeze from being so close to the lake.

"Fuck," he said again, turning back to the door and grabbing his radio.

"7312 to all units," he said. "Suspect is 10-8, leaving the victim's house. I'm 10-97 with the victim's spouse."

He didn't wait for a reply, but went back inside and reached around for another light switch. He found one, finally, and flipped it upwards, casting light throughout the back yard. Then he turned again.

Mrs. Cone was on the ground at the bottom of the back steps, crouched down as tightly as she could be. Her first name came to him at the best moment.

"Collette," he said, gently, seating himself on the stairs. She was trembling and said nothing.

He had no flashlight but activated the one on his iPhone, casting the broad but anemic beam across the back of her head and neck. She was bleeding, but not profusely, and was clearly still alive. Whatever injuries she had sustained were not likely to be life-threatening.

"Collette," he said again, reaching tentatively towards her. His hand reached her back and she jumped, falling backwards onto her behind and tentatively raising her head to face him.

Her face was much worse than what Siwel had seen from behind. The crucifix the killer was carrying had clearly made multiple impacts on Collette. Her blood was coagulating on her forehead, and one of her eyes was swollen shut. Her right eyebrow was a flap of skin hanging from her face. Siwel knew better than to touch her again, and focused his gaze on her unswollen left eye.

"Collette," he said. "You'll be OK. You're safe now."

He grabbed his radio again.

"7312, Central. I'm going to need an ambulance at this location 10-18."

"Safe?" she asked. It was a whisper.

"Yes," he said. "You're safe now. I won't let anything else happen to you."

She nodded and with one hand pushed her bloody hair out of her face.

Margaret excused herself from the Coroner's Training Room and grabbed her phone, dialing Clarence.

"Hey," he said. "Blair is back."

"Good," she said. "I've got the go-ahead to air the video you got from the convenience store and to identify the woman in it as a suspect. Her name is Donna Douglas, and she's the wife of Major John Douglas."

"Holy shit," he said. "OK."

"Did it digitize well enough when we uploaded it."

"Yep," he said. "It's grainy, as you know, but it'll work."

"Get your story online," Margaret told him. "Embed the link. Make sure Blair has it, too."

"Will do," he said. "By the way, Blair has some pretty blockbuster stuff, too."

"Great," she said. "Did we ever get a sat truck?"

"Setting up at the Harbor now," he said. "Blair is about to head that way."

"Fuck," Margaret said. With only minutes to get this video on the air and lives on the line, she wasn't sure how that would work. "OK," she said, letting out a deep, frustrated breath. "Email the video to Blair AND to the station downtown. Then get it on the newspaper website."

"Got it," he said, and hung up.

Margaret walked back into the room where the cops, Coroner's inspectors and the woman in the clerical collar were watching the tape, rewinding, and watching again.

"That's definitely her," Leveque said. "That's definitely Donna Douglas."

"Good thing," Margaret said. "It's about to be on the air and the web."

"Jerod, how are you so sure that's her?" Leslie asked.

He let out a shallow sigh.

"She was my Sunday School teacher when I was a kid."

The 10 p.m. newscast began as usual, with the standard

music and graphic flourishes, ending on the anchor's face.

"Good evening. Our top story tonight is another violent day in St. Tammany Parish. We're going straight to Blair Francingues, live at the Mandeville Harbor."

"Thanks, Charles," she said, her pretty face now filling the screens of nearly a million viewers. "It has, indeed been a bloody day, and it's far from over. There was at least one other attack today, this time targeting a prominent doctor near Slidell, but before we get to that, we've just received video of a woman detectives say is a suspect in the serial killer slayings."

The screen cut to the grainy image of Donna Douglas leaving the bathroom hallway at the Quik-n-Easy.

"Authorities haven't said much so far, but only minutes ago authorized the release of this tape, which was acquired by our partners at the Advocate," Blair said over the image. "Investigators say her name is Donna Douglas, wife of Sheriff's Office Major John Douglas. Major Douglas commands the Special Operations Division at the agency, and we saw him yesterday morning, right here, as investigators were pulling a body from Lake Pontchartrain near the Causeway, about three miles from shore."

The screen cut again to B-roll of John Douglas taken the day before. The major could be seen pacing along the dock before Moreau took the boat out to recover the body.

"Major Douglas was here early yesterday morning but then vanished, and we haven't seen him since, even with multiple other crime scenes unfolding. If you've been following this story you know the entire family of Phillip Prescott was found slaughtered in their Slidell-area home last night after an anonymous tip.

"That video you saw of Donna Douglas earlier was taken right after she, herself, made the anonymous call to 911, tipping authorities to the Prescott mass murder," Blair said. "Then, this afternoon, a Slidell doctor was attacked in his own home, and based on information we've acquired there's reason to think Douglas is responsible for that attack, also.

"We're working on getting a better photograph of the suspect, and we hope to have that ready by the morning newscast. I would encourage viewers to check our website often, as well, and we'll post updates there as we get them overnight."

The shot went back to the studio where the anchor himself looked pale and disturbed. These sorts of things just didn't happen here.

"We're about to get really busy here," Leslie said. "Dora, please call DeMarco and get his lazy ass moving this direction. Where's Christian?"

"Asleep," Dora said.

"Wake him," Leslie said calmly. "He's either well enough to work or sick enough to go to the hospital. Find out which one and take care of it."

Nick, Jerod, Karly and Rooney all headed for the door.

"Not so fast," Leslie said sharply. "I said we all need to communicate better. Where's everybody going?"

"Back to Mandeville," Rooney said.

"Covington," Nick said.

"The Radio Room, Covington," Karly said.

"Slidell," Jerod said. "Just in case."

She knew – they all knew – that he needed to go home to Terry.

"Good," Leslie said. "Does anyone besides Margaret and her staff have the ability to scan our channels?"

"Negative," Jerod said.

"Then cancel this fucking radio silence," she said. "We don't need any more disappearing acts."

"What about me?" Roxanne asked.

"Ready to call it a day?" Leslie asked.

"No way," the pastor said. "I'm here to help. I've come this far. Let's see it through."

Leslie regarded her carefully.

"OK," she said. "Please stay here with me for now. Everyone else, get out."

Margaret stood to join the others.

"And you," Leslie said.

Margaret turned.

"You thought we'd forgotten about you. I haven't. So, thank you. You did a good thing tonight. You did the right thing."

Margaret said nothing as she headed for the door.

The one thing Donna hadn't considered was what she would do with herself once she was finished with everyone else. This mission had been in the works for months, and she had been so focused on the process and incremental progress that she hadn't really thought about her own denouement.

Now what? she thought, as she drove her husband's Sheriff's Office vehicle out of Old Mandeville. She knew no one was paying attention to her at all. The only thing potentially suspicious about the SUV was that it wasn't northbound like every other Sheriff's Office vehicle. No one was going to stop her to figure out why. She was moving with impunity now, just as she had when she had driven to each of her murder scenes, just as she had when disposing of the bodies, including when she took her husband's Sheriff's Office boat into the lake along the Causeway. She felt both invisible and tremendously powerful at the same time.

Eventually, she knew, they would figure out it was her, if they hadn't already. She wasn't afraid of going to prison, although it didn't appeal to her. There was plenty of the Lord's work to do behind bars, but teaching people about sin and redemption had grown tiring over the years; she was on a roll, administering divine retribution and posthumous redemption with ferocious fervor in recent weeks. She was glad this part was over, but she was ready for her next assignment whenever God chose to reveal it.

She reached for her weapon on the passenger seat and gripped it tightly. She wiped it off on the fading upholstery, smearing blood, skin and a small amount of grey matter onto the seat. Then she held it in front of her.

"Here I am, Lord," she said. "Send me."

"Do you think she's done now?" Leslie asked.

"Based on what we know, I think so," Roxanne said as they sat in the doctor's office recliners again, sipping coffee.

"Are you OK?"

"Not really," Roxanne said. "But I will be – and I'm in better shape than a lot of people here right now."

Leslie said nothing for a moment.

"You've done a great job," she said. "You've been a real asset to this investigation."

"Thanks," Roxanne said. "I'm glad. But I don't feel like it's done. I don't feel like I'm done."

"What do you mean?"

"The killer has been identified, we're pretty sure she's finished, but we still don't know where she is," Roxanne said.

"True," Leslie said. "They'll find her, though."

"I know," Roxanne said. "I just hope it's soon enough... and I've thought about what you said earlier. I am part of this now. I want to help."

They were silent for a moment.

"Doctor, would you mind if I go sit by myself in your Grief Counseling Room for a little while?" Roxanne broke the silence. "I need a little solitude and some prayer."

"Help yourself," Leslie said. She stood and reached into her desk, then tossed Roxanne an electronic key, about the size and shape of a credit card. "Here," she said.

"This will open every door around here. Make yourself at home."

Sean watched as the paramedics removed Major Douglas from his home, down the hall and out the front door. There was no way to perfectly preserve a crime scene like this when emergency responders had to enter and remove a still-breathing body. The sad irony, Sean thought, was that Douglas was going to die anyway. He had seen enough battery victims to know one didn't survive a head wound like that, and if he did he would wish he hadn't.

He walked back to the garage, the street glowing with red and blue lights as his coworkers seemed to fill the whole block. There was an officer down and this is what they did, all of them, all the time.

He had a sudden thought. The killer would've known that. How best to keep cops occupied? Injure one of their brothers or sisters, then make sure they knew about it. Douglas had obviously been in no shape to call for help himself, so the killer had done it. He looked around for the ranking person on the scene and found the shift lieutenant, walking quickly towards him.

"Lieu," he said. "There's nothing else to do here. We need to be on the streets."

"Stay in your lane, deputy," the lieutenant said.

"Yessir," Sean said. "But I think the killer called this in so we'd all be here instead of wherever she is."

The lieutenant looked at him, a bit angrily at first and then more calmly as he considered it.

"Maybe," he said.

"And lieutenant, where's the major's unit?"

He was caught up short.

"The garage was empty when I got here," Sean said. "There are no other vehicles. Nobody has seen Major Douglas since yesterday morning. I think the killer is driving one of our marked vehicles."

"Fuck!" the lieutenant said, and grabbed his radio before Sean could say another word.

"3201 to all units," he said. "Be on the lookout for a Sheriff's Office SUV. License plate should read '9101.' I think the killer is driving it. Consider armed and dangerous."

He put down his radio and looked at Sean.

"There you go," he said. "Just in case. Can't hurt."

"Yeah, it can," Sean said, disgustedly.

"What?"

"If the killer has that SUV she also has a working radio in it and just heard everything you just said," Sean said. He turned and headed back to the house, stopping at his trunk to get Crime Scene tape. He was seething and couldn't help himself as he turned around and shouted, "You stupid motherfucker."

He strung the tape and went back inside.

Siwel heard the BOLO and stiffened. This explained the Sheriff's Office SUV he had seen down the block. Collette had blacked out and he was still waiting on an ambulance. That wasn't shocking, really; with Cone attacked, Douglas attacked, and half the damn Parish down with an illness, waiting for help was the new norm. It was the perfect time for a stealth attack on cops – or on anyone, really. Anyone at all.

Simon DeMarco was having a devil of a time sleeping. He was genuinely tired and he wasn't stressed about anything in particular, but he was wound up for no reason he could determine. After tossing about for several hours in his bed, he got up, threw on his gym clothes, and jumped in his car. Maybe physical exertion would help him rest.

Unlike the last coroner, this one hadn't seen fit to give him a marked vehicle, instead rewarding him with a vehicle allowance. It was fine, but while his Mercedes was more comfortable than a Crown Victoria, he missed the prestige of having a Parish Seal on the door of his work vehicle, and the ability to drive as he saw fit without fear of being pulled over.

It was a short drive from his house to Pisces Fitness in Lacombe, the 24-hour gym that he accessed with an electronic key card; he kept it on the same keyring as the one that opened the office, so he never had to worry about getting them confused.

If it weren't 10 o'clock he might've thrown scrubs and Crocs into the vehicle, just in case, but he had no expectation of being called to work mid-workout. The gym was mostly deserted, and only a Sheriff's Office SUV was in the parking lot. He thought little of that; it might be a deputy working out when he was supposed to be patrolling, or one stopping to write a report between calls, or even one sleeping on duty. It was none of his business and he genuinely didn't care. He left his cell phone in the console of the car, taking only his keyring, and put himself in the frame of mind to exercise.

Inside, there was no one else using the equipment. He started on the treadmill, manually adjusting the speed and incline until he was running at 6 miles an hour. When his heart rate was suitably elevated he got off, shook off the dizziness, and moved to the seated bench press. A few minutes later, the next part of his routine took him to the rowing machine. He closed his eyes, sweat dripping from his face, and counted his strokes.

He didn't expect the blow from behind that knocked him immediately unconscious, and he didn't feel the other ones at all.

Donna didn't have to go through his pockets for what she wanted; DeMarco had left his keys conveniently in a cubby by the bathroom and water fountain. She took the keyring and went to the Mercedes and started the engine, driving towards the center of death.

Christian stretched, yawned again, and splashed cold water on his face. He had been asleep for nearly 24 hours. He felt better but he was also starving, which was a good sign. Dora had awakened him, checked his vitals, and told him to get ready to work as soon as he could. She said she was going to sterilize the autopsy suite before DeMarco got there; it wasn't her job, but at this hour there was no one else to do it. Since late-night autopsies were rare and DeMarco generally did his cutting in the mornings, backup staff weren't around.

The building was dead quiet. He knew it would be a while before the next bodies arrived, and even longer until DeMarco got there, so he had some time. He started coffee in the break room and grabbed an apple from a basket on the table, biting into it as he walked down the back hall towards his desk. He was so hungry, he had almost finished it by the time he reached his work station. He stretched again and turned on the monitor, wondering what electronic paperwork he had left unfinished when his fever had gotten the best of him yesterday.

He was going through tasks when he vaguely heard the back door chime open, but he didn't turn around. In a time like this, anyone could be coming and going. When he saw the reflection in the monitor, though, he spun around to see who it was.

The crosspiece of the crucifix came down on the crown of his head. There was no frenzy to follow; once had been enough.

Nick pulled up to the Douglas house, her wig-wag police lights concealed in her headlights adding to the glow. Most of the patrol cars were gone now, deputies fanning out to look for the killer and Douglas' stolen unit. She saw Sean's car in the driveway, and a semi-marked car behind it. The lieutenant saw her coming and climbed out, walking towards her.

As exhausted as she was, she was also livid. She didn't

recognize him in the darkness and amid the strobing of police lights, but at this moment she didn't care who he was. Her patience with bullshit and incompetence was long gone. Nick headed towards him at a half-run and landed her fist right in his chest.

He recoiled, almost falling, but caught himself.

"You," she said, rising as much as her tiny frame would allow, "are one stupid motherfucker."

"Ma'am, I –"

"You're what? You're sorry? You just blew the only advantage we had left and God knows yet if you got anyone killed. Fuck you. Get out of here. Go do something useful."

She didn't wait for a response, but headed for the garage. Sean met her at the tape and silently handed her two latex gloves. She nodded thanks and put them on, walking around him and into the house. He followed, saying nothing.

Donna didn't know her way around the Coroner's office and the odd design of the building made it difficult to determine where to go next. To her left were two doors with windows in them; lights were off behind them. To her right, another door and wall of glass gave her sight of what was clearly the lobby. She wasn't sure where anyone would be, but headed in that direction. A magnetic click let her know the door had opened as she neared it, courtesy of a motion sensor, and she turned the handle. The hinges creaked only slightly as she crossed into the waiting area. She inched forward.

To the left, now, was a door with no window and a sign indicating "Authorized Personnel Only." To the right, a short hall with restrooms on the right, an unlabeled door to the left, and a large classroom straight ahead, its door propped open.

Dr. Wilson had been staring at the fountain for what seemed like forever. She wanted to give Roxanne her space, but she was growing impatient – not with the pastor but with what seemed like perpetual silence in the isolation chamber of an office her predecessor had built. She hated solitude and silence.

She turned from the window and looked at her computer screen. The surveillance system in the building was open in the background, as always, and a light was blinking on the bottom of the screen indicating movement. At this hour it automatically did that, and Leslie at first assumed it was Roxanne, Dora or Christian moving about. Then she remembered what had been happening and decided not to assume.

She sat and maximized the cameras' views. Her heart jumped.

On the lobby camera, she saw Donna Douglas clearly recognizable from the footage she had seen earlier. The woman looked lost, confused. A large object in her right hand was dripping blood on the floor.

"Fuck," she said. "Fuck fuck fuck."

Dora would be in the morgue, Roxanne in the Grief Room, and Christian – if he was awake – at his work station From the look of Donna's weapon, at least one of them had already fallen beneath her rage. She scanned the other views; the building was littered with cameras, but not every inch of the facility was covered. On the frame that included the Inspectors' work stations, she could barely make out Christian in his chair. He wasn't moving, but that could mean he was passed out asleep again or engrossed in his work. In the Morgue, she saw movement and shadows; Dora still lived. There was no camera in the Grief Room, which was closest to where Donna stood. She took a deep breath. There were no weapons in the building, and no cops, either.

"Fuck!" she said again, grabbing the phone but not taking her eyes from the screen. She called 911.

"911, where is your emergency?"

"This is Dr. Wilson at the Coroner's Office. We have an intruder, armed and dangerous. We need help ASAP."

"10-4, doctor," the woman said. "Do you want me to stay on the line with you until someone arrives?"

"Fuck, no," Leslie said. "I've got things to do. Tell them when they get here to kick in the fucking doors." She slammed the phone down.

Donna took two steps towards the Training Room and Leslie saw on camera as she pushed open the door to the room where Roxanne was in prayer.

"Oh!" Roxanne said, opening her eyes and lifting her head abruptly at the intrusion. It took half a second to realize who stood across from her, blocking the only way out of this room. She started to panic but gathered her wits quickly. She was going to need a steady voice, and she realized it in an instant.

"Hello!" she said. "You must be Donna. I bet we have a lot to talk about."

The killer was taken aback, not only by Roxanne's words but by her visage itself, a pretty young woman in a clerical collar – a "priest's outfit" she would've called it before her conversion. She said nothing.

"Please," Roxanne said. "Have a seat."

Reluctantly, the killer pulled out the chair across from the clergywoman and took a seat. Then she looked around, seeing the religious symbols on the wall.

"Idols," she said, jerking her head towards the wall.

"Oh, I agree," Roxanne said. "In fact, why don't we just take these down." She stood and began disconnecting the Crescent and Star of David from the wall.

"Jesus is the one true way," Donna said. "Sinners must be punished."

"Oh, yes," Roxanne said. "Absolutely. This isn't my office, though, you see. I'm just using it tonight."

As she pulled down the Crescent, she nonchalantly walked around the desk to place it on the side table. She realized she was putting herself closer to danger, but she was also putting herself closer to the door. Donna's arm shot up, the large bloody cross still in her hand. It wasn't an aggressive move, but it had its intended effect.

"Relax," Roxanne said, as easily as she could. "I'm just putting these other symbols over here. If they need to accommodate any pagans they can put them back up later."

She returned to her seat.

"Now," Roxanne said, pleasantly. "Why don't you tell me what's on your mind?"

She did her best to keep her eyes locked on Donna's, even as she saw a figure move in the darkened hall.

"I've been doing the Lord's work," Donna said.

"Oh, yes," Roxanne said. "I've noticed. We've all noticed. I think you've got your message across."

"They think I did wrong, though," Donna said. "You don't, do you?"

"Well, no," Roxanne said. "You followed your call."

"Exactly!" Donna said. "I'm glad you understand."

"Oh, I do," Roxanne said. "I really do. So what brings you here tonight?"

"One final mission," Donna said.

"Oh? And what's that?"

"I prayed earlier, when I finished my last job. I said, 'Here I am Lord! Send me!'"

"Isaiah," Roxanne said. "One of my favorite passages."

Donna smiled a bit.

"Yes," she said. "Isaiah. My favorite prophet."

"And what did God tell you?" Roxanne asked.

"He said, clear as a bell, 'Let the dead bury the dead.' That could only mean one thing."

"Well," Roxanne said, "that's what Jesus said when his disciples wanted to stop and bury the dead before doing more of His work."

"Right," Donna said. "I can't wait around while they

deal with those other bodies."

"The ones you killed?"

"Yes," Donna said calmly. "Some of them deserved it and needed cleansing. The other ones needed protection from shame."

"I see you took care of all of that," Roxanne said. "So God told you to let the dead bury the dead and now ... you're here?"

"Well, of course. This is where the dead come, where they get sent, before they're buried. They shouldn't be doing that. Jesus said to let the dead bury the dead. This place is just a sin factory."

"Hmm. I understand," Roxanne said, although she didn't. "That's all the more reason those unchristian symbols I took off the wall belong on that table behind you and not on this hallowed wall."

She saw Leslie look around the corner stealthily and silently, the doctor's eyes jumping to the table just inside the door. Roxanne still kept her eyes on Donna's.

In one quick move, Leslie stepped through the doorway, grabbed the metal Crescent and brought it down hard on the back of Donna's head. The killer's eyes widened in shock, and then she fell over backwards. Leslie made no effort to catch her.

Roxanne let out a breath she didn't know she'd been holding.

"Are you OK?" Leslie asked.

"No," Roxanne said. "Not yet. But I will be. Thank you."

"You're quite welcome," the doctor said.

"Is she dead?"

"No," Leslie said, leaning down to take Donna's pulse. "I didn't hit her that hard. I think Christian is injured, though. Go get Dora and check on him."

Roxanne hesitated.

"I gave you a key card," she said. "Dora is in the morgue. She's a trained paramedic. Go!"

The pastor left, heading towards the autopsy wing.

Leslie ripped the phone cord from the wall and bent down. She rolled Donna onto her bloody face, bound her hands as well as she could, and then threaded the cord around the woman's ankles, leaving her hogtied on the floor.

"Fuck you, you crazy fucking bitch," she said.

Epilogue

September 10

Sheriff George Stewart King was feeling much, much better. He had been detoxed and sober for 60 days now. He had followed instructions, obeyed his doctors, done his exercises – both physical and emotional – and was ready to go. Not so fast, they had said. He had committed to 90 days, but they could shave two weeks off the end if he kept up his work.

That was agreeable. He felt ready, but he was also clear-headed enough to defer to their judgment.

He wondered if anything big had happened while he had been gone.

Nick sat at her desk in the Sheriff's Office Slidell Complex. It had taken more than three weeks, but she thought she finally had all the paperwork needed to complete the full report on Eau. It was a lot, and she had organized it into a large three-ring binder with tabs.

Patrol deputy reports were in one section, detectives' resumes in another, Coroner's Office autopsy reports in a third, and her own summary next. The latter included her assessment of their failings, things they'd simply lacked the manpower or time to do: They hadn't listened to Karly's 911 tapes as a group; they hadn't concluded with certainty how Eau knew her home address or Jerod's, although it was likely she had accessed her husband's staff roster; they hadn't visited employees or collected tape from Pisces Fitness when they first discovered the link; they hadn't processed all the crime scenes in the last 24 hours of the investigation. They simply couldn't. Eau had moved too fast. There were others shortcomings, but they had done their best.

The report included printouts of radio logs, a CD of all related 911 and radio calls, and Karly's own, very brief, input. For the first time in her career, she had also created a tab for "Media," and had compiled printouts of every report in print media and a DVD of every TV story. Most of them were Blair's and Clarence's. She had even invited them – and Margaret – to submit their own reports for inclusion. Roxanne had also sent in a report, which read more like a lengthy journal, but since the pastor had been present for much of the final days of the case and had been witness to Dr. Wilson neutralizing Donna – Eau – her perspective was important. All of that would be helpful to the D.A. if Donna Douglas was ever sane enough to prosecute, which seemed unlikely.

Fred was due to return to work the following Monday, and she wanted all of this done for his review as soon as he was back. Once he signed off on it, it would go to the D.A.'s Office for review.

The dead who could be disposed of were all buried. John Douglas had succumbed to his injuries about an hour after being carted away, as Sean had foreseen. Christian had died at his desk, head slumped over on his keyboard and his brain spattered on the monitor. The Prescotts had been claimed by out-of-state relatives. The first and third primary victims had all been identified with the help of John Douglas' email accounts. The aliases were traced to IP addresses, which led to physical addresses, which led to identities and more death. It had been physically and emotionally exhausting.

The wounded were recovering. Cone was not only

alive but back at work. His wife's injuries would require reconstructive surgery but she would live – in another state and with a new name, far from her cheating husband. DeMarco had some rehabilitation ahead, but his physicians said he would recover for the most part. His hands might not be steady enough again to hold a scalpel, but his mind was intact despite the blow to his head.

Her desk phone rang and she answered quickly.

"Captain Brooks," the deputy at the secure front door said. "I have a delivery here for you."

"Thanks," she said. "I'll come get it after lunch."

"Captain," he said, "I think you should come now, if you can."

She didn't like the ominous tone of that, so she hung up and walked briskly to the lobby. Her husband stood there with all of their children. He held a large bouquet of flowers and each of the kids was clinging tightly to a single helium balloon.

She grinned and went to greet them, dropping her "cop mode" completely.

"Well, hello," she said, standing on her toes to kiss her husband on the lips and then crouching to greet the children. "To what do I owe this great surprise?"

"Nothing," Clay said. "Absolutely nothing. We just wanted to come tell you we love you and we think you're the best mommy in the world."

She grinned.

"Thank you ALL so much! I think you're all pretty terrific, too!" She moved to Clay and stood tall to kiss him again. "Especially you."

"Oh," he said, "and we got some mail today I thought you'd want to see ASAP."

He handed her an envelope the size of a large greeting card, already opened. It had a return address that looked vaguely familiar and the front was addressed in precise calligraphy. She reached inside and withdrew a wedding invitation.

"Dr. Terry Mozingo and Captain Jerod Leveque request the honor of your presence as they commit their lives to each other in holy matrimony. Saturday, November the 12th, at 4 p.m., at the Metropolitan Community Church of New Orleans. Please join Rev. Roxanne Clement in celebrating and solemnizing this significant moment."

She smiled again.

"Well," she said, handing it back to him. "It's about damn time."

Karly dropped off her retirement papers at Human Resources without fanfare.

"Are you sure you want to do this?" the H.R. Director asked. "Everyone knows how much you love your job – and you're good at it."

"Thanks," Karly said. "I'm sure. I'm going to go do something safer and less stressful – like ordnance disposal."

At the Coroner's Office, life – and death – slowly returned to normal, although it would be a while before anyone got near Christian's work station.

Sean Baxter was promoted to lieutenant, replacing the idiot who had tipped their hand and, quite possibly, cost Christian his life and DeMarco his career.

Dan Moreau was made Major and head of the Special Operations Division, replacing John Douglas – whose name was not mentioned again.

Robbie Silver and Michael Siwel went back to their jobs chasing thieves and burglars, far from the bloody messes of the summer. Many hoped that when Fred and the Sheriff returned, they would also be promoted.

Blair won an Emmy, and Clarence and Margaret shared a Pulitzer for series coverage and breaking news.

Chief Tom Richard and Officer Rooney went back to

Mandeville P.D. where most of their excitement involved setting up Neighborhood Watch programs and responding to false alarm calls.

Roxanne was putting away communion wafers after Sunday service when her cell phone rang. Ever since Eau had entered her life through a back door, she had been reluctant to answer a phone at this hour on a Sunday afternoon, but she did it.

"Roxanne, this is Leslie."

"Dr. Wilson?"

"Well, yes, but just Leslie," she replied.

Roxanne giggled.

"What's up, doc?"

"Ha," Leslie said. "If I had a nickel for every time I heard that. Listen, I'm sorry to bother you but I had a thought as I was leaving mass this morning and I figured I'd strike while the iron was hot."

"Uh-oh," Roxanne said.

"I know," Leslie said. "My thoughts often elicit that response. I'll be blunt, as usual, because you'd expect nothing less: I'm wondering if you'd agree to be the Coroner's Office Chaplain."

Roxanne paused.

"I'm honored, but I'd need to know more about what was required. I don't do things halfway."

"Of that, I am well aware," Leslie said. "That's why I'm asking you."

"Could we meet and discuss it?"

"Of course. I'd love to take you to lunch and twist your arm. You're really good at this, you know?"

"At dealing with death and crime victims? No, thanks!"

Leslie chuckled.

"No," the doctor said. "At dealing with the living. Around here, we know how to handle the dead. We need somebody like you to handle us."

Roxanne sighed.

"Lunch tomorrow?" she asked.

"You bet. Southside Café at noon."

The doctor hung up. She really did need help dealing with living, breathing people, Roxanne thought. Roxanne was here to help.